D0340030

MURDER

AND

A MUSE

Also by Gillian B. Farrell

Alibi for an Actress

Published by POCKET BOOKS

MURDER
AND
A MUSE

GILLIAN B. FARRELL

POCKET BOOKS
New York   London   Toronto   Sydney   Tokyo   Singapore

POCKET BOOKS, a division of Simon & Schuster Inc.
1230 Avenue of the Americas, New York, NY 10020

Copyright © 1994 by Gillian B. Farrell

Library of Congress Cataloging-in-Publication Data

Farrell, Gillian B.
    Murder and a muse / Gillian B. Farrell.
        p.   cm.
    ISBN 0-671-75710-5
    1. Women detectives—United States—Fiction. 2. Actresses—United States—Fiction. I. Title.
    PS3556.A7675M87   1994
    813'.54—dc20   93-38696
                                                                                    CIP

First Pocket Books hardcover printing March 1994

10 9 8 7 6 5 4 3 2 1

POCKET and colophon are registered trademarks of
Simon & Schuster Inc.

Printed in the U.S.A.

To Connie Jean "Willie" Snyder—the Willie of Willie's on Tenth, the location of several scenes from this book and its predecessor, *Alibi for an Actress.* It was a special place. Unfortunately, it will continue to exist, if it all, only in the pages of these and future books. So if you haven't been there, you missed it. Hopefully, Willie will start someplace new. I look forward to it.

MURDER
AND
A MUSE

1

I'm standing there. In my lover's office. It's not much of an office. I wish I could say he's not much of a lover. But that's not true. The office is pretty typical of what a detective's office is supposed to be. A midtown rental on a long-term lease.

He's been out of town. That's what he says. On a job. Detectives go out of town, on jobs. They work strange hours. Lots of nights. I know that. This gives him lots of opportunity to—have affairs. I've been waiting for it to happen. Or perhaps I should say, I've been waiting to have something rub my face in it so I could not maintain my suspension of disbelief. Waiting is not the right word. Waiting implies anticipation, positive anticipation, in some sense. Fearing? Dreading? Experiencing foreboding? Suspicioning?

I'm also waiting for him to return. From out of town. If that's where he is. One of his favorite one-liners is—Was, he no longer says it in front of me, when did he stop? was that the point where the joke was no longer funny? if I could fix that moment would I know something more about what I don't want to know?— "under five minutes and out of town doesn't count."

I'm not dressed for this kind of confrontation. If I had known, what would I have worn? Something provocative and sexy? Something competitive? Or severe and businesslike—but still flattering and competitive? I unconsciously check my hair and makeup.

Then the door opens and he comes in.

What am I going to say to him? What are the first words out of my mouth going to be? "Hello, dahling, so glad you're back, missed you terhibly." How about, "You two-timing son of a bitch, get out of my life and stay out...." I rather wish that he were some one-night, or five-night, or some other kind of part-time thing, so that I could dump him. But he's not. He doesn't just drop in to put his head on the pillow and his boots under the bed. He lives in my life. The closets are full of his stuff. My life is full of his stuff. And my son, who is not his son, dotes on him. I could say, "You've been lying to me." But none of that comes out.

The way it comes out is this:

"I did something I shouldn't have done." Let's start there. I don't want the way I found out to become the issue. Because that is trivial and beside the point. Or am I being insufficiently confrontational? If I were a guy, would I just slug him when he came in?

"Oh," he says. Neutral. Putting his brain in calculator mode.

"But I was worried...," I say, explaining how it came about. Though the evidence, the thing itself, is sitting there, a square plastic lump, on the desk beside us. "You didn't call. You weren't at your hotel. The one you said you'd be at."

"Uh-huh," he says. Does he know what's coming yet? Is that guilt I see in his eyes, or just gathering strength to lie and deny?

"I came here," I explain.

"I see," he says. Cool and male. Logical and collecting evidence.

2

I lay it on him: "I played your answering machine." The bomb.
"Yeah, so?"

"You know what I heard," I say. I can't believe his response.
Nothing. Mr. Cool. Stonewalling.

He shakes his head "no." As if he doesn't know.

Is it possible that he doesn't know? "You haven't heard your
messages?"

He shakes his head again. More "no."

I blurt out, "I wish I'd never come." But how do I feel about it?
I feel about eight things at once, most of them going in different
directions.

"What's on it?" he asks.

I don't know if he knows or doesn't know. But he is good at
this "handling the problem" mode. It's one of his logical, let's
examine the evidence, just like they would in court, things. It's a
device for diminishing emotion and controlling situations. I don't
answer him. We both look at the machine. He goes over to it. The
moment is charged and the tension grows. He almost hesitates.
Then he pushes play. We listen to the tape rewind, set up, there
is that moment of live "tone," just before a voice comes on. In
that moment neither of us is breathing.

"I don't like these things," his mother's voice comes on. A
comic anticlimax, hah-hah, not funny to me, I forgot that message was on there. He looks over at me, raises his eyebrow as if
to say "is that the problem message?" He knows it's not. "Please
call your mother," the machine says.

The machine keeps rolling.

There's one from his uncle. Another anticlimax. If he smirks
I'll lose it. He'd like that. Once I lose it, he can get calm. Hysterical woman, logical man—we know who wins that one.

"Oh, Tony," her voice comes on. Panting, syrupy. "Please, call
me. Please. As soon as you get back. I need to talk to you. To see
you."

"So," he says. I knew it. Cool. Nothing's happening.

"What's going on?" I say, matching his cool, but letting him
know I'm not letting it go.

3

"Nothing," he says. Yeah, right.

"Don't lie to me. I can stand anything, but not lying."

"Come on," he says, "I have a client. She happens to be in-clined to hysteria. She hates her mother. . . ." Like I care about her problems. I know who she is. And I know two things about her. Neither of them things that I like. She's younger than me and she has lots of money. And one other thing, and I know it, no matter what he says, she wants my man. "She feels guilty about her father . . . ," he prattles on. "She doesn't trust her law-yers. She feels she has no one in the world to turn to, except me. So she sounds like that. And I get paid very, very well. Triple what I get from some of the assholes I work for."

"If you are not honest with me, if you don't tell me the truth, we have nothing. I want the truth."

"If I'm being unfaithful, you want the truth?"

"Are you? I want the truth."

"What if I say I'm screwing her?"

"Then go right ahead. Go right ahead. Pack your bags, get the hell out of my house, and screw your little prick off."

"Fine," he says. "I will."

Then he starts to take his shirt off. Which is about what? His pectorals are not what our relationship is based on. "What are you doing?"

"Goddamn shirt is bleeding through again," he says.

Bleeding? What is this. Time for the sympathy vote? He's not going to get it, but I am going to find out what's going on. "Are you all right?"

"If you want to fight," he says, doing this awkward, pain-ridden dance of undressing, "we'll fight. But there's nothing going on." He sounds tired, pathetic. Sincere. Do I believe that? I can't stand watching him struggle with the stupid shirt. So I help him with it. It's possible that what he says is true. That that girl, his client, is hung up on him, without his having anything to do with it. Without his sleeping with her, anyway. It is pos-sible for desire to flow one way. There are bandages. And blood seeping through. Contusions. I'm the one that's there for him. I'm the one that he'll come to for care and healing.

"Baby, I need you," he says. He better deliver that line convincingly or he blows his whole scene.

"Do you?" I say. "I hope you know that." Which is revealing far too much truth about myself. Far too much.

He's got another line. But it doesn't matter because they're not auditioning Tonys, they're auditioning Glendas.

It was, my agent told me, "a significant part," in a "major project," with a "name director," which could make it a "key career role." She was very proud of having gotten me to be seen.

The name director was Alan DeLucca, known as the "Italian Alan," as opposed to, or in reference to, Woody Allen. This was not intended to imply that he was the sort of man who would have an affair with his lover's adopted daughter. As far as I knew he was married in a quite normal fashion, had been for some time, with two children actually from that marriage, everyone in one household. It was a reference to the subject matter of his work and the way he worked. The other currently famous Italian-American directors—DiPalma, Scorsese, Coppola, Cimino—have all made their reputations with operas of violence, full of blood and gore, gangsters and war. Not DeLucca. A lighter, more comedic touch. No giant mega hits, but all money-makers, and with a certain consistency. By the evidence of his films, a very good actor's director. The kind of director New York critics like—"like Woody Allen."

It had a New York producer who answered to an entity called Quad Star in Los Angeles who was producing it in association with one of the major studios.

This was DuLucca's first flirtation with murder. An adaptation of a detective novel called *Free Ride*, by Larry Rhinebeck, which had won an award. I had never actually heard of the book, though I was told it was a cult classic. It must be a very small cult because I'd never met anyone in it.

5

There are two secrets to know about auditions.

The first is that nobody ever gets hired from them. I've been on hundreds. In fifteen years, I've only gotten a part that way once. In reality actors get hired because someone has worked with them before and likes their work, because they're a star and will bring people who pay money to see the production, because they are having sex with someone who does hiring, is the child or spouse or other blood relation of someone who does hiring, because they did a shtick in their last movie and the director or producer wants that shtick repeated in this production.

The second is that we all go and do auditions anyway. More than that, we go and bleed. We prepare, we plan, we dress, do our hair and nails and get cosmetic surgery. Then we get judged. Not merely rejected. Judged. That judgment is then passed on to our managers and agents. We actually ask them to find out why we didn't get the part and to tell us. We know why we didn't get the part. Because nobody gets hired from an audition. But that's not what they tell us. They tell us it's because we're too short/tall, soft/loud, sexy/plain, boring/magnetic, American/exotic, because our voice is too shrill, eyes too old, manner too girlish, walk too stiff, knees too bony, attitude all wrong, because we overacted, underwhelmed, were the wrong type, were just not what they were looking for.

Yet it was an important audition.

The Italian Alan was an important director.

My agent and my manager would both be watching to see "how I did."

If I got it, it would put my career back on track. It would be the crack in the process where I could stop auditioning and get parts because someone saw my work.

And it was an opportunity to work with talented people in a first-class situation.

So I put effort into it. I had two days to prepare. The first problem was to get information.

No script was available to the actors. Just the two-page scene we were supposed to "do." To top it off, legend had it that the scenes DeLucca gave out for auditions were never actually scenes from the movie. This was part of the DeLucca method and mythology. It was also one more thing that encouraged parallels with Woody Allen. It's the sort of practice that encourages people who have gone to school too long to write pretentious commentary about auteurs. These theorize that actors are mannequins and imagine that the quality of a performance is determined by camera angles and the lighting. That to achieve—for example—an expression of fear, a director should lock an actor in a real cage with live and maddened birds and let them peck her to hysteria, rather than have the actor act.

I am tired of practices and theories that diminish the actor. I take them personally.

The entire description of the character as crafted—presumably—by DeLucca, handed down—through a personal assistant or a production secretary or even an executive producer—to the casting director, distributed to key agents and from them to designated actors like myself was: "Glenda—thirtysomething."

What was that? Insult? Negligence? Total insight? Zen koan?

If the Italian Alan didn't want to let me peek at his script, let alone his intentions, before I auditioned, I would go to the source, the novel, and find out what this character was like, what her life was about, and add some dimension to it.

I tried three bookstores in a row without finding it. A friend, who reads that sort of thing, recommended a special mystery bookstore. It was called Foul Play and located in the West Village. A very enthusiastic and knowledgeable bookstore person informed me that it was out of print. That it had gone out of print shortly after coming in to print. "Surely with an Oliver," I said, "someone would want to print it."

"A what?" the store person said.

"The award it got," I said, suddenly unsure of its name.

"Oh. An Edgar, you mean."

"Yes, that's it," I said.

"It did get one."

"I guess it's not an important award."

"Oh, it's very important," the store person said. He was very upset that I thought it might not be. "It's named for Edgar Allan Poe. It's the equivalent of an Oscar for mystery writers. It's really quite an honor."

"But not important enough to keep the book in print?"

"No," he sighed. "Not that important."

I turned to go.

"There's a sequel," he said.

"Will it tell me about the characters?"

"Oh, yes," he said knowledgeably. "It's a continuing character. I guess that's implied by its being a sequel."

"And is the character of Glenda in it?"

"The girlfriend?" he said. "Yes, she is. I'm sure you'll like it." He got it from the shelf for me. It was called *Bought and Paid For.*

Yes, she was in it. Apparently playing the same role that she had played in the first one—although one thing I must say for the author, he never threw in one of those "as happened in my last adventure" summaries. The so-called hero was the sort of angst-ridden, self-indulgent man who easily confused lust with love, who would destroy a relationship—not just with Glenda, an attractive, intelligent woman who was altogether too good for him, but with her son, who hero-worshipped him, as well—because he liked the way a younger woman's buttocks looked going upstairs in jogging shorts.

I pieced together that that's what he did in his first book. She took him back so he could do it again in the second book.

All I can say is that I would never want to be one of that author's women.

By the time I was halfway through—doing quite a lot of skimming—it was time to go to work. I brought the book with me.

My place of business, that particular night, as many nights, was an aging Cadillac, as dense inside with cigarette smoke as a performance by James Dean. Its name is the Silver Bullet. It's owned by Sonny Gandolfo.

We were on a surveillance job for Duke Investigations. A marital. When we're on a marital, Sonny likes to call us the SAD squad. Special Antiadultery Division. Except these two weren't actually married. The client was Rudi Dietz, a German-American businessman. The subject was his mistress. An old-fashioned word, but according to what the Duke told us, appropriate. Dietz paid the rent on her high-rise apartment on Third Avenue between Seventy-eighth and Seventy-ninth streets. In addition, he gave her $8,000 a month. Her name was Elissa.

We were to commence watching the building at 7:00 P.M. Mr. Dietz was going to meet us there to give us final instructions and photographs.

Sonny and I arrived a few minutes early. I got in the car beside him. We speculated—who wouldn't—on what sort of man felt he had to spend that much money to have a girlfriend. Sonny's various girlfriends are as likely to spend money on him as he on them. I've certainly never had anyone be quite that generous with me. I've never even had anyone offer. That includes one ex-husband. Would Rudi be a sort of elephant man? Or some other sort of physical grotesque?

At 7:05 a chauffeured Lincoln cruised past us and stopped. The back door opened. An extremely well-groomed man in his late forties or early fifties got out. He had silver hair, a dark blue banker's suit with pinstripes, a white shirt with a starched collar, a silk tie with discrete colors, and Bally shoes. He was neither fat nor skinny, tall nor short, ugly nor handsome to excess. In short, a very normal sort of rich man.

"Mr. Gandolfo? Ms. McGrogan?"

"You got it," Sonny said, through the open window. "You Dietz?"

Dietz nodded and got in the backseat of the Silver Bullet as if this were the way he normally took a meeting. He looked at his watch. "I am on my way to the airport," he said. His English was excellent and only faintly accented. "To Frankfurt. Elissa knows that I am going. Of course. Her friend will come over here between 7:30 and 7:45. Here are the pictures." He handed us an envelope with three snapshots. Two were of Elissa. The other was a three-shot. Rudi, Elissa, and a younger man. "That's her friend, Stephen," Rudi said. Stephen was a typically East Side male in his mid to late twenties, light brown hair, sharp nose, large eyes that were of indeterminate color in the photograph. I tried to define what the quality was that made someone "East Side." I decided it was to have more money than could possibly come from a salary, and time with nothing to do but spend it on self. "They will do a little bit of marijuana. Then, at 8:30 they will leave and go to Mortimer's. They will walk. Unless it rains, which is not predicted. If it does, they will take a taxicab, of course. They will have dinner. Then they will come back."

He seemed to know everything that was going to happen. What did he want us for?

"What I want to know is what they are like together," Dietz said.

"Anything else?" Sonny said. The limo still waited outside. Two tons of patience and obedience.

"I want to know if Stephen goes home. Or if he spends the night." He looked at his watch again. "Good night and good luck," he said. Cheerfully. Then he got in his limousine and departed for his flight.

"Well," I said, "he seems to have that down pretty pat."

"Whatcha reading?" Sonny asked.

I explained about the audition and having to read the book to get even a glimmer of what the character was about. "I don't know what they're going to do about her in the movie, but the character is impossible in the book. This guy goes out and cheats on her every time another woman smiles at him. She gets a little annoyed, but takes him right back. Are there really women like that?"

The moment I opened my mouth, of course, I realized that I had just asked the Pope if there were really Catholics.

Sonny has a wife, Cindy. Together they have two children, Sonny Jr. and a girl. The three of them live on Long Island. Their daughter, Annette, is eight. It has been seven years since Sonny has lived there. They are not divorced. He has a regular girlfriend in New York. He has another regular girlfriend in Miami.

This is more typical than not. Duke DeNobili, the Duke of Duke Investigations, has a wife in Staten Island with whom he has two children, a regular girlfriend in Manhattan, plus a standing arrangement with the Hotel Rensselaer for whatever comes up.

Then there's Tommy Zee and Tommy Martini, two other detectives, best friends and partners, who went down to San Juan on a job and both came back with girls named Maria—who stayed in New York to be their main girlfriends. Tommies Zee and Martini both have wives and children. But that's in Queens.

The list goes on.

"Well, did you ever think about it," I said. "I mean the other side of it. Why does Cindy stay with you?"

"Why not?" he said.

"Doesn't she want a full relationship, full time with a guy?"

"For what?"

"Right," I said. "For what?"

"There he is," Sonny said. "Right on schedule."

It was 7:30. The boyfriend had appeared. The doorman nodded to him in polite recognition and swung the glass door open for him. The lobby was open and well lit. We could see the deskman also give the boyfriend a friendly greeting. He didn't call upstairs to find out if company was expected.

"You see," Sonny said, "different women want different things. You take Cindy. She's happy, she's got the kids, the house, child support. She's happier I'm outta the house. Some women, sex, it's like a burden to them. Particularly after they have kids."

"It wasn't before?"

"It was always a little bit like that. That's why we got married. Cause she didn't wanna until we got married. It was pretty good at first. But then we had kids. Now, Mercedes," he said, referring to his regular girlfriend, "that's different. There's a woman really loves it."

11

"Why does she put up with you seeing other women?"

"Well, she doesn't know for a fact that I see other women. She knows it as a fact of life, but she never actually saw me with another woman. Also, she's Spanish, you know, and they know that a man is a man."

"What's that mean?"

"Men got urges, you know that. They're more animalistic than women. Women are, most of them, more moral than men. I unnerstand it's not supposed to be that way, but it is that way."

"What about this one, here, that we're supposed to be watching?"

"I didn't say all women, all the time. Most of them, most of the time."

"Does Mercedes ever ask you about what you do when you're not with her?"

"Uh-huh."

"What do you do?"

"I lie."

The kept woman and her boyfriend came out of the high-rise exactly when Rudi Dietz said they would. It was a dry, pleasant evening. They walked. We drove along slowly behind them. They were arm and arm, a little high and giggling. They stopped once. He leaned over as if to whisper something in her ear, but tongued it instead. She rubbed up against him in response.

They stayed at Mortimer's until 10:18, eating and drinking. Then they walked back to the apartment. They went upstairs.

Different people have different expectations and desires. Some women love men who cheat, take them back again and again. But is that about putting your love in the wrong place? A belief that love once given is truly irrevocable? Or is it that the pledge, the promise itself, holds them in place? Or is it a different set of expectations? Or does the cheating add necessary conflict—conflict creates anger and anger is the closest form of excitement when a relationship gets old?

I didn't care for myself. Just for how I was going to play the character. I didn't have a relationship with those sorts of problems. Nor did I intend to.

The boyfriend stayed the night.

I got a couple of hours' sleep before the audition. Enough that I looked fresh. Appropriate application of makeup helped. Then I selected my wardrobe. I wanted her to be attractive. But she couldn't be drop-dead sexy. That was the part for the Other Woman.

The key to Glenda, in the scene and in the book, is that she wants to lose the fight. She just wants a lie strong enough to believe. Once I knew that, I had a through line to play. When she's attacking, her biggest fear is winning. If winning means exposing the truth—that he is sleeping with his client—and then simply throwing him out, or if she must waffle, forcing him to choose.

He knows that. Either instinctively or with callous calculation. Just like Sonny knows that his women want lies. That's why they teamed up with a chronic liar. Sonny's a dear and wonderful man. I love him in many ways. And like him more than 99.5 percent of the other men I know. But becoming sexually involved with him would be an act of prime silliness. So Cindy and Mercedes and Caren all actually want a cheatin', lyin', three-timin'—though very masculine and charming—man. There's some place in them that chooses that pain.

Now I had several layers to play with: what Glenda says she wants, what she thinks she wants, and what she really wants.

The Italian Alan was not at the audition.

After I was kept waiting for about forty-five minutes among a constantly diminishing, but always replenished, group of women, all approximately my age, height, and weight, I was sent in to meet the casting director, Fernando Howard. I am told that he is known to his intimates as Fern. He was dark and sufficiently overweight that his fat cells seemed to puddle on his body.

He said, "Yes?" as a sort of general interrogatory.

I gave him my name and my head shot.

He gestured at a pool of light and a stool. There was an inexpensive video camera pointed at the spot.

"When I say 'action,'" he said, "you say your name, then commence the scene."

"Commence the scene?"

"Right."

I sat. He switched on the camera. A little red light came on on the side. He said "action." I commenced the scene. He read all the Tony lines and the answering machine lines in the same tired monotone. I tried, as we all did, to imagine that we had some dynamic leading man, full of delicious passion, rough but with a special sensitivity, masculine and tough—in short, a much younger Sonny Gandolfo—playing opposite me. Instead of the weighty figure of indeterminate sex who was very, very tired of reciting these lines and could not have given a good goddamn about me, the reading, or being an inspiration.

I read, the next day, in *Variety*, that Lucy Kohl had been cast in the part. Lucy's grandfather had been one of Alfred Hitchcock's producers. His wife had been a bosomy starlet who never quite made it to the screen in spite of extraordinary good looks. Their son, Lucy's father, was a motion picture banker. Her birth mother was now a studio executive at MGM. A few years ago, back when I was living in Los Angeles, Lucy had a series of leading roles. She had played the true love of an ill-fated rock star, the cute young partner of a gruff old cop in a buddy-movie-variation that never got released, the daughter who got killed in order to set an action adventure hero off on his trail of revenge. You must remember her. She's the one who always made you say to yourself, "What's she doing in this movie? She must be someone's something." Then she disappeared from the scene. Now, having been seen around town for a couple of years in some of L.A.'s more prestigious twelve-step programs, she was considered employable again.

That may sound catty, but every word is true.

2

The Dietz job, we figured, was a one-night affair. We watched, we saw, we reported, we went on to other things.

I auditioned for a sitcom about a woman who was a very severe female banker now, but in a previous incarnation had been the keeper of a fifteenth-century London bawdy house. She would flip back and forth at critical moments. This made her feel disoriented and was the source of much of the humor. Oddly enough, this bawdy house, as written in the pilot, did not seem to include the concept of prostitution. I auditioned for the part of a modern female lawyer who was the incarnation of a seventeenth-century French countess, who, to escape a fate worse than death, had run off, disguised as a man, to join the musketeers. She would flip back and forth. This was the source of much of the humor. I also went up for the part of a woman in advertising who was the incarnation of a fifth-century barbarian warlord—a male. She would flip back and forth in a humorous manner. I also read for the part of a female scientist who had been reincarnated many times and who was liable, at any moment, to become someone else in a far-off time and place. The inappropriateness of her responses each time her world changed was the wellspring of many hilarious situations. Then I auditioned for the part of an Egyptian princess from the XII dynasty, Theban, approximately 2,000 B.C., who had been reincarnated as a Jewish American Princess in contemporary Great Neck, Long Island.

I began to grow depressed. It was one thing to audition and audition and not be cast. But to suffer that rejection for parts that I would have been embarrassed to perform in public if I had been cast in them was doubly painful.

The office of Duke Investigations is in Queens, just off the Long Island Expressway. Oddly enough, I have never been there. I knew it had to have a mailbox, a telephone, an answering machine, possibly a file cabinet, a secretary named Brenda, and, in all probability, many framed photos of the Duke either receiving medals—from when he was a cop—or with celebrities he has known.

The Duke actually conducts his business from his car phone and from the Stuyvesant Room, a bar and restaurant, in the Hotel Rensselaer on West Forty-fourth Street. The car is a Seville. At those times that he needs to meet in a formal setting, the meeting is at the office of the client or, more often, at the office of the attorney that hired him. I, and other investigators like Sonny, are rarely present at those meetings. When it's time to take credit for things, the Duke shares 50 percent less than is absolutely, inescapably necessary.

However, both Sonny and I were called to a meeting at Rudi Dietz's office.

The office was on the twenty-ninth floor of a glass tower that occupied a block between Park and Lexington avenues at Fifty-third Street. It was expensive. It had a view. Mr. Dietz may have only been one person, but he was, according to the sign on the door, several companies.

Mr. Dietz had returned, that morning, from Europe. Although the Duke had faxed him a clean and typed version of our report ten days earlier when we had made it, he made us go over everything in detail. How had they held hands? How did Elissa react when Stephen put his tongue in her ear? Had we been able to get into Mortimer's and how did they behave there? What about when they went home—were they in a rush?

Then he called Elissa on the speaker phone.

"Darling, I have returned," he said.

"Oh, Rudi, I have missed you," she said. We all heard her voice very clearly but with those peculiar hollow tones that speaker phones produce.

"Have you really?" Dietz said.

"Oh, very much. Rush right over."

"What about Stephen? Didn't Stephen keep you from feeling lonely?"

"Oh, don't be ridiculous. He's just a friend. This jealousy of yours is absurd."

"Is it really?"

"Yes, Rudi. It really is. I want you to stop it."

"Didn't you go out with him the very night I left?"

"Just to dinner," she said.

"Oh, just to dinner?"

"Yes. Just to dinner. Do you want me to eat alone? There is nothing more pathetic than a woman out for dinner alone. People snicker behind their hands."

"But wasn't the walk over romantic . . ."

"What are you talking about?"

". . . with his arm around you. Making the stop to slobber his tongue in your ear?"

"Rudi . . ."

"You rubbing yourself against him. In the public," he said, his syntax slipping and a German accent beginning to emerge. "On Lexington Avenue!"

"You have jet lag. You're dreaming." Most people having this conversation would have snapped at Dietz to stop sounding like the Wizard of Oz and get off the damn speaker phone. But it didn't seem to bother her. They were a strange pair.

"Then after dinner," he said. "Tell me, what happened after dinner?"

"Nothing."

"What does nothing mean?"

"Nothing!"

"Nothing?"

"Oh, now you want me to walk home alone. At night. In New York City. And get raped and accosted and worse. Oh, you really do care for me."

"*Ja, ja, ja.* Then what? He stay with you?"

"No."

"All night? *Ja?*"

"No."

"Are your sure of that?"

"You bet I am and . . ."

"You liar! I can prove you are a liar!"

"Oh, yeah?"

"Yeah! I had detectives watching you."

"How dare you, you son of a bitch," she said. She sounded really outraged.

"They saw everything. The tongue in the ear, you squirm like a streetwalker, they saw Stephen go up to your apartment . . ."

"What an absolutely unspeakable, filthy, disgusting thing to do. Detectives!"

". . . und dey vatched all night." The angrier he got, the more German he got.

"Snoopers and peepers. You are vile. You'll never touch me again."

"Und all night, Stephen stayed. He's no friend."

"I can't believe you did that."

"So you are a liar."

"Go to hell."

"I have the detectives right here. Duke, tell her."

"Uh, yeah," the Duke said. "I, uh, had two operatives on you the entire night. And what Mr. Dietz says here is totally verified. Two witnesses signed, sealed, delivered."

"What a slimy way to make a living," she spat at the Duke. "Does your mother know what you do?"

"You leave my mother out of this," the Duke said. "My mother is a saint. Her name should never cross the lips of someone like you."

"Go ahead, Mr. Gandolfo," Dietz said, "tell her what you saw."

"How many goddamn people you have there?" Elissa said.

"Yeah," Sonny said, "if you want exact times, I'll have to check my notebook."

"I'll give you exact times," Elissa said. "You want to know how many times? I'll tell you how many times. I'll tell everybody. You want me to do that, Rudi?"

"I want you to admit you are a liar and a cheat and I have the witnesses in writing to prove it. They're right here. You're a liar." His English was getting better again, although he sounded quite angry. It had been when he spoke about sex that he lost linguistic control. This must have meant something. I wasn't sure what, but I filed it in my bag of acting tricks.

"Why don't you invite everyone over," Elissa said. "Have the whole crowd watch. You are despicable. Having me followed."

"I order you to stop seeing him."

"I order you to go to hell. I order you to get out of my life. I order you to never, ever have anybody spy on me again."

"I can cut off your lease. I will cut off your credit cards. I will cut off everything. You are cheating on me!"

"Go right ahead. See if I care," she snapped back. The delivery was great. But nobody believed it.

"Why did you cheat on me?" he asked her. It gave her some sort of out.

"You left me alone. I was lonely. I'm sensitive. I get lonely when I'm all alone."

"You mustn't do that."

"You mustn't have me followed."

"If you swear to stop, I will forgive you," he said.

"I'll swear to stop. Stephen's not so hot anyway. But I'm not about to let you back in, either. How dare you have me followed! Do you open my mail too? Listen in on my phone? How about my underwear? Do you check my underwear? Hey, everybody, does he check my underwear?"

Sonny looked over at me and rolled his eyes. People do do that. Check underwear for semen and blood and have them typed to see if they're the right DNA. Duke likes to have that done. It's ultramodern, very high-tech, and he can bill a lot for it.

"I had to do it," Dietz said. Talking about the surveillance, not the underwear. "And you see I was right. Listen. Forget about Stephen. I will be there early tonight. We'll have a special night."

"If you come here, I won't be here. I told you . . ."

"*Liebling* . . ."

"I don't forgive you!" she shouted. All of this was still on the speaker phone.

". . . I'm sorry. I'm sorry," he said, "that I used detectives."

"You had better be."

"I really am."

"If you ever do that again, we are through. You'll never touch me again. Ever."

"No more detectives. I promise."

"Swear it!" she cried.

"I swear. On my honor," he said.

"All right," Elissa said. "You can come over."

"Six," he said.

"Fine," she said.

"And no more Stephen," he said.

"I promise," she said.

He hit the button that shut off the speaker phone. "Thank you very much," he said to us.

"You're welcome. Duke Investigations is glad to be of service. Duke Investigations always delivers," the Duke said with an absolutely straight face and total sincerity.

"I am going out of town again on Friday," Dietz said. "I want you to watch her again."

"Sure," Duke said.

"Can you get pictures this time?" Dietz said.

I saw with some sort of regret, perhaps envy, that *Free Ride* had started rehearsals and was scheduled to begin shooting in a matter of weeks. Alan DeLucca was one of those old-fashioned directors who actually believed actors could and should rehearse, as if by trying things out, trial and error, work and thought, they can grow in their parts, add layers, find more ways to communicate, actually get better. This is not necessarily the current practice. It's more of a problem on big-budget films than small-budget films. The reason is that what makes a film big-budget—thirty, forty, fifty million dollars—is the cost of the star actors and directors. But the bigger—and more expensive—they are, the less time they have available. So an actor who's getting scale, six hundred and something a week, has the time to put in a year rehearsing if you want him to. And so do all the other actors in that film. But on *Bonfire of the Vanities,* for example, the actors may fly in from their previous film, put in a day of script reading, wing their performance, then fly off to Rome for their next project. Plus, the film schedules around them. So Melanie Griffith does a Melanie Griffith bit, Morgan Freeman does a Morgan Freeman imitation, and Bruce Willis does what he did on television.

Woody Allen and Alan DeLucca rehearse. They get performances.

My auditions seemed to be coming in waves. Perhaps it was some sort of psychic phenomenon. The reincarnated female professionals disappeared all at once. Suddenly there was a great need—out there in TV-land—for women to discuss various aspects of feminine hygiene.

Now I knew that both my agent and manager were working very hard to get me these auditions. They considered them important. After all, a national commercial pays a lot of money. And frequently continues to pay it for quite some time. Plus, this was getting me known among the casting directors. Yes, they were beginning to ask for me.

Being rejected took its toll. But I worried more about being accepted. Did I want to be on national television saying: "When I want to be really fresh—Ocean Spray, deodorant douche. Fresh as an ocean breeze. Tangy as a cranberry treat. Sprightly as a citrus tree. Now in five natural aromas.... Just for girls who are—really fresh." This last was supposed to have at least a triple meaning. Then there was: "I used to worry about those heavy days. Well not anymore! Now heavy days are wonderful days and Just My Secret." And who could ever forget: "This is not your mother's tampon."

On Friday, Rudi Dietz left town. Once again, he scheduled an 8:30 flight. This time to London, I believe. For the weekend. He left Elissa's apartment at 7:00 in the Lincoln limousine. He stopped by our car. "Good luck," he said.

"Thanks," Sonny said.

"Pictures?"

"You bet," Sonny said. We had a 35mm Nikon with high-speed color film and a Sony camcorder. They were on loan, direct from the Duke DeNobili family collection. Fortunately the DeNobili family had not misplaced the instruction manuals.

"Could we get a camera in the apartment?"

"We could, but not now," Sonny said.

"I wish I'd thought of it sooner," Dietz said.

"Next time," Sonny said.

"Have the Duke fax me in the morning," he said.

As soon as he left, Sonny and I went back to reading the manuals. They were in English, which helped. At 7:30 Stephen showed up. At 8:30 he and Elissa came downstairs. They walked, with their arms around each other, to Mortimer's. Sonny drove slowly behind them. I took the pictures. I was new to this and quite nervous. At a traffic light they stopped and kissed each other.

We cruised along behind them, the Cadillac gliding at a pedestrian's pace. It was not exactly subtle. But they never noticed. They never really looked. How could they not suspect that they were being watched? Did she believe that Rudi Dietz's word was that much more reliable than her own? Maybe she didn't care. Maybe it was a game.

They went to Mortimer's.

This time I had the foresight to have made a reservation. So Sonny and I spent $189.50, plus tip, on dinner for two and watched Elissa and Stephen drink and bill and coo and make frequent trips to the bathroom. We put the video camera on our table and pointed it at theirs. The Duke had suggested a piece of blank tape over the red "on" light. This worked very well. The food was certainly adequate. The service was exceptionally rude. I was not dressed to East Side standards. Sonny didn't even look rich.

We left while Elissa and Stephen lingered over after-dinner drinks. We waited outside in the Silver Bullet. When they came out, I followed them on foot while Sonny drove the car back to her apartment building. We guessed that they would stay true to form. They did. They went upstairs together.

Sonny found a spot to park by a fire hydrant. I joined him. We settled in for a long night. At about 6:00 A.M. I went out and got us coffee, donuts, and the morning papers. I knew Sonny would grab the *Times*, at least for the crossword puzzle, so I also got the *Post*. In "Tina Talks" there was this item: "Guess which little twelve-stepper just took two giant steps back? Little Lucy Kohl on her way to LAX—for her comeback appearance in the latest DeLucca—was driving just a little bit out of her lane, and into her lane, and out of her lane. Along came CHPs—ever so cute, always so arrogant, with leather boots and such big bikes—and arrested her for DWI and then: possession of a controlled substance! When will they never learn. Tsk-tsk-tsk. What will the completion bond company say?"

3

One would think, wouldn't one, that enough was enough and that Rudi Dietz would have been finished with Elissa. But he was not.

Rudi had truth—that his girlfriend was unfaithful, that she lied about it, that she would continue even after being caught, and that her promise was worthless. Rudi had proof—still photos, very grainy but all the more authentic-seeming for it, and he had videotape, with that "Top Cops" documentary look, lots of irrelevant action crossing through the foreground, hand-held jostling, and off-level framing that is the virtual definition of contemporary reality. Now he wanted insight—why did she do it? was it love? or youth? or something even more peculiar. I was assigned to get it. He wanted me to make Elissa's acquaintance, become her pal, share confidences with her, "what you call girl talk." Rudi had a plan, which he explained to the Duke and the Duke then explained to me. I should meet her at the beauty salon. Her haircutter was Rudolpho himself of Rudolpho's on Sixty-fourth Street and Madison. The trick was to have me there at the same time. So I couldn't use Rudolpho but I could perhaps get Eduardo, who, for certain hair types, was said to be even better than Rudolpho. While I was at it, if it was appropriate, I could get my nails done, fingers and toes. It sounded to me like a real long shot, the sort of thing that would only work in a movie. Would she recognize me? I hadn't actually spoken to her, but she might remember my face from Mortimer's. Or might she suddenly flash on a face that had been following her around the East Side and put it together with the face at Rudolpho's?

On the other hand, I would be paid to get my hair and nails done at one of the most expensive salons in town. A dream job for a girl detective.

Everything would be billed directly to the account of a buddy of Rudi's named Jürgen Bürger. Since the cost of my maintenance was being charged to a man who did not appear to be related to me, Elissa and everyone at Rudolpho's would assume that my profession—which was the catty way to say it and perhaps I should say *situation*—was the same as Elissa's.

Rudi knew Elissa's schedule and I made an appointment to match hers. They told me that I was very lucky to get an appointment with Eduardo, or anyone at Rudolpho's.

What does today's kept woman wear to the hairdresser? Actually, to judge by Elissa, the au courant East Side mistress dresses like an old-line WASP who studied art history at a university in Boston because anything else would have been too, frankly, commercial. Have they always done this or did the Mayflower Madame, Ms. Biddle Barrows, set a trend? Was this how Elissa wanted to appear to the world or was it how Rudi Dietz, her patron, wanted her to appear? The look required clothes that were simultaneously expensive and very boring. I didn't have them and thought that $400 for a skirt and $195 for a blouse might be pushing my expense account privileges beyond the bounds.

I went over what I did have and decided to go for a look that was actually a bit flashier—and a lot less expensive—than the real thing. I did have a good silk blouse, a delicate but provocative shade of rose, and I wore it with a wide belt, a short tight skirt, boots with heels, and pantyhose with a pattern. It made me feel sexy and dramatic and attention-getting. Sort of keepable. I wore a trench coat over it because I didn't feel like being accosted in the street. I don't mind the occasional glance, perhaps a head turning as I passed, but nothing loud, extravagant, or obscene, please.

I went in early. In case Elissa got there early, and we would both be hanging around with nothing to do. Just like an audition. Of which I had another with the dread Fernando Howard. I didn't understand why I should bother. I knew he didn't like me and that he wasn't going to like me anytime in the near or distant future.

When my time came—still no Elissa—Eduardo looked me over with a manner designed to convince me that he was Michelangelo and I was a piece of marble. A nice piece of marble perhaps, pure and white, but nothing until he cut away the dross and made the soul of the stone appear.

"What am I to do with you? What am I to do," he sighed. Not to me, to the muses of hair creativity. "Who . . . never mind . . . it is better I do not know. . . ." He circled me. After all, sculpture is a three-dimensional medium. When he had come around 360 degrees and was facing me again he said, "I have a cut for the East Side, very severe, very puritan, you burn with suppressed fires of ownership. What do you think?" He did not wait to find out what I thought. "No, no, no. No, ess you. Eduardo ess psychic, you don't know this of me, because you have just first meeting. Ess espirtual, you understand?"

"Absolutely."

"Your hair must be an espression of your espirtual nature. You are of artistic nature, you are of the etheric plane, I think so, yes. Eso not eso much cutting but body and luster in your hair. Rudolpho has developed his own line of conditioner and shampoo. They are very specific. Maria, Maria," he called to a young woman who was deeply cosmetic. "You go with Maria and she will prepare you. Maria, you must use conditioner number four on Anna. Leave it on for esix minutes, essact."

Maria shampooed and massaged me. She was attentive and chatty and I enjoyed the luxury of hands massaging my scalp. I would have to give her a very good tip with Mr. Dietz's money.

Finally, my time had come. I was led to the chair.

"You have a no need to tell me what you want," Eduardo announced. "I know already what it ess you want."

These words filled me with terror.

"No . . . ," I said.

"Yes," he said, eyes gleaming with creative fire.

"But . . ."

"Ahhh, you are really a blonde."

"You won't cut off too much, will you?" I asked weakly. I feared that Eduardo had an avant-garde streak in him that unleashed itself from time to time in cuts of dramatic severity or sent otherwise placid women home with hair that was defiantly punk, full of angularity and spikes. I just wanted him to leave enough that I could have whatever he did to ruin me corrected by someone else. If need be.

"You use henna," he said conversationally. "This ess good. But I think a lighter shade."

Elissa finally came in. I smiled at her. She looked at me like I hadn't been properly introduced to her. So much for that.

When Eduardo left the room for a fresh scissors or whatever he left for, I said, "Excuse me. I'm in a panic. I'm always in a panic when I get my hair cut. Especially by a new person. I can never bring myself to tell them I hate what they're doing." Time to throw in some flattery. Tell a woman you like something about the way they look and they always like you. It's instant. It's guaranteed. "Your hair looks really nice. I really like it, I do. . . ."

"Thanks," she said, as warm as a customer speaking to a waiter whom she was about to tip significantly less than fifteen percent.

27

"Anyway," I continued, "it's my first time with Eduardo. Is he good?"

"He's fine."

"Thanks."

"You're welcome."

My, she was friendly and forthcoming. Never mind. Ever resourceful, I had another trick up my silk sleeve.

Eduardo returned. He posed theatrically, as I imagine the nineteenth-century imitators of Edmund Kean must have done at the commencement of some bloodcurdling melodrama or the start of one of Shakespeare's scenes of multiple homicide. He held his glittering scissors in one hand, a comb in the other. He stood behind me so that I could see in the mirror how he looked standing behind me. If *Thus Spake Zarathustra*, the theme from *2001: A Space Odyssey*, had come over the sound system, it would not have been an overstatement.

With a graceful stroke of his comb, he swept the hair away from the right side of my face. He followed that with several swift, finicky gestures that separated out the twenty-eight strands that he was going to cut first.

I twitched my nose, quivering it like a cartoon bunny. "Is there," I asked, "a cat in here?"

"No," snip, snip, Eduardo said.

I brought my hand to my nose as if to quiet it, but quivered more violently than ever, building and building tension that it could only release with a sneeze. I confess that though I can cry on cue, I cannot sneeze at will. The sneeze was produced by a powder given to me by Henry Neimark, thespian, magician, and dear friend.

"There must," I declared, "be a cat here."

"Never," Eduardo said. "No ess any petses. No cat, no dog, no bunny rabbit, not even no gerbil."

"Then why did I sneeze?"

"Ahh." Snip, snip. Snip, snip. "This I do not know."

"I'm allergic to cats."

"No ess any cats here."

"Maybe a cat was here. Or maybe there's one of those dreadful people who carry around pets in their pocketbooks here. Aside from being really cruel to the pets it's really dangerous to people with allergies. Please. Please, stop cutting. I can't handle cutting when there's a cat around."

"Ess no cat," Eduardo said.

"Stop cutting," I cried, beginning to panic as allergic people do when they're trapped someplace, locked up with whatever causes their reaction.

"Look at Elissa over here," he said. At last. "She is allergic to cats too and she no ess esneezing."

"Really?"

"Elissa," Eduardo said, going over to where Rudolpho was snipping at Elissa. "You are allergic to cats, are you not?"

"Yes," she said. I knew that. It was one of the things that Rudi had told us about her. I also knew that she was a Sagittarius with a moon in Scorpio, who couldn't drive a stick shift and wore A-width shoes. My plan was working.

"If there ess a cat here you would be reacting? Ess true?"

"Absolutely," she said

"Oh, it's such a trial," I gushed at Elissa. "People just don't understand. Have you always been allergic to cats? . . . How does it affect you? . . . Do you get all clogged up?"

She nodded, the most minimal form of response that politeness required. My plan wasn't working. My carefully prepared common ground, the mutual suffering that would bond us forever in friendship, had not worked its congealing magic.

Meantime, I had to keep an eye on Eduardo's endeavors, lest I emerge like a victim of mange or a schoolchild who'd recently been through a particularly vigorous cure for head lice.

In spite of my fears, Eduardo seemed to be operating with some degree of restraint. My fears appeared to have been exaggerated. I realized that over here on the East Side, hairdressers were likely to save their greatest dramas for themselves and keep them off their customers' heads. So I tried to come up with a new approach: *Oh dear, it's so expensive here. However do you afford it? I couldn't except that I have a wealthy older friend who helps me out. How about you?* Too direct. *Have you seen the new exhibit at the Whitney? Modern art has grown so unmodern so quickly. I yearn for ferment and excitement in pigment, don't you?* Too much like a man's pickup line. Maybe she just didn't like to talk to women. Maybe a guy would have been better for this job.

The receptionist, Mahina, came in with a message for Eduardo. On her way out she somehow knocked over my bag. The contents tumbled out, spreading fanlike, each item cutting a trail through the litter of hair on the floor.

I turned to look. We all turned to look. Among the items facing us was the large, sandwiched-in-plastic card with the small black-and-white photo of my face and my right thumbprint on it. The one that identified me as a detective. I didn't think Elissa could read it from where she sat. But if someone got to it before I did, they would certainly notice it.

I started to get out of the chair.

"No, no," Eduardo said. "Esit, esit, we will get it. Not to worry."

"Very sorry," Mahina said, in a distant, weary way that made me think that she wasn't sorry at all, except about having to squat on the floor in her tatty tight skirt to pick up after herself.

I tried once again to get out of the chair.

"Esit, esit," Eduardo said. "I will help."

What was the first thing that he grabbed? My ID card. Did he quietly and discreetly put it back in my pocketbook, preserving my cover? No. He did not. "A detective," he shrieked. With glee. "Oh my God. Just like 'Charlie's Angels.' A girl dick, how positively divine. Is it true? Are you really a detective?"

How was I to deny it? With him holding documentary proof in his hand, screeching loud enough for the neighbors to know, and blowing my cover with Elissa forever. "Well, yes, I am," I said.

"You must tell me your greatest adventures. Do you carry a gun?"

"I'm a private investigator," I said. "I don't go around shoot-ing people."

"Excuse me," Elissa said.

"Yes?"

"Do you, like follow people?"

"Yes," I sighed. So she figured it out.

"Like husbands and wives, girlfriends and boyfriends?"

"That's not all we do," I said, hoping to preserve some shred of dignity. "But we do that too."

"Could I hire you?"

"Yes." I assumed she could. I certainly couldn't imagine Duke turning away a paying customer.

"There's someone I'm . . ." She paused, searching for exactly the right word, precise and descriptive, that would say neither too much nor too little. She finally came up with, ". . . seeing. Something is going on with him, I think. Sometimes when I see him, he's light and wonderful and charming. Then the next time he'll be dark and . . ." Once again the pause while she consulted her mental thesaurus. ". . . difficult. Could you investigate him and find out?"

"Well, it depends," I said, realizing that maybe there was such a thing as a conflict of interest. If we were watching her for Rudi and Rudi for her.

"His name is Stephen," she said.

I sat in Fernando Howard's waiting room. It was aptly named. I had rushed from Elissa to be at the casting in time; he was making me wait. It was Glenda again. Lucy Kohl was being replaced. They were re-casting on both coasts. I suspected that, once again, they would pick someone from L.A. even though DeLucca was a "New York director."

None the less, there I was. The primary feature of the waiting room was a lot of chairs. Six against the wall where I sat. Four across from me. Two flanking the entrance, two flanking the door to Fern's inner sanctum. On the wall across from me was a two-foot-by-three-foot blowup of a head shot of a very pretty young actor, clean shaven, with limpid eyes under relatively long lashes, looking out longing for something. A part, perhaps. I figured it for Fern's current lover.

It had been my intention to dress down as I had for the first audition. I'd visualized this woman, Glenda, as going over to her live-in lover's office after work, a little frazzled, a little stressed out, and in a hurry to get home to pick up her son, after school or from day care. I hadn't worked out which. In any case, I saw her as garbed for functional respectability, not for sex or glamour or even comfort. Sensible brown leather shoes with low heels. Plain panty hose. A simple, pleated gray skirt—hemline below the knee. Matching gray jacket. Light blue blouse, buttoned to the neck. Ever so boring.

But Elissa wanted to tell me all about Stephen. So intuitive, sensitive, yet really cold and distant, which she loved in a man, she hated men who were all over her, all hurried, heavy and moist. Stephen had a way of dressing, no matter what he wore, it looked elegant. Then she wanted to know how I would follow him and if we should shoot pictures of him or even videotape. And she wanted to know how long I'd been a detective and what I did.

In the end, there was no time to go home and become drab. I looked—if I'd gotten my character right for the morning—like the sort of woman a German businessman would spend $6,000 or $7,000 a month plus perks to keep in New York—who had had her hair freshly done. Nothing sluttish, mind you, but hardly Glenda the dreary.

A guy walked in, looked around at the choice of seating— alone, alone, alone, alone, or next to me—and chose next to me. He was slender, tall, about forty-five, and meticulously neat. He wore brown loafers, shined; summer-weight wool pants, freshly pressed; a belt that matched his shoes; striped shirt, ironed; his hair had a business clip; and he was closely shaved. We all read character from clothes, rightly or not. This man was more obsessively neat than very trendy, so I didn't think of him as gay, perhaps just anal-compulsive or Italian.

"Hi, how you doin'," he said.

"Fine. Yourself? You here for the auditions?"

"Yeah," he said.

"What part?" I asked.

"I might do a bit. Maybe one of the lawyers. But I told Fern that I might help out with the readings."

"You know him?" I asked.

"Yeah," he said.

"Do you like him?"

"Yeah," he said. "Why?"

"Then I better keep my mouth shut."

"Why's that?"

"I shouldn't say anything about Fernando Howard. It's not that he's worse than other casting directors. He's probably not. Sometimes I think they hate actors. How else could they treat us with such disrespect? It might be OK if they knew anything about acting. But most of the time they don't."

"You don't think so?"

"I'll give you an example. Take this audition, I'm supposed to do a scene about being betrayed by my lover and then fooling myself into forgiving him."

"Is that what you think the scene is about?"

"You know the scene? This Glenda, Tony, and the answering machine thing?"

"Yes," he said.

"Don't you think that's what it's about?"

"It could be about her seeing that Tony is hurt and realizing that she loves him more than she's angry," he said. "And that their love is more important than whatever else is going on."

He was totally wrong and I told him so. "No. Not at all," I said. "If he weren't bleeding, she'd find some other excuse to back off from the confrontation. She may not be conscious of it, but she wants to lose the argument. She wants to be convinced that he's not cheating on her."

"Well, of course she'd rather think that. Anyone prefers to be convinced that their lover is loyal, if they are."

"No, I don't mean she wants to be reasonably convinced. I mean that no matter what, she's going to find a way to take him back. If he wants to lie to her about it she will accept that as the way. If he doesn't, she'll find some other way. The only thing she really doesn't want to happen is for him to say: 'Yes, I'm having an affair. I like it better with her. I'm leaving you.' "

"So that's how you'd play it."

I shook my head. "That's just one level," I explained. "She may not even know this about herself. Or know it, but not allow herself to see it. There are still other levels."

"Like what?"

"I may be making this up. But I have to. I don't have the script. That's part of the DeLucca mystique," I said with some sarcasm. "Or the casting director's contempt for the actor. If they thought of the actor as a creative person—the way they think of them-selves—they would give us material to work from. To give us just these two pages, that's saying we're objects to be used."

"What do you mean?"

"That we're just a 'look,' a 'sound,' that fits certain lines. Not someone capable of creating a character in relation to the whole story."

"Maybe you could get the book," he said. Challenging me. "If it matters to you so much."

"The book," I announced, "is out of print. But I did get the sequel." I'd expected that I would have to wait and I'd brought *Bought and Paid For* with me to pass the time and see, as well, if there was some striking moment with Glenda that would inspire my audition. I showed it to him. "I have to tell you, this guy Rhinebeck doesn't really know women all that well. He knows them as sex objects. This is a very self-centered hero he has here."

"I thought of him as sort of noble. In that cynical American, Bogart, Sam Spade kind of way."

I didn't reply to that. I just said, "At least I got some insight into Glenda. What she says she wants is middle-class respect-ability. She wants a guy who comes home at a reliable hour, who makes a reliable salary, who'll buy a condo. But that's not what she wants. I bet that's what her first husband was. She wants a guy who's wilder than that. More dangerous. More masculine."

"Sure. I see that."

"I'm a detective . . ."

"You're a what?"

"A private investigator. I'm an actor first, but that's how I make a living. Most of the guys that I work with, they've been on the force fifteen, twenty years. Most of 'em, they've worked homicide, up the two-three, the two-five"—he looked blank—"that's Harlem and Spanish Harlem. They've been shot at, stabbed, in fights. They've shot, even killed people. They're very masculine. That's very attractive to a certain kind of woman."

"Is that the kind of woman you are?"

"But they are all unfaithful, constantly. They're all married, plus they have a girlfriend. Sometimes the same girlfriend for fifteen years. Maybe even have two sets of children. Plus they go out with any female capable of the word 'yes.' The wives and the girlfriends put up with it. Why?"

"Why?"

"Good question," I said.

"Do they know? That these guys are screwing around?"

"They're women. Of course they know."

"So? Why?"

"A lot of them just believe that 'Men are that way.' Part of it is that they figure that somehow that's part of the package. Sort of 'If you want a real man he's not going to keep it at home.' "

"You think that's true?"

"I think that if you want a good woman, you better worry about being good enough to keep her at home."

"How about dinner tonight?" he asked.

"Who are you?"

"I have to work tonight. But we could have a bite together before that."

"I don't know," I said, reflexively. I'm not wild about "dating."

"Is Glenda one of those women? One of those cop's wives?"

"I don't know. I think underneath she wants to be what he is. She would really prefer the roles were reversed. But she's afraid of that much chaos."

"And you can project all of that into this little scene?"

"If I'm a good actor, yes, I should be able to."

"So what's wrong with Fern?"

"Instead of having an actor in there to read with me, he reads the lines himself. So I have to play what's really a love scene with a very overweight homosexual. He's busy looking at the script, so he never even looks at me. Plus, as soon as I finish my line, he's right there with the next, so I don't get a chance to work with silences."

"Did you notice that photo?" He pointed at the wall.

"Yes."

"Do you know who that is?"

"No idea," I said.

"That's Fern. Twenty years ago," he said.

"Wow," I said.

"If not dinner," he said, "how about lunch?"

"Why?" I asked. "Why me? Do you have a need to feed someone?"

"Yes," he said. "I do."

"Maybe you should feed some of the homeless?"

"Why are you giving me a hard time?"

"Why do you want to feed me?"

"Because," he said, giving exactly the right answer, the most right answer, "I'm loving listening to you. I want to hear more. I like people who have something to say."

"OK," I said.

"Which? Lunch or dinner?"

"Dinner's fine," I said.

"Where would you like to go?"

I thought about it. He was an actor. Who was working nights. At what? How much could he afford? "Do you know Willie's on Tenth?"

"Never heard of it."

"It's at Tenth and Thirty-third. My friend Willie runs it. It's like an old-time saloon, but the food's fabulous and reasonable. It's fun."

"Great. Five o'clock?"

"Sure," I said.

"I have to be on set at seven," he said.

"Oh, it's an acting job?" I'm always glad to hear of an actor working at acting. It's sort of like hearing that a pair of giant pandas have successfully mated or that a scenic wetland has been saved from development—a sign that something precious has not yet totally disappeared from the earth. "What are you shooting?"

"I want to hear more about your theory of casting directors."

"Oh." A sound of surprise from another voice and a different direction.

I looked up. It was Fernando Howard, waddling out from his inner office. In there he had sat in shadow. Out here, where the light from the waiting room hit him more harshly, I could see that he wore a toupee. I thought of cleverly cruel comments I could make about it—afterward, when he rejected me again.

"I didn't realize you were here. You should have said something," he said and sounded genuinely concerned.

"I was exactly on time," I said. I stood up, ready for my reading.

"Not you," Fern said. Cold to me. "Alan. Come in, please. I wish I'd known." Polite, even fawning, to him.

"That's OK," Alan said, "I was having a good time."

I was ready to point out that I had been there first. That I had the appointment. That this was no way to treat an actor. And that, frankly, Fern, baby, I'm outta here. "Come on," my new dinner date said before I had a chance to speak. And he gestured for me to go with him. He graciously stepped aside and let me enter Fern's office first. I like men with manners. Most women do and most men don't get it.

"Can I get you something?" Fern said. "I have Perrier and soft drinks and I can order out for coffee."

"How many people do you have scheduled today?" my date asked. "For Glenda?"

"About twenty, twenty-five," Fern said. "And three more to-morrow who couldn't make it today."

"I think this girl should do it," Alan said. "I'm sorry. I don't even know your name."

"Annie," I said. "Annie McGrogan."

"Hi," he said. "I'm Alan. Alan DeLucca."

"Oh," I said. In all the pictures I'd seen of him, he'd had a beard. A very neatly trimmed beard.

"What about the other . . . shouldn't you . . . don't you want to . . . ," Fern said.

"No," Alan said. "We'll use Annie."

"I didn't recognize you," I said. "In all the photos, you always have a beard. It was a nice beard," I added inanely.

"I shaved," he said.

"I see," I said.

"Get with her agent," Alan said to Fern. "Make a deal. If there's any questions about the deal, you see Dan Ginzburg . . . he's one of the producers," he added for my benefit. "Then get with Mitzi. Mitzi'll take care of getting her to wardrobe and all the rest of that and making her a schedule."

"What should I do about the rest of the auditions?" Fern asked.

"Go ahead with them," Alan said. "In case something doesn't work out."

"I hate that," I said. "Every actor does. Auditioning for a part that's already been cast. That's not right."

"You have a lot of opinions, don't you?" Fern said.

"Is there something wrong with that?" I said.

"I have to get some rest," Alan said. "I have a dinner date and then on set at seven. I'm glad this is settled."

He walked out without another word.

"Was that really Alan DeLucca?" I asked.

"Yes. And I'm really a casting director. The very incarnation of evil," Fern said. "And now you're really Glenda. Who's your agent?"

Willie's on Tenth is two different places, depending on how you approach it. If you walk from the subway—the closest stop is Penn Station at Thirty-fourth and Eighth—you make your way past dioramas of urban angst as they might appear in the Museum of Natural History if, alongside the stuffed bison and antelopes, the curators built an exhibit of New York in the late eighties, early nineties, nouveau noir, crack smokers in boarded-up doorways and between parked cars, obviously diseased prostitutes on the sidewalk, gaps in the backdrop where old tenements have been torn down giving city streets the derelict look of collapsing Halloween pumpkins. If you come that way, then Willie's is a warm oasis, a symbol of hope and optimism, cash proof of faith that the city, which does have a history of reinventing itself, will continue to do so forever, or at least just one more time. If it does, then Willie is ahead of the curve and her saloon will be perfectly placed for the fun and profits to come. If she lasts that long. Running a restaurant is a tough racket.

On the other hand, if you arrive by limo, you might think you'd gone slumming. Her clientele, exhibitors at the Convention Center, construction workers, less than wealthy actors, and the steady, serious drunks from the neighborhood, might not appear to have the same good cheer and welcoming warmth that they do if you have just survived arriving by foot. Especially now, since Willie had redecorated. Since I'd last been there, she'd taken down all the paintings on the long wall over on the restaurant side, then ripped off the floral-pattern pink-and-lavender wallpaper, and, on the bare plaster, she had spray-painted in large black letters: *Fuck the IRS* and *Fuck Mayor Dinkins.*

"What do you think?" Willie said to me. "Do you think it's too much?"

Willie is one of my dearest friends. If I had known that Alan DeLucca was Alan DeLucca, would I, should I, have said Le Cirque? Café Des Artistes? Petrossian? Willie's is a place to go to when you're spending your own money, not dipping into the bottomless well of a motion picture studio expense account. How would *Fuck the IRS* and *Fuck Mayor Dinkins* affect Alan DeLucca's opinion of me? "Not at all," I said. "It's not too much at all."

"Really?"

"Really."

"Well, it's what I wanted to say."

"Then you should say it."

"You're right, Annie," Willie said. "Thanks. Order anything you want. It's on the house."

"I'm expecting someone," I said.

"Who's buying you dinner?"

"I expect so."

"Is he cute?"

"It's business."

"Too bad."

"It's a part."

"A part?"

"In a major film."

Willie squealed and hugged me and grabbed the first three passing people. One of them a waiter, whom she knew, and two of them customers, whom she probably didn't. "This is my best friend, Annie, and she's the best actress in the *world* and she just got a part in a major motion picture. A big part." She looked at me. "It is a big part, isn't it?"

"Reasonable."

"Not the lead?"

"No."

"But with lines?"

"Yes."

"How many lines?"

"I don't know. Pages of them."

"Ohhh." She hugged me again. "I'm so proud of you. I'll send over champagne."

"Maybe I should wait and see what he wants."

"He'll want champagne. Trust me. Is he on expense account?"

"He must be."

"I'll put one of the Frenchy labels on the bottle then. One of those fancy ones with a date."

She was reacting just as I would have hoped. There was one other person I was hoping to find at Willie's to share the news with. "Where's Andrew?" I asked her.

"He's taking some time off," she said.

"Has he got a part?" I asked hopefully. He's a good actor. Like many good actors and bad he has to support himself doing something else. So did I. Up to this point.

"No," Willie said. Roland, the bartender, was yelling at her. "I don't know. He's been very difficult lately. Moody." She finally turned to Roland and screamed across the room, "Tell 'em I'll call back." Roland said something I couldn't hear. Willie yelled, "Tell him to go 'F' himself. And then tell him I'll call back. And tell him to never, ever come in here with a gun again. In the meantime send over a bottle of champagne."

"Never, ever walk in here with a gun again?" I asked.

Right about then the long, gray Lincoln Continental limousine slid into place outside the front window. An un-uniformed chauffeur jumped out to open the door, but the passenger hadn't waited and was letting himself out. A sign in the window blocked our view so we couldn't see who it was.

"I hope it's a guy. Alone," Willie said. "I could use a guy with money."

"What happened to . . ." I paused for a moment to remember the name of the man who I thought was her current beau. It's not that she turns them over so fast that it's hard to keep up, because she doesn't. Since David Kay, the elderly Jewish Mafioso who kept her in style for ten years, they last at least ninety days and often a full year. It's just that next to Willie's own flamboyance and emotional extravagance none of them seems like much more than a gray shadow trailing on the wall behind her.

"Champagne's on it's way, sweetie," she said, rising to meet and greet whoever it was that had arrived in style. Her impressive breasts led the way and I understood that they would, in many ways, define her, from first impression to last, to any man who met her. I had large breasts once. It was in a play called *Bazaar and Rummage*. I was having immense difficulty with the character, an agoraphobic lounge singer who hadn't left her house in three years. I just couldn't find my way into her. Sometimes, when you can't work your way from the inside you have to work your way from the outside. I decided she must look like a Holiday Inn nightclub version of Ann-Margret. With a powerful push-up bra and a lot of stuffing, I created size and cleavage. It made me a different person. One of the other actresses in the show had an eleven-year-old son. From the day I came to rehearsal wearing my new and improved breasts, he began to follow me everywhere. And whenever there was any sort of elevation from which he could get a sight line from above them— scaffolding, ladder, the balcony—he would inevitably mount it and gaze down. And his palms would sweat. The response of adult men was indistinguishable except that if they were more than five feet five inches tall they didn't have to find something to stand on first.

It was Alan who had arrived by limo.

It was with a profound sense of something—relief? hope? anticipation?—that I saw he was able to stand in front of Willie and have Willie point out my table without seeming to be mesmerized by the size and prominence of the bosom before him.

Although film directors are, by definition, obsessed with the visual image, many of them seem to revel in ignoring their own physical appearance. Several who are among the most demanding about their actor's looks, fitness, wardrobe, makeup, are, themselves, less than in shape and downright slovenly in their dress. Alan DeLucca was not one of those. He was wearing a brown cashmere sport jacket over a blue turtleneck, loose camel-color slacks, and casual Italian shoes. His clothes draped on him as if they had been custom tailored, which they may have been, and had come fresh from the cleaners. His shoes were polished. He was trim and had a very erect posture.

He smiled when he saw me as if what he saw pleased him very much.

I smiled back. My heart went pitter-pat, pitter-pat and tried to make my brain forget that I knew that he was married.

He was still smiling when he sat down. Then the champagne came and I was sort of embarrassed and tried to explain that I hadn't ordered it, I wasn't trying to trick him into buying me an expensive bottle of wine, that Willie had made that decision, and having met Willie, if only for a moment, he could probably tell that she was a person that it was terribly difficult to say no to.

"Do you like champagne?" he said.

"Well, yes," I said.

"Then it's fine," he said. He took the bottle out of the ice bucket. It opened with an excited *Pop!* and foamed in a very satisfactory way. When he poured it into our glasses it fizzed and sparkled. Obviously the refraction of light is governed by the amount, and type, of emotion in the immediate atmosphere. He raised his glass. I did it too. I thought he would make a toast. Something sweet and corny, maybe something slightly suggestive of emotional entanglements to come. Maybe something about working together, or my career, or the movie we would both have a part in creating. But he was much cleverer than that. He said nothing. He just looked me in the eyes. His were brown, something between tan and chocolate, shiny and somewhat strange. The toast was silent and vastly more powerful for it because we were each able to make it mean all the possible things we might want it to mean. The moment was so intoxicating that I drank to clear my head.

I tried to think of something to say. Normally I don't have any trouble at all thinking of something to say. But what I meant to say I couldn't bring myself to say, which was: *When will your divorce be final?* Which would have been more than pushy, it would have been foolish, for as far as I knew he hadn't even started to get divorced. As far as I knew he was still as married as when the Sunday *New York Times Magazine* had done a cover story on him two years earlier. Since I couldn't say that, I considered announcing that I never, ever, go out with married men and would certainly never, ever, have an affair with one. That would have been a bit presumptuous, since he had done nothing that could be construed as a pass or proposition.

So I said, "Uh, I guess I should, uh, take this opportunity, uh, being with the director, uh, over dinner, to get some insight into the part. I would really like to know more about your, uh, approach to the film." And maybe that was why he'd asked me to dinner. So we could exchange views and he could get some understanding of my approach to acting while he conveyed to me his approach to directing.

"I brought you your pages," he said. He handed me a slim manila envelope.

It was not nearly thick enough to hold a whole script. I got very suspicious. "My pages?"

"Yes."

I looked inside. There were about fifteen or twenty pages. I had heard that he did this sort of thing. "I'd like to see the whole script," I said. I said it in a very open, nonconfrontational way.

"For the most part," he said, "I only show actors the scenes they're in. I don't give out scripts."

That really is an outrageous way to work. It's a puppeteer's attitude. It denies that actors have the creativity and intelligence to understand the whole without its corrupting the way they approach their own part. It suggests that they are blind creatures who must be manipulated by some greater intelligence in order to achieve anything of value. It is blatant power-tripping and, in principal, makes me livid. But still, I knew that Alan and I *connected* and that I could work with him. Perhaps he just needed to have how I felt explained to him, and then he would understand.

"I like to think of myself as a collaborator," I said. "Working with the director, making a contribution to the creation of the writer. If I don't have a vision, if I can't share their vision of the work as a whole, then my work might not be in tune with what they're doing."

"We're blind," he said. "In real life, we're blind. You don't know what I did before I walked in the door. You won't know what I do when we part. I don't know what you did before you came here tonight. I can guess. I might guess wrong. And that's important. That I guess wrong. Because I am going to act here, at this table, based on what you seem to be bringing with you to this table.

"If actors know the whole story—everything that 'really' happened in rooms where they were never present—it takes the life out of it. If they know how it will end, it takes away the fear. And the hope."

"That's *really* patronizing," I said. "That's saying that actors don't act. That they just 'act out' or something. Acting is an art and a craft and I trained very hard to be able to seem to be totally in the moment, just as if what's happening is really happening, even though I know what the other actor is supposed to do next. That's an actor's job. And the more I know, the more I can bring to it. Would you direct without reading the script? What would you do for pacing and rhythm and intention and buildup and all those things?"

"You've seen *Casablanca?*"

"Yes."

"There's a great mystery there. Because everyone involved thought it would be a kind of mediocre B movie, or at best a very pedestrian A picture. The mystery, and every one has their own theory, is why it became the iconographic piece that it is. I personally think that not knowing how it would end had a lot to do with it. It took what might have been some very sappy scenes and gave them a tension, an edge.

"I think that every moment on film should be *Casablanca.*"

"There are lots of movies where nobody knows what's going on," I said. "Let alone how they'll end, and they don't become *Casablanca*. Probably most movies where nobody knows what's going on don't get released."

"All of mine do."

Oh yes. He was *the great director*—and he was, innovative, daring, true-to-himself—and I was *just an actress.*

Then he said, "I don't think of actors as puppets. They save my ass all the time. I just try to come up with enough material for them to work with. Then I hope that they can do the miracle that actors do and do it in front of my cameras so that when they're done, I have a film to cut.

"That's why I cast you. Because I think, I'm betting, quite a lot actually, that you can do those kinds of miracles and make this part a happening part. Because if you don't, the movie is going to be like a lame man running."

Wow, did he redeem himself. I gulped down my champagne and glowed. He poured some more. I drank the next one with a little more restraint. The un-uniformed chauffeur came in carrying a cellular telephone. The art director and the producer both needed to speak to Alan.

"Let me take it in the car," he said to me. "It's just too noisy in here. I'll be back in five minutes. I know it's rude. But they'll get all tied in knots if I don't call them back. Is it all right with you?"

"Of course," I said.

"Would you mind ordering us something to eat while I'm on the phone?"

"How do I know what you'd like?"

"Be daring. Be decisive. I love daring, decisive women. How wrong can you possibly be? It's just food."

The minute he left, Willie rushed over. She asked why he was leaving. I explained about calling from the car. She seemed very relieved. "I didn't think he would up and leave you here. He's sweet on you."

"He's married," I said.

"Oh, Annie," Willie said, as if I'd dropped in from a forgotten century.

"Going out with a married man is like taking a trip to nowhere," I said. "It's full of anticipation and planning and what ifs, but when you stop to look around, you are still sitting in your apartment by yourself waiting for the phone to ring."

"Can I ask you something? Did the nuns tell you that in Catholic school?"

"No. Not really."

"Did they tell you that if you wore patent leather shoes, boys would look up your dress in the reflection?"

"Well, yes," I said. They did say that.

"Did you ever look at a pair of patent leather shoes?"

"I guess so."

"Do they reflect good enough that a boy could see all the way up your leg right to your whatzzis? Of course they don't. And who cares if they do?" She helped herself to some of our champagne. She drinks pretty steadily. Mostly wine. And smokes a couple of packs a day. She has a rasp in her throat and a hell of an attitude. I think she's a good antidote to me.

"What are you trying to say?"

"I'm trying to say that I could see from across the room the way he was looking at you. Plus I could see the way you were looking at him. Plus he's good-looking and he has really great taste in clothes. Plus he's a famous director who works all the

47

time and you are a wonderful actress who doesn't. I don't mean to be mercenary about this, honey, but there is no reason you can't be to him what Diane Keaton was to Woody Allen."

"What if I turn out to be Mia Farrow?"

"If you're gonna fall in love with a guy, you're gonna get fucked over. That's just the way it is. None of 'em are any damn good over the long haul. But if you can get five or six great parts out of the guy—and have a little fun—before he fucks you over, you're doing better than most of us. You're an actress. What's getting your heart broken, compared to playing the lead in *Broadway Danny Rose* and *Purple Rose of Cairo?*"

Alan came back in the door before Willie could say anything more subversive except, "It's so exciting."

I really don't know what we ordered for dinner. I certainly didn't taste it. We did go through another bottle of champagne. Which is quite a lot for me. When we were done Alan offered me a lift home in the limo. I went. Even though I don't go out with married men. When I was married and I met a single man who liked to go out with married women, we created a lot of turmoil and pain. I still feel like I wear a scarlet *A* on my breast. Even if that feeling is old-fashioned, arcane nun-school baggage, that is what I feel. Alan was, however, a perfect gentleman. We just talked and laughed. We laughed a lot, more than I had since I couldn't remember when.

When the limo pulled up to my door, he leaned over and kissed me. It was a very light kiss. Not dry. Not wet. It left me wanting more. Much more. But it was over as quick as it started. And that's all there was that night.

From her name on down. Glenda. You can tell from the cadence and sound of it, the glutinous *G*, like glockenspiel or globule, that this is the doormat at home, that out there, in the exciting, sexy part of the script, there is the Other Woman, hot, independent, witty, stimulating, provocative, tough, and endearing, everything that *Guh*-lenda is not.

I was in seven sequences.

I first appear in scene ten.

INT: TONY'S BATHROOM, EARLY MORNING
Shaving cream squirts out of a can into a small hand. The hand belongs to WAYNE, not quite six, Glenda's son. He solemnly puts the shaving cream on his face as if he actually needed to shave. He hands the can up, which reveals . . . TONY, standing beside him. Tony lathers his face. He opens the medicine cabinet, takes out a bladeless razor or razor

with a guard over the blade, hands it to Wayne, then takes a bladed razor for himself.

GLENDA enters with a freshly ironed shirt on a hanger. She looks at the two of them. With a straight face she walks between them, picks up the shaving cream.
She lathers her face as the other two watch. Everyone keeps a straight face. Tony hands Glenda a razor. Tony looks in the mirror, tilts his head to begin shaving. Glenda and Wayne follow suit, precisely.

Cute.

Note the freshly ironed shirt. A woman caring for her man. And how will he pay her back?

In the next scene, which Alan was magnanimous enough to let me have, even though I didn't appear in it, Tony explains to Wayne, in a manly way, that he's going off on a case. Then Tony says farewell to Glenda. What does she do? She begs him not to screw around because she figures he subscribes to the theory that "under five minutes or out of town doesn't count." Why does she think he has such an insensitive attitude? Because he goes around saying so.

Is she right?

Well, even as their conversation at home continues as a voice-over, the action reveals that one of Tony's bosomy ex-girlfriends is at the airport waiting for him. They exchange significant glances. This isn't even the main Other Woman that Tony—I am certain, even without actually seeing the whole script—has the hot sex and slobber scenes with.

So as I'm reading my very first lines of dialogue, I feel like yelling at the character, "Kick him out, or any grief you get, you deserve." I can tell a man wrote this.

The next sequence I appear in, scenes eighty to eighty-three, takes place in the country. Glenda, Tony, and Wayne have a picnic that turns into a food fight. First she "tsk-tsks," but then she joins in. She isn't a total drip, but would be if she could be. Then she and Tony have a sunset and a kiss.

Then there is a scene in which I receive a phone call from him. Nothing in my "page" of the script to indicate what it's about.

Then my big scene, the one that I did in the audition, in which I discover that he's making it with his client. That Other Woman, who gets all the hot scenes. But I make myself pretend that it's not happening because he bleeds a little. I don't like this person being perpetuated on the screen.

Finally there is a set of scenes that begin with my watching Tony put my son, Wayne, to bed. Then I tell him, actually it's more like begging and nagging, to quit the case because of the Other Woman. Then I find out he's going to spend a weekend with her. I warn him not to. And *at last,* I pack his bags for him and hand them to him.

I happened to know from reading the sequel that she takes him back. The movie doesn't even bother to show that. And why bother. It's obvious from everything that she is just the sort who would.

What did I want to do? Did I really want to understand this woman and tell the audience about her?

"I'm going to change her. Right now," I said to my agent, Martha Fiel, who was happily faxing contract revisions back and forth. At last I was justifying the four hours and forty-five minutes of overtime she and her office had invested in my career. I had left her, to move upward, and be represented by the legendary, and oily, old Viennese schmoozer and deal slicer, Bobby Motzkin. Actors always believe that if they just had a powerful enough agent it would finally make their career happen and they would, at last, get the parts they deserved. Those great, meaty, glamorous parts, that, in addition, also happen to pay oodles of money.

Part of being a legendary agent seems to be that you don't actually busy yourself with actually doing business unless it involves an immediate deal with at least six and preferably seven figures. The day-to-day business of trying to get auditions for actors who just wish they were working, on anything, as anything, is left to subagents.

What I didn't know was that Bobby had a sort of sublegend about his subagents. He hated to pay them a lot of money, so he didn't. As a result, they were either terrible and after a brief stint he fired them, or they were good and could get more money if they worked somewhere else and, being agents, they realized that, and quite promptly went somewhere else.

The most recent hireling was Martha, the agent I'd left to join his agency. My Great Leap Upward had taken me right to where I'd jumped from. I don't know what that proves. If anything.

"Don't," Martha said.

"Don't what?"

"Don't change her."

"She needs changing."

"It would be good if this were the first of many roles."

"Of course it would. And the sun rises in the east."

"You're a wonderful actress, really you are," Martha said. "I felt that when you were with me before and I feel it now."

"Thank you."

"But you know how businesslike Mr. Motzkin is."

"How businesslike is Mr. Motzkin?"

"I'm going to let you in on something."

"OK."

"But not a word of this outside this office, all right?"

"Sure."

"Well, when Mr. Motzkin hired me, at a very attractive salary, I might add, he did so because he wanted me to shape up this office. That is, cut out the nonproductive clients. That's the hardest thing in the world to do. Because you are all people, all of you actors. But when the numbers speak, they don't lie. What I had to do was calculate each client as revenue, if you know what I mean, revenue generated, versus overhead incurred and, well, make sure all our clients had right equations. Right up until you got hired for this job . . ."

"Yes?"

"You had a bad equation."

"So?"

"So you have a chance. Take it. Don't rock the boat."

"Who do you think I am? Guh-lenda?"

"Huh?"

"You think this is about business and deals and getting along. Well, maybe for an agent it is. And it should be. But not for a true actor. I don't act to put things out there that shouldn't be out there. If something needs changing, I'm going to stand up for it."

"Here's a deal memo," Martha said. "We probably won't get the actual contract for a week or so. You have to call the production office to get your schedule."

"Fine," I said, determined to do everything in my power to improve this dreadful character. I just couldn't bring myself to like her. She was a masochist and a female masochist, which is the worst kind.

"You know, when I look at you," Martha said, "I get this terrible feeling that I'm watching Dustin Hoffman in *Tootsie*. Someone who's so sure they're right about Art and Acting that there is absolutely no restraining them."

"I admire Dusty. And people like Robert De Niro. Because there is no restraining them. They know that if it's not worth doing right, it's not worth doing." I didn't mention the conversation outside Fern's office, the dinner together, and especially not the kiss in the car. That was personal between Alan and me. I knew that Alan understood me and respected my dedication to exactly that, acting as an Art. Though we hadn't said so explicitly, I knew this was going to be a true collaboration.

"Look, I'm going to say this because I care about you and I think you could have a career. *Tootsie* was a movie. This is real life. Integrity is good. Working is better. Find a way to combine the two so that everyone around you is happy."

I managed to smile and say, "Thanks for handling all of the business end of it."

53

"You're welcome," Martha said.

What did she know? Before she was an agent she was a stewardess.

Production offices are usually temporary places. They exist from preproduction through wrap, sometimes through postproduction, sometimes not. They're invariably frantic and full of coffee. They used to be full of smoke and ashes, but not so much anymore. As anyone who reads the credits on a film must realize, it has become normal to form a company almost every time a film is made. I don't understand why, but that's how it seems to be done. This one was called Free Ride Pictures. They rented space in the Film Center building on Ninth Avenue between Forty-fourth and Forty-fifth streets. There was a cheap coffee shop downstairs and there used to be a wonderful New Orleans style restaurant as well, called Jezebel's. But Jezebel went to Paris.

Directors and assistant directors have the same word in their titles and they are both in the same union, but they are very different creatures indeed. Directors must have charisma, or at least enough salesmanship to have convinced one or several people to let them use huge amounts of money to make a motion picture. They have to have done this at one point when they have never made a film before, and then again, in all probability, after that first film lost every nickel invested in it. They are supposed, especially by French theorists who call them *autuers*—literally authors, a concept that screenwriters in particular resent—to be the heart and soul of the collaboration that is a motion picture. They must be able to recognize or to create a story that is cinematic, have an ability to tell a story in visual images, possess a knack for selecting actors as well as art directors, composers, editors, and then be politic enough to work with all of those people while somehow convincing the very nervous people who put up the money that it's all right.

On the other hand, the most important quality of an assistant director is to display no fine feathers, never to give any sign that he or she wishes to rise above his or her station. ADs are there to translate the director's wishes into orders that a variety of technicians, performers, and traffic managers will then carry out. They are rather like mobile executive secretaries, same functions, but no desk. Second assistant directors work for the first assistant director. They do a lot of clerical work, they cue extras and hold traffic. They make a lot of money compared to most normal jobs, not much compared to directors.

A second AD named Eddie was there to give me my schedule. He seemed very nice and very calm as well. He had schedules and call sheets for me. I was to go out to the studio in Astoria, Queens, immediately. That's where the film was presently shooting. But I was not going to see Alan. I was going to meet the heads of the wardrobe, hair, and makeup departments.

"Plan to stay late. Joey Branco, he's the second unit director, he'll shoot some screen tests of you."

"Screen tests? Am I cast or not?" Does it never stop? Was this one of those *yes, you're cast, but not until after the* . . . I'm slender and have light eyes that change color with their environment. I have red hair and a redhead's complexion. A few years ago I was sent on a call where the character was described as slender, gray-eyed, fair, and redheaded. Out of the hundreds of skinny Nordic and Irish and Lucille Ball types— many of them, obviously, red for that day only—I was finally cast. So the casting director told me. But by the time I got to my agent's office and she called to confirm it, I had been uncast and replaced. The film was made. One evening, when a social situation made it impossible for me to avoid viewing it, I discovered that the person who had replaced me was Whoopi Goldberg.

"The tests are for wardrobe and makeup, not for you."

"Oh, fine. I thought, maybe . . ."

"Oh, no. Not at all."

"Good. When am I meeting with Alan?"

"Let's see, let's see," he said, looking through his pages and notes. "You're back in tomorrow—maybe—after they view the dailies on your tests. That's Wednesday. Then you've got two days of shooting, Monday and Tuesday, that's scenes ten and twelve. Then . . . nothing, nothing, until the following week, the upstate location, we'll go up by bus or limo . . . that's your scenes eighty, eighty one, two, and three. It would be simpler, and cheaper, to . . . but Alan likes to shoot as much in sequence as possible. Then you have a week off and you're in the studio the following week."

"What about rehearsals?" If it had been another director I might not have expected or asked for them. Strange as it sounds, a lot of directors just sort of throw actors onto the set, like tossing dice down on the felt of the craps table, and figure that out of the tumble and roll they'll come up with something. But years of publicity had nurtured the legend of DeLucca the actors' director who *rehearsed*.

"Rehearsals?"

"Yes," I said.

"Well. Rehearsals."

"When do I have them?"

He looked through his schedules and notes. He didn't seem to be finding anything.

"Walk-throughs? Run-throughs?"

"Uh, perhaps . . . I, uh . . . on set. Go right from rehearsals to shooting," he said. He wasn't sure if he'd made a statement or asked a question.

Was the legend a lie? Was it the force of circumstance? Or had someone forgotten? Or had the person who was responsible for scheduling decided that it was one more headache best left ignored and let the actor scramble to get out of the pit by herself. "What about meeting with Alan?" I asked.

"Alan?"

"The director."

"Oh. Mr. DeLucca. Uh . . . let me see . . . I . . . uh . . . don't have anything."

"Don't you think I should speak to him?" Something must have been misplaced or overlooked. I understood that he was directing a film and had a lot to do, but I also remembered the touch of his lips on mine. I knew Alan would want to see me as much as I wanted to see him.

"I don't see how that . . . there's nowhere on the schedule . . ." He continued to go through his various papers. They had looked very neat and organized when we began. "I guess I could talk to Mitzi. . . ."

"Mitzi?"

"Mitzi's the first AD. Alan uses her on all his pictures."

He said that with a certain obedient awe. Clearly it was Mitzi who had hired him and clearly he hoped she would hire him again.

"Oh, here," he said. *Here* was a scrap of yellow paper, a piece of Post-It.

"Oh, good," I said.

"I'm supposed to arrange for you to rehearse with Rain."

"Rain?" All my scenes were with Tony and he was being played by Choice Wardell. Who the hell was Rain?

"Rain Popko," Eddie said as if it answered my question. "Over the weekend."

"Why on the weekend?"

"He has school during the week."

"School?"

"His mother prefers that he not miss school unless he's actually shooting."

Oh, yes. I'd forgotten. The Wayne character. Glenda's son. It's not that a woman's son is not important to her. It's just that Glenda had all of two lines with her son: "Stop that." And "Wayne!" It wasn't much to rehearse. Plus, I must confess, I am not all that fond of children. I didn't like them when I was one. I didn't like them now. I didn't look forward to having one or, God forbid, more, of my own. On those occasions when I have inadvertently spent time with them, they've been loud, messy, and frequently illiterate. When they appear in public places their primary interaction with adults seems to involve whining, crying, and screeching performed in such a way that the adults whine, cry, and screech in return. On stage or on set, they're usually little hams, using cute the way Barrymore used to use his eyebrows, to upstage and undermine anyone else who had the temerity to try to act in his vicinity. I was desperately in need of time with the star, the person with whom I really played my scenes, and with the director, who I hoped would help me, or at least allow me, to actually make something of this pathetic, begging, beige-wearing, wimp of a woman, and the second assistant director had nothing for me but a scrap of colored paper with stickum on the back that was instructing me to go off and play with a six-year-old.

Eddie issued me some petty cash to take a cab out to Astoria.

Alan would be out there and once he saw me we could begin to put things right. On the cab ride over I took a pen and notebook and made notes about Glenda.

When I arrived in Astoria I was sent to another temporary production office. This one had the old-fashioned reek of tobacco. I was eager not only to see Alan, but to see how this legendary director worked. But it was a closed set.

At least, I thought, I would catch up to him when they broke for lunch. But at lunchtime he and the cinematographer and the producer went to look at dailies. Lunchtime also meant that the heads of the makeup, wardrobe, and hair departments could break from set and come to the insert stage to examine me and attempt to determine how I should be rebuilt. They all brought food with them. I thought I caught a glimpse of Alan's head passing the other way down the hall. It might have been someone else. Was I reading him so wrong?

I was suddenly inundated with attention. Not as a person or actress, but as an object to be photographed. The hair person, crunching through a salad with rabbit intensity, wanted to plop variously colored wigs on my head. Neal, head of makeup, had a pastrami sandwich thick as a forearm with a whole kosher pickle on the side. It crunched as loud as a cartoon apple each time he bit into it. Fanchon, the stylist, and Rubio, the head of wardrobe, both had plates of an unidentified trendy-food. They all drank coffee, except Rubio, who had blackthorn tea, and talked to each other about me.

The second unit cameraman snapped a couple of shots of me, using a Nikon with a Polaroid back. Then he told the gaffer to tell the electricians to move some lights.

A wardrobe assistant rolled a wheeled table covered with blouses and fabric swatches alongside me. He held them up below my chin, one after another, while Rubio and Fanchon argued which color and fabric made me look best and if best was indeed what they wanted.

A pockmarked man with piercing brown eyes walked up and stared at me. I have never heard of brown eyes described as piercing. Piercing eyes are always blue or black. I have never heard of cold brown eyes either. But these were brown, piercing, and cold. I would have cast this guy as a serial killer and I felt like the victim-to-be. "Good afternoon," he said in a cultured voice that sounded strange in his hit man face. "I'm Joey Branco, second unit director. I'm going to work with you on the screen test today. It's primarily for them." He gestured in a way that made them seem less important and reassured me. "Are there any particular lines you'd like to work with?"

"Lines?"

"Yeah, lines. Might as well get your voice down on tape. Sound man's request."

"I guess I'll do the scene I auditioned with."

"Fine. You know the lines?"

"This all just happened . . . I . . . Nobody told me . . ."

"Don't worry about it. We'll do like a couple of lines at a time. That good for you?"

"That'll be fine."

I knew that Fern had gone on auditioning after I'd left. I knew that Lucy Kohl would pull every string she could to get her part back, if she got out of rehab. Why wouldn't Alan see me? The more everyone reassured me that the test was for my clothes and makeup, the less I believed them. The less I believed, the more Glenda eluded me.

My first day's shooting was a disaster.

6

The party, although it was a gracious gesture, courtesy of Willie, did not relieve my anxiety. She invited a bunch of our actor friends and some of my detective buddies. Andrew was there, not working, just to see me and congratulate me. Sonny came because he's my partner and partners care. Duke came because he figured there would be actresses there who would be more like what he thought actresses were than what he had discovered I am. That is to say, people with large breasts. Most of the detectives have an old-fashioned ideal of femininity.

"So I guess I'm gonna lose my partner," Sonny said, holding a double Scotch in a large hand, a voice as full of gravel as Lee Marvin's. There were thick rings on his fingers, heavy gold around his neck and his wrists. He was doing all right at the track, nothing was in hock. Smoke curled from his perpetual cigarette.

"Well," I said, thinking of my screen test, "I might be back before you know it."

"Nah. Once Hollywood discovers you, you'll be making too much money for the SAD squad."

We raised our glasses and touched them together. "To the SAD squad. Special Antiadultery Division."

"Your friend Willie," Sonny said, "I think she's interested in me."

Some women might have said, *How's your wife?* or *How're Caren and Mercedes?* That's what Glenda, President Emeritus of the League of Whining Women, would've said. What I did say, finally, was "Sonny, you gotta help me here. Help me to understand. How do they . . . why do they accept it, Caren and Mercedes, and your wife, knowing that every time you're not actually in their sight, you're with some other woman?"

"What's to understand?"

"I would leave you in two seconds flat."

Sonny looked thoughtful. He's a determined underachiever but he's very smart. He swirled his Scotch, took a healthy swig of it. "What I think you gotta realize, Annie . . ."

"Yeah?"

"You're my friend, you're my partner. I told you, you're the first woman friend I ever had, I wasn't making it with. Caren, Mercedes, my wife, Duke's wife, all of them, they're regular. The thing is, it's *you* that's different."

"What does that mean?"

"You got a boyfriend?"

"Uh, not right now."

"Not right now. You looking?"

"I have had boyfriends. There's nothing wrong with me. I'm just not in the market for one right now."

"Most women, if they don't have someone, they're in the market. Lots of times even when they have someone, they're in the market. Actually, women, when they set their minds to it, they're better at cheating than men are. All the plotting and organizing. They have the minds for it, and the time for it, especially if they're not working."

I didn't understand. I didn't agree. I gave him a kiss on the cheek and said, "I'll miss you."

I wondered if I would indeed miss being a detective. It had started as a way to make money that was a lot more interesting than being a waiter while I waited to get working at what I actually am, which is an actress. And, if things followed here in New York the way they had in L.A., then once I started working as an actor, I wouldn't stop. There are two talents involved in acting. One is doing the job, the other is getting the job. There are lots of ways to approach both. I'm not good, normally, at auditioning and hustling and shmoozing. Virtually all my work— with the exception of Glenda and my first job when I went to L.A.—had come from jobs I'd done before. Either people I'd worked with or who had seen me. I had left L.A. for personal reasons, not career reasons. After I broke up with my lover, the lover that I'd broken up with my husband to be with, I wasn't going to be comfortable with less than a full continent between us. Women are like that. In my opinion. Which seemed, at the moment, to be different than everyone else's.

"Whatcha worryin' about?"

"This part," I said. "I still don't think I have a handle on it."

"You'll figure it out."

"What if I don't?"

"Don't worry about it," he said. "Do what you do, and you'll do all right."

The detectives were so different from my actor friends. From anyone I'd known in my life, for that matter. Actors live on dreams and hope. A callback is cause for celebration. The first and last time I got excited about a callback in front of Sonny he said, "So how much they pay you for one of these callbacks?" I guess dealing with corpses has a way of deflating your excitement over the possibility of getting to play make-believe. It works the other way too. Every time an actor gets a part he treats it like it'll make or break him. Like it's life and death. Which of course it is emphatically not. Detectives know better. Even if they screw up a homicide investigation, which even the best do from time to time, it doesn't shake them up too badly. They know another corpse'll come along soon. My association with Sonny and Duke and the guys didn't just alter my behavior around them, saving my actorish reactions for my actor friends, it changed me, and something ever so slightly bleaker, and more clear-sighted, entered my soul. As the night went on, I watched Sonny smoking and drinking, the way that he probably had every day of his life since puberty. He seemed untouched by it. But I knew, and he had to know, that it would turn and smite him all at once, heart attack or cancer or the like, taking some quotient of his life away. Was I too romantic if I thought that he thought that that was probably all right, that he was surprised enough that he'd lived as long as he had, that he'd just figure he'd done all right making it however far he made it?

Andrew was the only one of my actor friends that I told how troubled I was about doing Glenda and whether or not DeLucca, who had still not spoken to me again, had someone else in the wings. Should I have done something else, something more in the backseat of that limo? Thrust my tongue into his mouth? Hiked up my skirt and ripped out the crotch in my pantyhose and screamed, "Oh, Mister Director! I want you! I need you! Stick your dick in me! I don't know where it's been, but go right ahead. I'm just a slut of an actress and you know we all fuck for parts." Was that what this was about? I would have talked to Willie about it also. I trust Willie with feelings of confusion and anxiety. In many ways that's what her life is about, and very loudly as well. But she was too busy running the bar and having both Duke and Sonny trying to work their way to direct contact with her breasts, for serious girl talk.

Andrew was very sympathetic. He offered to go over the part with me and rehearse with me and whatever else I wanted.

In the end, Willie went home with nobody and I shared a cab to the Upper West Side with Andrew. Away from the din and the smoke and booziness, I realized that he seemed profoundly uneasy and distressed. I asked him what was wrong. He said he was just feeling moody. I didn't believe him. The cab stopped at his house first. I'm not sure why, but when he got out, I said I'll get out too, and I sent the cab away.

"What are you doing?"

"I'm not going away until you tell me what's wrong."

He invited me up to his apartment. A studio in a brownstone. It was clean and tidy, rather like Andrew himself, with two modern paintings hung on the wall and several old-fashioned prints in frames. He had shelves and shelves of books. He poured us each another glass of wine. An unremarkable Chablis, I think. Finally he told me the last thing in the world I wanted to hear, that he was HIV-positive. "I'm so ashamed," he said. "I don't know how to deal with it. I'm too ashamed to talk about it." Which meant that he wanted, above all, to talk about it. It made my problems seem as trite as they were. We talked. We cried. Finally, Andrew decided he would pretend he could cope with it.

The sky was getting light when I left and it was dawn by the time a cab brought me home. When I got upstairs I found a message on my answering machine. Alan had called. He wanted me to meet him for breakfast. "How about 7:00?" the tape said, "at the Omni Hotel." I looked at the clock. It was 6:15. I hadn't slept and I assumed that I looked it. I have to admit I am past the age, if there ever was one, where a girl looks better for not having slept all night.

It was time for a shower and serious makeup work. When I got to breakfast I would have to see to it that I sat with the light behind me.

7

Alan had fresh-squeezed orange juice. It has a special color. Different than the stuff that's had its water removed, different water put in, pasteurized, and put in a container with a shelf life that's as long as it takes to sell it. He had a bowl of fresh fruit—oranges, apricots, grapes, and peaches—a slice of dry toast from some sort of stone-ground health loaf, and a cup of very aromatic coffee. I had the same, except that I had an herbal tea instead of the coffee.

He asked me who my ideal was. Before I realized that he must have mean *as an actor*, and must have expected a reply like Laurette Taylor, Bette Davis, Eleonora Duse, someone like that, I blurted out, "Saint Joan."

"Why?" he asked. Taking me seriously. Not laughing or making a joke because I'd suddenly revealed a part of me that was real. The realest real parts are not for public viewing. The truest aspects of ourselves are all fools, each and every one of them,

vain and posturing, too good for this world or lowly and cow-
ering, devastatingly childish, weak, fearful, and crude. Husbands
and wives are not to be trusted with them. That's weapons-grade
uranium. Stuff to bust open the best defenses, blow up the stron-
gest egos, make desolate the tenderest of loves. It's not for casual
acquaintances—or even for friends—it's the mask of truth, it
marks you as weird, and turns them away.

No. There are only two places for naked revelation. In performance, where there is the pretense of making the revelation
about someone else, some fictional, non-existent person who
won't have to bear the pain and embarrassment of their truth
being known, where not making the revelations is to fail. The
other is when you're falling in love. Or infatuation. Not *in love*,
then it's too late. In that initial period when you're still strangers
and too flush with desire to perform cruel acts of judgment.

I found myself talking about the growing up in Catholic
school. I didn't tell him the usual stories about how parochial
parochial school was, bigoted and dogmatic, destructive of intellectual appetites and a child's eager curiosity and interest in
the world. I told him about when I was too young to know that,
when I believed in their magic and I looked for signs from God
and more than once fell down on my knees in a great empty
meadow in visionary ecstasies.

Of course I moved away from the Church. And was very
angry at the nuns who slapped me and taught me to diminish
myself and tried to turn us all into sexual cripples. But I do have
a spiritual life. What might be called New Age. I had one boyfriend who called me a Shirlite. A Shirlite—he made this up and
thought it was very clever—was anyone who could read Shirley
MacLaine and believe it. It's easy to mock, but it's clear to me
that the spiritual dimension exists, that it is very important, and
to live without it would be empty. There must be roads to it and
they must be many and various.

Alan didn't mock.

He told me a story about a story. When he was young and in
college, in the days of Timothy Leary, *turn on, tune in, drop out,*

when hallucinogenics were regarded as divine wafers—as well as fun, he admitted—he'd partaken and from there flirted with Eastern religions or at least with their ideas, in the mode of Leary's partner in research, Richard Alper, who became Baba Ram Dass and wrote such books as *Be Here Now.*

"Have you ever read Rudyard Kipling?"

"No," I said.

"He's not fashionable. But he is a wonderful storyteller. I came across a story of his. This was at a point where things had gotten pretty intense. Pretty mystical in a drug-induced sort of way. And dropping out was a very attractive option. I read a story called *The Miracle of Purun Bhagat.* It starts out by saying that Purun Bhagat was Brahmin of the highest caste. This is the India of the early British Empire. Purun Bhagat was wealthy and educated and became the prime minister of one of the native states. He was cultured and multilingual and progressive. He went to England where he was honored by the learned societies, he was given honorary degrees and a knighthood. But then, in his sixtieth year, he did something that no Westerner would ever dream of doing.

"He walked away from it all. He put aside power and wealth and worldly honors. He shaved his head, put on saffron robes, and took up the begging bowl of the *saddhu.* For—and this is the key thing—'he had been, as the old law commands, twenty years a student, twenty years a warrior, although he had never held a weapon in his life, and twenty years the head of a household. Now it was time to put worldly things aside and commence the final journey. . . .'

"This struck a powerful chord in me. There was something in me that said that the acid road, turn on, tune in, drop out, was too easy. Even the spiritual road, without acid, was giving up, not walking away from. I would have to win on the material plane in order for me to embrace the spiritual and know that I was not doing it because I was afraid to compete. I had to know that inside.

"Of course the danger in winning is winning. It's easy to give up worldly things when you don't have them, when you're a loser. It's harder when you're a winner. It's very easy to get attached to wealth and glamour and power and sex and all of this—which I admit I love—that comes with making movies, with being a successful filmmaker. You know what's the most seductive of all—the joy of making things. Things that are hard to make. Both technically and artistically difficult, and dancing over the abyss of failure and making them happen and when you're done: there is a book or a bridge or a movie or jet that exceeds the speed of sound. They're all things that could—even should—crash and burn. But they don't—because you managed to make them work.

"So maybe I am caught in the dance.

"My hero—in this Western material world—was always John Huston. He never stopped making movies. They had him breathing from an oxygen tank, riding in a wheelchair, and that beautiful sonuvabitch of a dirty old man with that wicked gleam in his eye was making movies almost till the day he died.

"Maybe when, as the old law commands, I'll have been twenty years a student, twenty years a warrior, and twenty years the head of a household, I'll be able to walk away and take what's left and go on the spiritual journey. And maybe I won't. Maybe I'll be weak and say, 'No, I want to make more movies, more money, more love.' I truly don't know."

Gosh. Wow. What was I supposed to say after that. Aside from, *I wish you weren't married so I could fall into your spiritual arms right now.* I think I gazed at him for rather a long time.

It was Alan who broke the silence. "Would you like some more tea," he said. "Or something more to eat?"

I pointed weakly to where the baked things were displayed. There were croissants and brioches, Danish and fruit tarts and custard tarts. There were honeyed rolls and crispy pastries in a variety of shapes laced with cinnamon or raisins or chocolate.

"Which?"

"The chocolate," I said.

The waiter came and told Alan there was a phone call for him and mentioned a name. Alan apologized, said he had to take it. I said I didn't mind. I was actually grateful when he left. It gave me time to regroup, think of the things that needed to be spoken of, and be prepared to be businesslike about it. I retreated to the Land of Preoccupation, which is where most of us live most of the time. Sometimes I think of it as a funny little country that has a border with border guards. They stand around and operate our eyes and ears and they make speeches for us so that we can appear to be present while we're actually somewhere inside worrying about laundry and bills and errands and love and life and death and betrayal and bounced checks.

When Alan returned to the table he too had gone back to Preoccupation.

"I want to talk to you about the part of Glenda," I said.

"Of course."

"As written . . ."

"What?"

"As written, what comes across is a typical female of insecure proportions. A clinging vine type and filled with anger. A masochist who just isn't enough to herself so she can't possibly be enough for her man, or any man actually. She wants to be punished. She is intelligent but has not yet been enlightened to anything. No sense of humor."

"Is that how you want to play it?"

"No."

"Good."

"This woman is at a turning point," I said. He nodded. An *ummm* nod, a nod devoid of meaning. "This woman," I went on, "who appears coldly in control has something unspeakable going on in her heart or head, in her soul."

"Torment?" he said, casual as a cop being clever during an interrogation. The sound was so neutral it filled me with confusion and—although it's a very strong word—fear. Was I being judged still? Again? The endless audition? One wrong move and phone Fern and pull another Glenda out of the lineup?

"She needs to be made sympathetic."

"Of course," he said. Still with that utter neutrality.

"This woman is the epitome of inertia," I said. "Women like this have a tendency to just sit on a page and take up space. Where is the glee or bumps or surprise? Suburban beige, natural base, a little earthy shadow, lipstick the color of the inside of the lower lip, clear nail polish, taupe stockings, a muted mind, and brown eyeliner.

"Is that what I am? The wife in *Fatal Attraction*, there to make it obvious that her guy has *got* to screw around or die an early death of boredom.

"Is that how you want it played?" I asked.

"Is that how you see playing it?"

"It's your movie . . ."

"It's your part . . ."

"I thought you might want to tell me how you want it to work with your movie."

"I thought you were going to tell me how you were going to make the part yours."

"You're famous for working with actors and actually doing rehearsals," I said.

"I know. Fifteen years ago I had a PR guy, Ralphie Rosenberg, tell me, 'Tell 'em you love actors. The New York critics'll eat it up. Think you're serious. When you're in L.A., tell 'em you hate actors, you love stars. In L.A. they'll eat that up, because they think stars equal box office and box is what movies are about. In France tell them you hate everything and they'll think you're very deep.' Good advice."

"So it's just public relations?"

He looked at his watch. He had to be on set soon. It was only a question of how soon. "This weekend," he said, "why don't you rehearse with Rain. He's a good little actor. He's eight, *going on nine*. Wayne was originally six. We changed it because we liked Rain so much. Dennis Murphy will set it up for you." Murphy was the production manager.

It wasn't what I hoped to hear. "I'm sorry," he said, "that we couldn't spend more time talking about the role. I know that's what you want. Maybe before we do the next sequence you're in, the out-of-town scenes. I should be more disciplined about my time but I wanted to get to know you. And then that damned phone call. I am sorry that I had to take your time to deal with it. I really did have to take it. It was my attorney. It looks like my separation is turning into a divorce." He sounded regretful.

"Oh. That's too bad," I said.

When Rain Popko smiled the whole world smiled too. Although his smile was innocent, it was also amoral. The only other actor, the only other person, I've ever seen that had a smile that was so completely without shame was Harpo Marx.

"How do you want to work on this?" I asked him.

Since we only had two lines together, but both had additional scenes to play with Choice, we decided that we would each play Tony for the other. "Then I'll play Glenda," Rain said, "and you play Tony."

That sounded like something to do.

When Rain played Tony he did a Choice Wardell imitation that belonged on "Saturday Night Live." It was hilarious. It was deadly. He had the voice, the heir-of-Brando stare, and the I'll-out-Pacino-you-Al attitude. I was in stitches.

When we switched I tried to top him, but I couldn't. He knew it. It pleased him immensely. He was smug about it. But he was eight, going on nine, and I had to let it not bother me.

Then he played Glenda. His imitation of me playing the part was as deadly as what he had done with Choice. So I got him back with a Rain Popko doing Choice Wardell imitation. It was the most fun I had had acting in years. Before we even knew it, our four hours were up. His mom came knocking on the door and took him away.

We did it again on Sunday and this time I was looking forward to it. Rain was lovable. And he knew it. That's what he kept that smile around for. I was sort of infatuated with him. There was a great relief in having loving feelings toward someone that didn't involve sex. And especially didn't involve sex with someone else's husband. Just looking forward to hanging out, having fun, doing actor stuff. I could see where I would enjoy going to the park or the museum with this kid. Or going to the movies or sneaking chocolate bars.

It opened a door in me that I didn't even realize I had shut. Behind it was the love room. Place of light, delight, turmoil, disappointment, betrayal.

We decided to do some improvs, extending the scenes we had. First there was the opening shaving scene. Then Tony sends Wayne off to school, then Tony says good-bye to Glenda.

We restructured it this way—Tony says good-bye to Wayne at home. Then Wayne stays and watches Glenda's good-bye. Then, we improvise Glenda sending Wayne off to school. The first time it was kind of cute—*I want to be a detective just like Tony, chase bad guys, he's just like a hero on TV* and his mom says, *That's nice but it might be better to be a lawyer or doctor or college professor*—but boring, boring. "Let's find some more conflict," I said. So we tried it again. This time we had a little confrontation about what he should be when he grew up and how much he had to study in school. Which I understand to be pretty standard mom/son dialogue. Boring, boring, and boring.

"You want real conflict, some real nitty-gritty?" my adorable little guy said.

"Sure," I said. "Go for it."

He flashed me that imp's grin and went to the far side of the room. He put his arm against the door frame and leaned his forehead into his arm in a moody and dramatic pose. Just as I realized he was doing Burt Reynolds in *Deliverance,* which was the last time Burt tried to do serious drama and be one of the heirs-to-Brando, Rain winked and flashed me that smile. Then he went back into his pose

When he came out of it he wasn't smiling. His lower lip stuck out. Pouty. Not pouty sexy like a male model in a jeans ad, pouty obnoxious like a kid.

"What is it?" I—Glenda—said.

"Nothin'."

"Wayne, tell me what's bothering you."

"Nothin'."

"Come on, Wayne," I said in a motherly way, patronizing perhaps, but he was eight. I squatted down so we'd be eye-to-eye. "I'm your mom, you can talk to me."

"No."

"Wayne . . ." I said, patient as only a mom can be.

"All right. Don't blow this, bitch!"

"What?"

"You heard me."

"How dare you speak to me that way."

"First you tell me I can talk to you," he said in that horrid mimicky-mocky way that children have, "and then you say, *How dare you speak to me that way.*"

"All right," I said, getting hold of myself like a caring mom would and trying to find our why her son is so angry. "Tell me why you're so angry."

"I told you."

"Explain it a little better."

"Don't blow it, bitch. Don't nag at him, don't bitch at him, don't drive him away, like you did my dad."

"I didn't drive your dad away. . . ."

"Fuck you, you did too. Now I got a new one and I don't want you to blow it."

"I don't think it's up to me . . . I mean up to you to tell me . . ."

"Bitch, bitch, fucking bitch," he yelled at me, snarled at me. "You're going to do it. Drive him away. Well, I'll go with him. I don't want to be with a whiny nag, can't keep a man."

"It's a lot more complicated than that. . . ."

"The fuck it is." My adorable imp was a loathsome troll, vicious and mean. I was as hurt as if he'd spoken to me that way.

"And don't use that language."

"Fuck you, *Mom.* Get Tony to shut me up, cause you can't do it yourself."

That was it. I went to slap him across the face. Like my mother or father would've done to me.

The thought grabbed my arm and held it. I would not be them. Not even in an improv. That wasn't who I wanted to be, who I wanted Glenda to be. I forced myself to reach past the defiance and provocativeness of my son's attitude and look at his pain with love. I breathed deeply. I calmed myself. I squatted down again to be at his eye level. He wouldn't look at me. I reached out to put a reassuring arm on his shoulder.

He hit it away.

I was aghast. They're supposed to respond to love. Make nice, get nice back. It's supposed to be simple. I reached out, he slapped me down, well the hell with him. But not if I was Glenda, not if I was his mom. I would have to reach, and reach, and reach. My pain didn't, wouldn't, count. Only his. It wasn't stupid, like giving a man-lover that much power. It was necessary. Maybe I should have known all that, understood all that, simply by being told we were mother and son. But I've never been a mother and I didn't know it. It was obvious, but I'd been looking in the wrong directions—at actor things, at my career, at my feelings for Alan, my fears, at Glenda's relationship with Tony.

"What do you want me to do," I said, feeling inadequate and inept.

"Just keep him here," he said as if it was obvious. His attitude was whiny and resentful. It was ugly.

"I'll try," I said.

"You'll fuck it up," he yelled at me and ran away, into the other room. He sat on the floor and started to cry. I didn't go after him. I sat down on the couch and waited.

I didn't have to wait long. I heard some throat-clearing and some sniffling-back noises and after about a count of ten he came back. He was looking cocky. "What do you think? Pretty good? Intense, huh?"

"Yes," I said. "Very good."

"Pretty precocious."

"Very," I said.

He nodded. Very satisfied with himself. He came over to the couch and sat down beside me. I waited for him to say something more but he didn't. I put my arm around him and he accepted it. He leaned against me, then he started to cry. I just held him. I had rarely held a crying child before. After a while he stopped. "It would be really cool," he said, "to have a dad like Tony."

"It would?"

"Sure," he said. "To do guy stuff. Play ball. Show me how to shoot a gun. My mom's all right but . . ."

"But?"

"But it's a fucking revolving door when it comes to men. She doesn't think of me at all. She just thinks of herself. I wish she would find just one and keep him."

"Like Tony?"

"Yeah. He's a cool dude."

The next day we shot our scene.

8

I had been prepared to dislike Choice Wardell and I did. In person, he looked far too much like my ex-boyfriend, Rowdy Randolph. The one I left my husband for. The day after I arrived at Rowdy's house with my suitcase, he went off to a distant location to shoot a movie of the week. A bad one. He didn't invite me to join him on that distant location. But one of his tired old ex-girlfriends, more aggressive than me, paid her own airfare, showed up uninvited, and stayed for a week. The sort of friends who aren't really friends were quick to tell me about it and I knew about it even before he came home.

Actually, Choice was better-looking than Rowdy as well as looking better on film. At the moment, or when I last saw Rowdy, he could be described as a pretty boy starting to grow old. Although he had a perfect nose, there was also that heaviness at the bottom of his cheeks that made him look jowly. Perhaps as he ages he will look more and more like Richard Nixon. He deserves that.

I must admit that Rowdy was very athletic and had a terrific body, more so in person than on screen. Choice is the opposite, more screen presence than he has in person. Even if he weren't fit, he would have that ready-to-mix-it-up, tough-guy look.

Here we were, meeting for the first time. Like fighters at weigh-in. In a couple of hours we would be in front of the camera together as a couple. Two people in a sexual and domestic relationship, complicated and enriched by a child who needs us, loves us, both. It was our brief moment to get some kind of communication going.

He looked me over.

I don't know what he was looking for. An indication that he could have me the first evening he didn't have a poker game or a willing groupie? Whatever it was, he didn't see it and reacted to my greeting like a carnivore meeting a carrot. We went our separate ways and when we were called on set some hours later to be shown our places and do walk-throughs for camera, there was not a single spark between us.

It did not bode well.

There was a mirror in the shot. Shots with mirrors are complicated and time-consuming to set up. We spent another hour, at least, while the gaffers tweaked lights, the dolly grip moved the dolly, the construction grips moved the walls of the set, the prop people moved the props, wardrobe fussed with clothing, and makeup touched us up as we sweated under the lights. Actually, lights aren't as hot as they used to be because, a camera-person friend told me, the film is faster.

About halfway through Choice said, "Al, my man, don't we have a stand-in? Isn't that what money's for?"

"You're absolutely right," Mitzi said.

Choice walked off. Mitzi called the stand-in.

Ten minutes later, everybody was ready to shoot. Mitzi sent a production assistant to get Choice. He seemed irritated that he had to come back so soon.

"Places," Mitzi said. "Quiet and a run-through."

"You gonna shoot the run-through?" Choice said to Alan.

"I might," Alan said.

"Directors and their games," Choice said. "Directors are weird, you know that, Alan? You're a strange dude in there."

"Stand by," Mitzi called out, squaring her shoulder pads, daring anyone to be inattentive.

Makeup rushed forward and spread lather on Choice's face. She took away the barber's smock that covered him. Bare from the waist up, he stood in front of the set mirror. A lot of women find him very sexy. I didn't. But then, I was closer than they were.

"Camera," Mitzi called. Even if we weren't shooting film the camera crew would run through their move as a rehearsal.

"Speed," called the sound man, recording wild track and room tone even if there was synch sound.

"Action," Mitzi yelled.

Rain, as Wayne, reached out for the shaving cream. He was adorable. Then he turned his hero-worshipping eyes up at this jerk who played Tony. I really sort of loved the little guy—Glenda did love the little guy. I saw this egotistical, wiseass, cinema imitation of Sonny and Duke, through my kid's eyes. Sure, my little guy needed him. And I had brought him into the little guy's life.

Why? Because when I met him he . . . he made me hot. He made me feel womanly and sexy and other things I needed. He still did. Part of me realized I had trapped myself with the most obvious trap an actor can fall into—foreknowledge. I had been dealing with Glenda in terms of what was going to happen to her and how she was written to react. Hey, *Be Here Now.* Some past, no future, in the moment.

OK, Alan was who I really wanted, if I was to want someone, which I didn't because that room in my heart was more or less closed for the duration. But yes, I could see how I would want someone who would make me feel, make me feel, make me lose control. To keep him, I'd treat him right, just like any other woman who wanted . . . wanted to keep a man for the sake of her son who needed a role-model father figure . . . that was a cop-out excuse, that was bullshit . . . if I wanted the scene to play . . . just like any other woman who wanted . . . wanted love. Was willing to be hurt. Again and again. Didn't matter. Need that love. That wet, hungry, sleepy, weepy, cuddling, stupid, hot, and sexy love. I'd iron his goddamn dirty shirts for him.

I—Glenda—walked in with Tony's shirt in my hand. Crisp and ironed. Even though I had to get myself ready to go to work too. Didn't matter. I did it because I loved doing it for him. All that women's lib stuff has its place, in the checkbook, but not about ironing and making my man look good.

I saw, I could see, how my son, who was going to be a great big man some day, who came out of me in tears and pain, who has a smile that lights the world, I could see how he adored this Tony guy. Doing guy stuff with him. Pretending to shave. I loved my two guys. I picked up the shaving cream too and I put it on my face and I got a razor and Rain did an imitation of Choice Wardell doing Tony and I did an imitation of Rain doing Choice Wardell doing Tony.

I think someone was laughing—which was OK since it was not a synch scene—Mitzi hissed, "Quiet." Quite a hisser that Mitzi.

Tony thought he was just the sexiest guy in the world. Well, I was going to teach him a little bit about sexy. I took the shaving cream and squirted it on his chest. He looked down to see what I was doing, I turned to face him and rubbed my breasts against him. I wasn't wearing a bra and the shaving cream soaked my blouse and he had to feel me against him as clearly as if I were naked, except this way, of course, it was even more obscene.

"Mom," Wayne said. Eight-year-old boys don't like sex in moms. But if they want dads, they better understand it. That's what Glenda thought. I sort of agreed with Wayne.

The person that is inside of me that sits still and watches me, watched aghast. This was not something that I, Annie, would do, ever, in real life. It was also something that I disapproved of as an actor. An actor's art lies in the revelation of the layers and complexities of character, the nuance of voice, posture, timing, attitude, the trick of letting a person's inner thoughts seem to be legible on their face. It most emphatically is not about displaying body parts, wiggling your ass or throwing your tits around. People who do nude scenes and say they only did it because it was relevant, or in context with the character, or call it tasteful, are almost always willfully fooling themselves into doing what some salacious producer wants because he can't think of anything to sell tickets except T&A. So why was I doing this and where was it coming from?

Come on, kiss me, you fool, I thought at Choice, that is, Glenda thought at Tony. So she did have more going for her than I thought, glee and some bumps and she could throw a curve. Not bad for a too-tolerant, long-suffering, sort-of-nowhere woman who wore #10 makeup and had beige on her mind.

Yes, I said to myself, when Choice turned to face me. I turned my face toward him and—thinking of Alan—my lips swelled and moistened, my mouth opened, and both of us with faces covered with shaving cream, our chests wet with lather, sliding against each other . . .

"Mom," Wayne said.

He wasn't going to stop this. I picked up the can of shaving cream and—hoping there wasn't something horrible in it that would blind him for life—sprayed it in his face. He closed his eyes tight, looking funny as can be.

Then Tony and I kissed.

Wayne wiped the shaving cream off his face and, hands covered with white foam, watched us. Then he put his arms around the two of us and hugged us both. Hugged us tight. Hugged us as if he could hold us together forever that way.

The scene was over.

"Cut," Alan said.

"Cut," Mitzi said, louder for us all to hear.

Usually there is a sort of hubbub immediately after the director calls cut. Everyone relaxes, breathes, scratches, chews, or slurps. Everyone reports to someone else. Another focus check, a light meter reading on the background, did it look good through the camera? was the dolly move smooth? how was it for sound? how many feet of film were shot and how much was left in the magazine? another take? a different shot? do it the same? do it better? print it? any notes for the editors? it was good for me, was it good for you?

There was silence.

Then there was applause.

"I can't believe it," I said to Willie.

"What?"

"Any of it. That they applauded. You know crews. They are never impressed. I've near heard of a crew applauding."

"I told you you were great," Willie said. Dear sweet Willie.

"That wasn't me. That sex thing. When I think of it I'm . . ."

"What?"

". . . embarrassed."

"Little tits are cute sometimes."

"Willie!"

"You're such a prude, Annie."

"Yes, I am."

I could have been with a lot of people that night. I was suddenly very popular. Even Choice Wardell had altered his attitude toward me. He didn't get that it was Glenda who did that to him—not Annie—no way Annie would do that to him. Probably not in the privacy of her own home even if she were in love with him. I should have been home, getting beauty sleep. I had an early call the next day and the camera is very strict with people who don't get enough rest. I was full of excitement—and relief. I wanted to be with someone who would have loved me if I'd bombed. If I'd failed. A friend no matter what, not a newfound, who knows where they'll be when I'm down, friend.

"He really is remarkable," I said.

"Who? Choice? God," Willie growled, "I love his chest. Tell me what his kisses are like."

"No. Alan."

"Oh. Alan. Ohhhh."

"Not what you think . . ."

"Ohhhh?"

"As a director."

"Of course. As a director."

"I mean it, Willie. I thought he was just being another jerk who didn't know what he was doing. And leaving me to direct myself. But he kept telling me, over and over: 'Rehearse with Rain.' And that was the key, the way in. He really is a brilliant director. I mean it, Willie."

"Uh-huh. I thought you don't get involved with married men."

"I'm not talking about involved. I'm talking about an actor working with a director."

"Uh-huh."

"Besides . . ."

"Besides?"

"He got a call from his lawyer and . . ."

"And?"

"He's separated and now they're starting divorce proceedings."

"So you *are* going out with him."

"No."

"Seeing him."

"No."

"Well, why not?"

"Come on, Willie, he hasn't even asked me."

"Oh."

"Oh what?"

"And if he asks you?"

9

The next day we were scheduled to shoot scene twelve.

12: INT. THE APARTMENT, DINING AREA,
Glenda dressed for work. Tony is back to pick up his suitcase,
finish off a cold cup of coffee.

> TONY
> Hello, baby. Good-bye, baby.

> GLENDA
> Will you be good while you're out of town?

> TONY
> Whatever do you mean?

> GLENDA
> There is a certain school of thought,

among men, so I have heard, that out
of town doesn't count.

> ### TONY
> The line is, "under five minutes and
> out of town doesn't count."

> ### GLENDA
> I don't want a line. I want an answer.
> Are you going to be good?

> ### TONY
> Sure.

> ### GLENDA
> It's just that I seem to remember that
> you had an old girlfriend down there.

> ### TONY
> You have to stop being so insecure.
> It drives me up a wall. . . . Come on. . . .

He kisses her, a good erotic kiss, not a husband's peck. Glenda
responds but she also wants to keep talking about it.

> ### GLENDA
> I seem to recall it was one of . . .

EXT. NATIONAL AIRPORT, WASHINGTON, D.C. DAY
The dialog continues over, as TONY walks out of the airport,
to a waiting car, where Sandra sits. She is as described.

> ### GLENDA
> (voice-over)
> . . . your more intense infatuations.
> Sandra the therapist, smart and
> very buxom.

> ### TONY
> (voice-over)
> Buxom? . . .

GLENDA
(voice-over)
What kind of therapist was she?
A sex therapist?

TONY
(voice-over)
That was a long time ago. . . .
Before I even knew you.
Besides, she's happily married now.

GLENDA
(voice-over)
Make sure . . . you come back to me.

I had a lot of questions about the scene. Who is Sandra the buxom sex therapist? Is she really? Do they do it? Immediately? Or sooner? Am I a paranoid who happens to have real enemies? Or simply an insightful woman who knows her dog? Was I supposed to blend in with some concept of the film? Or chew up the scenery and act the other bitch off the screen?

When I arrived at the studio Alan didn't seem to be around. I found Mitzi, and I asked her if she could tell me about *this* Other Woman—who I suspected was not *the* Other Woman—or if I could ask Alan. Whatever I had done the day before, it seemed to have made a difference the morning after. "Sure," she said. "I'll tell Alan as soon as he comes in. That's the best time to talk to him. After that—clutter and clatter."

A little man, the sort who wants to be a big man, dressed in an expensive suit, came over. "We haven't met yet," he said. He stood as if standing straighter would make him unshort. It didn't. He held out his hand. I took it. "I'm Mitchell Du Bois. I'm the producer." He kept hold of my hand. "You know," he said, pulling me closer by hauling on my hand, "this is my project, my baby." He spoke intimately, intensely. "It was my energy, my vision, that made this happen." He grabbed hold of my elbow with his left hand. "It was my reader, in my development company, that first read the novel. It was me that negotiated it, that nursed it, that went after Larry Rhinebeck and said, 'Come to me, baby, come to me. Show me, make me see it, that there's a movie in here.' Cause what there was, was one terrific book, an exciting book, an action book. It won an award, a prestigious award. But that was after my option. I saw it first."

He vibrated constantly with suppressed energy or resentment. He released my hand only to swing around and take both my hands. "My project, my baby. I got Choice Wardell to say, yes, yes, I'll play Tony. Then I got Alan, I said Alan DeLucca, what you need, you need an action picture, action picture with a toucha noir, a toucha humor, a toucha smarts, with a twist or two, and have I got the book for you. Now I brought in you." He stepped closer and pulled me to him at the same time. There's a square dance step that's very close to the motion he created. "So welcome aboard. I want to tell you, I want to tell you, that was a hell of a scene, hell of an improvisation, you played yesterday. Saw the dailies, great dailies."

"Thanks," I said, finally easing my hands out of his grasp and stepping back. But that meant he could stare at my chest. Which he did.

"You wouldn't know to look at you, what a terrific body you have, terrific, and you wouldn't know to look at you. You save it for the camera, huh? I saw the dailies. They were great on camera."

Maybe I had made a mistake. Maybe sex scenes are so dominating to shallow minds that they are always gratuitous and that's why I've instinctively shied away from them. Would Mitchell Du Bois ever look at me and see an actor or would he always see nothing but creamed breasts?

He moved around to my side. He slung an arm over my shoulder. "You wanna know something about the story, about the characters, about who they are and what they do? Lemme take you to the horse's mouth, the man himself, who created them all and brought them to life on the page." He squeezed. "Come on," he said, sort of pushing me across the stage to the breakfast junk table where an apparently unemployed person stood in debate with himself, trying to decide, a bagel with a shmear of cream cheese and Nova Scotia salmon or the classical prune Danish, or perhaps, knowing they were free, whether it would look somehow undignified or too unrestrained to have both.

"This," Mitchell Du Bois said, thrusting me at the person, "is the creator, the man behind the story, Larry Rhinebeck, author and writer of *Free Ride.*"

"Oh," I said. One glance at him, thick, unkempt, and owl-eyed, made it clear that his novels, with their rascally attractive and sexually active hero, were exercises in pure wish fulfillment. It's not that being heavy or looking constantly startled disqualify a person from being attractive. He was, in fact, no rounder than Bill Clinton on one of his heavier days. There was simply no charisma.

"Uh, hi," he said.

"I tried to find *Free Ride,*" I said, "but it was out of print."

"Oh. I know."

"I got the sequel."

"Oh."

"I thought it was very well written. I don't read many detective books, but I thought it was well written."

"Oh. Uh. Thank you. Would you, uh, like a Danish or something, they're very good."

"No, thank you," I said.

He sighed deeply. "I don't understand why they put out all this food. I used to like it but, but it's been two weeks and I've gained eight pounds. I stand around a lot. I guess that's part of it. But when I write I sit around a lot, so maybe that's not it. They're very good and, you know, they're free." He took a bite, aiming for the prune part.

"Who is Sandra, the buxom sex therapist?" I asked him, though somehow meeting her creator made her not only less real, but infinitely less threatening. Till now I had visualized the sort of silicone someone who mesmerized Duke and Sonny the minute they entered a room. Now I suspected that Sandra was more matronly, pillowy and wide all over, waist, hips, and thighs. "Is she really?"

"Really what?"

"A sex therapist?"

"Uh, yeah. It's not that, that big a deal. Except to Glenda, of course. Labels are always, uh, better than contents."

"Does Tony do it with her? Immediately? Or sooner?"

"Do it with her?"

"Yes."

"Very, uh, euphemistic, aren't you?"

"No, I mean, yes, I guess so."

"Umm."

"So, um, do they?"

"No. Not right away. Not for a long time. I don't know if I should be telling you this. I know how Alan is . . . he likes to act like this could be like *Casablanca* and any moment could go any way. But, but I tell you, I wrote the book and then I wrote the screenplay, so I know, and I discovered it from experience, the story is tight, very tight." He held his hands up, fingers intertwined to show me how tightly woven it was. "It's tightly woven. Can't unweave without it falling apart. One thing leads to the next. One thing echoes another. You know what you got here—a foolproof screenplay. I know Alan is a good director. Great director. Great. But—a chimpanzee could direct this movie from this screenplay. I could direct this movie from this screenplay, and I ain't no chimpanzee."

Remembering my agent's words, remembering her clear and sincere warning, remembering that truth is not always necessary in every conversation, I said, "Yes, the little bit I read, is foolproof."

"See," he said to Du Bois, "see, everyone can see that."

"I can see that, Larry," the producer said. "I've always seen that. Haven't I always seen that, and said that?"

"So you see," the writer said, "the Sandra character is there to test Tony, and to let us see him say 'no' and be faithful." He put down what was left of the prune Danish.

"So he doesn't sleep with her and Glenda is paranoid."

"No," he said. He looked at the platter of pastries and the cherry Danish, bright red, moist and glistening, called to him. He picked it up, bit, chewed a bit, and spoke. "He does. But only after he sleeps with Christina. For Tony, sleeping around is a kind of breaking down. So doing it with Sandra, it's sort of symbolic of the downward slide."

"OK," I said.

"I, uh, liked what you did, yesterday."

"Thank you," I said.

He took a big bite out of the Danish. I started to go. Unable to actually form words with so much pastry in his mouth, he made a noise that let me know he wasn't done yet. I stayed. He chewed. He swallowed. "The, uh, shaving cream thing, that was good."

"Thanks."

"You know, it's something Glenda would've done."

"I'm glad you think so."

"Oh yeah," he said. "She was very straight, but capable of outrageous acts when I least expected it."

"You talk about her as if she was real," I said. "That's good, that's how I like to approach my work."

"Oh. She was real. Totally real. This book was based on reality. Not so much the violence. I'm not a violent person. That's where Tony differs from me. But all the sex stuff and the point of view, the biting sarcasm and the witticism, and all the sex, that's all real."

"I should have realized," I said.

"I could, uh, tell you how I see this next scene being played. I have it all in my mind. Alan has the name, so he has to be the director, I understand that, I have to make my bones somewhere else, but this screenplay is so, so cinematic—"

"It is," Mitchell Du Bois interrupted. "You read, and you see camera positions, you see angles. This scene, I see starting in tight, ECU, on you, tender caring face. Then I see slow pull back, and booming up, booming up. Higher and higher, so we're looking down on them. Down on the little people caught in a pattern, trapped in a pattern, of their own making perhaps, perhaps of a force beyond them. That's what the high shot does for you, it says patterns."

At that point Mitzi showed up and asked me if I were free to talk to Alan. I said yes and thanked both Larry and Mitchell for their input.

As we walked away from them Mitzi said, "Did you hear the story about Mother Teresa?"

"Do you mean a joke?"

"Yes," she said. "Mother Teresa died and of course she went straight to Heaven."

"I have to warn you," I said, "I don't get jokes."

"Saint Peter was waiting and everyone made a fuss over her. He immediately took her to see the Big Guy, who said, 'We'd like to do something special for you.' Mother Teresa, ever humble, said, 'Oh, no, just being here, that's enough for me.'

" 'No, no,' God says. 'We have to do something special for you. To encourage others, let them know there's a heavenly reward for saintliness.' "

"You won't be offended," I said, "if I don't laugh. I've never understood jokes. It's hard, especially with my Jewish friends."

Mitzi continued as if I hadn't said anything. " 'Really, there's nothing I want,' Mother Teresa says."

Nobody believes me about the jokes. I can appreciate witticisms and humorous observations. It's the formal, structured joke with a punch line that I don't get.

" 'Come now, there must be something,' God says. 'No, no, noting special for me,' Mother Teresa says.

"God says, 'I insist. We have to do something for you. Surely there is something you want.' Mother Teresa says, 'No, I have all I want.' God says, 'For me, tell me you must want something.'

" 'Well,' Mother Teresa says, 'I've always wanted to direct.' "

10

Alan's office was a no-smoking zone. His morning meeting was in progress. A storyboard of the day's scene was pinned to the wall. He had a legal pad with notes on it. Amy, the continuity person, what used to be called a script girl, was on his left. Mitzi resumed her place on his right, her note pad in front of her. Lazlo Viktorska, the cinematographer, was sketching out a shot. "Just do it," Alan snapped at him. "Do it both ways."

Lazlo made a very clear effort not to show that he resented Alan's tone. He was a tall, cadaverously thin man. He had a lantern jaw and large deep eyes. He wore his hair long, not long in back in the Los Angeles twinkie ponytail fashion, but on top and on the side, like classical musicians used to do when they were known as longhairs. It was lank and straight and jet black except for a shock of white about two inches wide on the right side, as bold and graphic as the stroke of a paintbrush.

Alan looked up. He turned from Lazlo to me and greeted me.

It was as if he intended to shift all his attention and concentration to me, but something so preoccupied him that there was sand in the gears and the shift wouldn't quite take.

"I was going to ask you about Sandra and Tony and what happens between them, but I ran into Larry . . ."

"Never listen to the writer," Amy said. "Especially if they did the book."

". . . and he told me." I shifted gears as Amy's remark registered. "Why? Has it changed?"

"No," Alan said.

"But what?" I said, hearing a *but* in his voice.

"Dammit, Glenda doesn't know what the future brings. You don't know. I don't know. The future is bitch. A traitorous, howling, sniveling, tricky bitch. Now I might change the script tomorrow. I might change it in the next two minutes. Just to be perverse."

"I've said it before, that's an actor's job, to make it seem . . ."

"That *was* an actor's job when actors worked on stage, doing the same damn play over and over, same damn play for years. But this is end of the twentieth century, we make movies now. We do them one time and we don't have to pretend we don't know how the story ends."

"But I do."

"Oh, do you?"

"Yes. She can't take it anymore and she sends him packing and then she takes him back."

"How do you know?"

"Because I read the sequel."

"I hate sequels," Alan said. "One thing I assure you I won't make is *Free Ride II*, or *Free Ride III* or *IV* or *V*. And just to make sure, at the end of this movie, Tony rolls himself a speedball, whacks the main vein, and then when he hits cruising speed, he eats his forty-five."

"Is that how it ends?" I was, frankly, shocked. Nothing like that had occurred to me. After all, I had read a sequel.

"You know why? Because of you. Because he needs Glenda.

But you're too much of an uptight bitch to take him back just because he does what guys do, which is dip his wick from time to time, it doesn't mean squat, but to you, because you're so . . . rigid . . . so monominded . . . and you take away the only thing that means anything to him . . .''

"Wayne," I said.

"Yeah. The kid. Yeah, you take away the kid, and you kill him with it."

"Oh," I said and sat down. I looked at the storyboard on the wall. It was just that day's scenes, not the ending. It started with CUs of Tony and Glenda, then boomed up to a high shot. "That's what Mitchell Du Bois said he would do, if he was directing the scene," I said.

Mitzi sneered. "Mitchell and Larry have seen the boards."

"Wow," I said and got ready to leave. "Thanks," I said for lack of anything better.

When I was at the door, Alan said, "Or maybe she just flat out loves him. Loves him so much that it just doesn't matter and she lets him come home. Maybe that's how it ends."

"That's not love. That's total lack of self-respect."

"Is it?"

"Yes," I said. No man would do that to me. And ever see me again, that is.

"Then play it that way," Alan said.

I went and looked at the set. It was, if I understood correctly, Glenda's apartment. Glenda and Wayne's. Tony had moved in with them. Decor tells a lot about a person. Just as clothes and makeup do. One thing I could say for the set was that it looked realistic. On television and in movies they're always showing city apartments with rooms as wide and high as the dining hall of a Southern plantation house, plus a view that looks out over the Hudson on one side and Central Park on the other. Somebody not only knew how big real apartments in the city are, they hadn't been so rich so long that they'd forgotten the size of the rooms that real people lived in.

What did the decor tell me? She—they—were middle-class, educated, neither garish nor exquisitely artistic. Beige. She was beige. There was a window, plants, a bucolic painting featuring English horses. There was no way I was going to get the set repainted. But it needed something. Flowers. That would give it some color, some life.

On the way to Astoria I'd seen a Korean market near the studio and they always had flowers. I went out and found it. I had thirty dollars, so I bought twenty-five dollars' worth. Far more than Glenda would actually spend, but this was a movie and I could overdo it.

Bobbie Leuci, the prop man, could have given me a lot of trouble when I asked him to find a vase and put the flowers on the set but all he said was, "I don't mind doing it for you, Annie, but that's an art director decision or the director."

I left the flowers with Bobbie and went to see Alan. When I got to his office the door was closed and there was a silence from inside. A kind of dead silence. Maybe I was imagining things, but there was a strange vibration, stillness where I expected energy and activity. I hesitated even to knock, afraid of what I would find. Then I decided all that was silly.

I knocked.

There was no reply for a moment, then Alan's voice, sounding very tired, said, "Yes?"

"It's me, Annie."

"Come in."

I did. He looked very tired, very worn. There was a glass of water and a couple of bottles of pills on the table with prescription labels.

"Are you all right?"

"Fine," he said. The way he said it, a monosyllable was all he had.

"I, Glenda, would have flowers. Especially because Tony's going away."

He sighed. He looked at his watch. It had to have seemed to him like just that last thing that was too much to deal with.

"I got them already," I said. "From the Korean fruit stand. Which is just where Glenda would have gotten them. Nothing expensive or fancy. Just what she would have, I just need your permission to have Bobbie Leuci put them on set." He didn't reply. "It's my apartment," I said. "That's the way I would have it."

"OK. Try it."

"Thank you," I said and left. I was worried about him. I wished I could help.

Alan didn't come out of his office. Mitzi, with her authority, and Amy, with her notes, ran the set. The crew called them the Two Witches, the most literate among them, the dolly pusher and Mr. Wardell's hair stylist, traded couplets from *Macbeth:*

> When shall we two meet again
> In thunder, lightning, or in rain? . . .
>
> Eye of newt, and toe of frog,
> Wool of bat, and tongue of dog.
>
> Finger of birth-strangled babe,
> Ditch-delivered by a drab.
>
> By the pricking of my thumbs,
> Something wicked this way comes.

We ran through the blocking. Lights were fine-tuned. The flowers were added to the set where Glenda would have placed them. We rehearsed the move for the master, a fairly complicated shot for camera that involved a slight zoom, a traveling shot, a boom up, and a focus shift. They stopped several times and the camera assistant ran a tape measure from the front of the lens to my nose. That made me very insecure as sometimes the skin on my left nostril erupts in an imperfection, a *thing*. I would have to check my makeup very carefully. With a microscope. That's not a neurotic level of vanity. The idea of one's face ten feet high with a *thing* on its nose would unnerve anyone.

Then we broke for lunch.

Still no Alan. I wanted to go back to his office. To see how he was and find out what was happening. He was a very powerful person, intellectually, artistically, and emotionally. But I didn't go.

Choice joined me at lunch. We both had salads. He wore a gun in a shoulder holster.

I didn't think it was right for the scene. I decided not to say anything. He was the star. I was a supporting player. If this was his Tony, then that was the Tony I would play to. He took it out of the holster and moved various parts of it around. It seemed to have bullets in it and it made heavy metallic noises when he pulled this and snapped that. I remembered from the second book that Tony didn't normally carry a gun. But, on the other hand, the detectives that I worked with, and they were all but one of them retired from the NYPD, carried guns.

"Sometimes, when you do a role," he said, "it just fits you like an old pair of jeans. Just slides right on. Or like really good custom-made shoes. When I do Tony, somethin' inside me says— this coulda been me. If things had gone down different, you know, if I'd grown up in Brooklyn, in the streets, instead of, you know, this is the way it coulda gone for me.

" 'Cause an actor, it's a lot like bein' a dick. You gotta live by your wits. Be fast on your feet. Tough enough to take it too, when you gotta take it. Tough enough to take it and get up off the floor and keep on comin'."

"Instead of . . . ?"

"What?"

"Where did you grow up?"

"Oh. Yeah. Beverly Hills."

"Oh," I said.

"Tony, he's like me. He's striving after a kinda truth. Can't help himself. He's driven. That's what it is with him and the women too."

"Oh, that's what it is," I said. If I still went to confession I would have to admit that I had an unclean thought. I almost said, "I thought it was his dick." But I don't say things like that.

"Yeah. It's not just a physical thing. Some guys, they're ruled by their dick. But not Tony. He's got this stream of romance runnin' through his soul, deep down and turbulent, you know what I'm saying. That's what it is, it's a reaching for ... for something. He doesn't care if it destroys him. He's gotta keep on reachin', searchin'—the case, and the women. Same thing.

"That's me. What finding the truth and justice is for him, that's what acting is for me. The search for truth and then bring that truth to the role. And women—oh hell, I know my reputation—but the truth behind the truth is that I'm not into screwing around. I want real interpersonal penetration. I want to reach inside and see where the love is."

"That's heavy," I said.

"Yeah," he said.

"Did you get the salad with tofu?" I asked him.

"Uh, no. I got the feta cheese."

"Oh, cheese," I said.

"It's goat cheese," he said. "Not cow's milk."

"Oh."

"On the coast I do the tofu thing. You gotta be conscious of what you're doing to your body. The body is a temple and self-respect starts with what we put into it."

"Absolutely."

"The feta, it's that Greek restaurant thing. Very New York. Well, you're a New York actress, you know that. Tony, that's what he might be having. My concentration, it's so intense, so goddamn intense it just spills right over into my whole life, even lunch."

"Wow. That's intense," I said.

"Yeah," he said. "Yeah."

When he took out his gun again I went to the dessert table. I brought back chocolate cheesecake and ate it in front of him.

* * *

I went back to the dressing room fifteen minutes before I was due back on stage. To check my makeup and my nose and to get myself together. Glenda was dressed for work. Businesslike and boring. What was I going to do with her today?

When I got out on the stage, Alan was there. He looked great. Energetic, but calm and relaxed.

Fernando "Fern" Howard, the casting director, sat off to one side. He had missed lunch but arrived in time to scrounge some dessert. He sat, hips spilling off the sides of his chair, with a wide slice of Sacher torte on a paper plate on his lap. What was he there for? After yesterday I'd been certain, absolutely positive, that I was no longer provisionally cast, but cast, so totally and completely cast that when the picture opened, my face would be projected on every screen where it was shown and at the end where all the names come up it would say: *Glenda—Annie Mc-Grogan.*

I tried to imagine that he was there for another reason. To discuss any one of twenty other characters. To talk about extras. To schmooze and remain on the director's good side. Try as I might, I couldn't imagine any of that.

What was I going to do with Glenda?

Alan, flanked by Amy and Mitzi, leaned over to Amy and asked a question. She looked at her notes and gave him an answer. He leaned over to Mitzi and said something to her. She was a short woman; her shoulder pads, an unfortunate choice, made her look wide and a bit like a truck, or a truck driver. A cute, freckled, blond truck driver. "Are we ready?" she called out, not screaming, but loud, penetrating, and very commanding. Camera was. Crane was. Sound was. Choice was. I wasn't. But I wasn't about to say so.

"We're shooting film, people," Mitzi announced.

Did Alan always shoot the first one? Did he play games about it? Was it because I'd delivered on the first take the day before?

"Camera," Mitzi called.

"Rolling."

"Sound."

"Speed."

"Slate."

The second camera assistant clapped the sticks, held them for a beat, then moved out of the way.

"And . . . action!"

Tony grabbed his suitcase, grabbed his coffee, said, "Hello"—slurped it, it was cold, grimaced—"baby. Good-bye, baby . . . ," and we were into the scene.

I was . . . how should I put this . . . adequate? boring? nowhere? I needed to look at my nose. Had the chocolate cheesecake done something horrible to me? Nose. The problem was that this scene was written to be played on the nose. There was no subtext. She was just being flat-out insecure. Whining. Make a joke out of it? Make it sexy? Like with the shaving cream?

"Cut."

The door to the stage opened and Dennis Murphy, the production manager, came in looking confused. Sonny strolled in behind him. What was Sonny doing here? Dennis went to Mitzi, Mitzi looked at me, Alan looked to Mitzi.

"It's someone called Detective Gandolfo, wants to see Annie."

By then Sonny had strolled over from the entrance. He had a knack of doing that, walking in and acting like he belonged wherever he went.

"What's up?" Mitzi said to me.

Sonny grinned at me and gave me a casual wave. The thick gold bracelet that one of his girlfriends had given him glittered when it caught the spill from the stage lights. Something about Sonny interested Alan. He got up and introduced himself and asked Sonny what he wanted there.

They shook hands and Sonny said, "I have to talk to my favorite partner over there"—he gestured at me—"about a matter that was unresolved. A case we was working on. I thought I might drop by, you know, and see how she was doing, doing a major motion picture. Kill two birds with one stone."

"Your partner?" Alan asked.

Now everyone was listening.

"Yeah, Annie and me, we done a lot of cases together. Good detective, Annie."

"She's a detective?"

Now everyone was looking at me.

"Sure."

I wasn't angry at Sonny. I could never be angry at Sonny. Like he said, he was my partner and he treated me right. But I suddenly realized: These people didn't know I was a detective, they only knew me as an actress, and I liked it that way. For a long time I'd thought I was getting terrific mileage out of being an actress/detective. Whenever I met casting directors, directors, producers, they were fascinated by my second career. They would spend time with me asking, "What was your most dangerous case?" "Do you carry a rod?" "Do you use disguises?" "Do you do divorces?" "How can I tell if my husband is cheating?" Now I knew that these people would see me in a new way and I didn't want them to.

Sonny had charmed Alan. As he does most people. "You ever been on set before?" Alan asked.

"Nah, I never," Sonny said.

"Well then, be my guest," Alan said. "If it's all right with Annie. Is it all right with you?"

"Yes," I said.

If there wasn't enough pressure already, this did it. After sitting for five hundred hours in a parked car and telling Sonny what a serious actor I was and how important it was to me and how it was a high calling—now I had to lay it on the line. It was like acting in front of my mother.

Alan had someone get Sonny a director's chair and a cup of coffee and sat him down next to his own seat.

Choice leaned over and said to me, "I didn't know you were a detective." He touched his gun as if for reassurance.

"Camera," Mitzi called.

"Rolling."

"Speed."

"Twelve. Two." And clap the sticks.

Tony was all business and excitement about getting out of town. I wasn't even in his consciousness. I was the goddamn couch. If I didn't stop him, "Hello, baby, good-bye, baby," was all I was going to get. When all else fails, Stanislavsky said, try a limp. That would do for this scene. So I grabbed him. As in: Stop. Pay attention. To me. Before you rush out to your adventure.

There was that holster that I thought was inappropriate and the gun that he liked to play with so much.

I played it like Glenda was trying to make light of it, make it sexy, but she couldn't help letting the plaintiveness show through. But when Tony said, "*The line is, 'under five minutes and out of town doesn't count,'*" I reached into his jacket and grabbed the stupid gun. I pointed it at him. *I don't want a line, I want an answer, are you going to be good?* I liked how that felt. I liked that it totally changed Choice's choices. He had to pay attention to me. He had to be in the scene.

What was I? A crazy lady? Or cute and ballsy? Sexy or threatening? And how was he going to get his gun back?

We did twenty-two takes of the master. We ad-libbed after a while: *Are you going to give my gun back? You can go, but your gun stays here.* Silly things like that, but it gave me room to be honestly plaintive with my last line: *Make sure . . . you come back to me.* Then we did the scene broken down into pieces, one-shots, two-shots, reaction shots.

I have to say that everything moved in a very smooth, businesslike fashion. There was no hysteria, no tantrums, no yelling. We quit at 5:00. A day at the office.

Fern was gone.

Sonny was there. "You done good," he said. Both Alan and Fern had told him he had a look and then they made him talk. "They like the way I talk," he said. "Said I sound like a cop. I said, 'Yeah, I see how that could be.' So anyway, they're doing a screen test for me. I think I'm gonna be in this picture wid you."

"That's wonderful," I said.

"I gotta talk to you about this Elissa and Stephen case. I been tailing him and we got some information to report. But what we figured, we figured it would be better you did the report to her, what with you being the original contact person and also she might recognize my voice or Duke's from talking to her on the phone, on behalf of Rudi, if you recall."

"I didn't know you went on with that. Isn't there an ethical problem?"

"I raised that with the Duke."

"What did he say?"

"When you're undercover, ethics is more elastic."

"Excuse me," Alan said. "Would you two like to come to dinner with me?"

"Gee, I'd love to," Sonny said. "But I got to go to the track. Do some business there."

"That sounds like fun," Alan said. "You mind if I join you?"

"Nah, not at all."

"How about you, Annie, coming to the track with us?"

We went to Belmont.

"Anyway, lemme tell you what we got to tell Elissa," Sonny said on the way out. "Me and Cowboy been sitting on the guy's apartment, lives on the East Side but like a fifth-floor walk-up, last of the tenements. So last night, we're in the Silver Bullet—I don't like to fight over what's on the radio but if I gotta listen to one more song about the cheating side of life, I'm gonna shoot the speakers in my own car—and our old friend Stephen comes out. He's walking against traffic, so we do like we do." Which is, the passenger gets out and follows on foot, the driver stays with the car, maybe drives around the block to see if he can pick up the action. If he can't, he goes back to the original location. The detective who's following the suspect stays on him until they stop somewhere, then he calls the office. The person in the car keeps checking in until he gets a message where his partner is and then joins him or her if possible. "I don't find them, so I go back to the apartment building, start doing the crossword puzzle. I'm not there ten minutes and Stephen comes out of the building.

103

"So I figure Cowboy screwed up, lost him or something. So I jump out of the car and I start to follow. He heads downtown, down to some club, Soho. Very trendy. You woulda liked it. So when we get there I go to the phone and Cowboy he's left a message for me, coupla messages, that he's at Kavanaugh's on Third Avenue and Stephen's eating the mussels marinara and drinking white wine and I should come on over.

"So I leave a message for Cowboy that whoever he thinks he's watching isn't our guy, 'cause I've got our guy and I can see him from the pay phone where I'm standing. And I know the guy because I've surveilled him before.

"Anyway, you gotta talk to Elissa, 'cause what I think is happenin' here, is we got twins, and I think she's maybe dating both of them and maybe doesn't know it."

We ate hot dogs with mustard and drank beer from huge waxed paper cups, we cheered the horses we'd bet on and tore up our tickets when we lost. I lost $40. Alan lost $900. Sonny won $800 and lost $750, and did his business, whatever it was, with some Damon Runyon characters who'd wandered off from the touring company of *Guys and Dolls*. After the one race Alan's horse won, he hugged me. That was the moment, it seemed to me, that the next step was taken. For the rest of the time at the track he touched me a lot, nothing specifically sexual, arm around me, my arm through his, brushing my hair back out of my eyes when the wind blew it around front. That sort of thing. Sonny, with whom I'd been relentlessly asexual, winked at me, like I was one of the guys and I was the one trying to score.

Sonny left the track in his own car.

I went back to Manhattan in Alan's limo.

We talked about movies and acting and the track, about my career as a detective, Sonny and Duke and the guys. At one point he looked at me and made love eyes, staring into mine and letting me look into his. I'm a sucker for that, no question about it. I'm not a sucker. I believe in it. You can really see someone in their eyes and the only way they can really see you is if they look in your eyes. But he didn't rush things or jump on me.

When we got to Manhattan he said, "I've moved out of the house, the apartment. I have a suite at the Pierre. You don't have to be on set tomorrow, would you like to come up for a drink? Or something to eat. They have great room service. Caviar omelets—what else can you eat after a night of losing at the track? Right?"

I said yes.

The limo stopped, the doorman opened the door for us, he smiled and said, "A lovely night, Mr. DeLucca." We walked in, my arm in his, and rode the elevator to the sixteenth floor. It was a lovely suite and looked lived in.

Alan gave me the room service menu. "Order what you like," he said.

I had no appetite. None at all.

I didn't know what to say. It had come, I guessed, to that moment. But there should have been lots to say. Or had we already talked as much as we needed to. Didn't he want to know about my . . . well . . . my childhood and there were several acting teachers that I had that I'd yet to tell him about and he hadn't told me anything, really, about himself, how he became a director, what his mother was like, how his wife was . . . better not think about his wife or discuss her, that can be very disruptive, disenchanting . . . couldn't we just have sat on the couch and chatted for a while longer?

He took me in his arms and bent to kiss me.

Then there was the most dreadful pounding on the door. Alan tried to ignore it, but a voice called out, "Open up, Alan, we know you're in there." The mood was not yet broken, but it was dented. Alan tried to kiss me, just, I think, to establish the fact, before he dealt with the door bangers. It didn't connect. He sighed and turned to the door. "All right," he yelled, "I'm coming."

He led me to the bedroom door and opened it. "Why don't you wait in here," he said.

That didn't seem unreasonable. I said, "OK," and he shut the door behind me. As soon as he did, I realized that I had a terrible headache, from the beer and from smoking cigarettes, which I do, sometimes, when I drink, which I don't do very often. Actually, I find neither alcohol nor nicotine the least bit addictive. Purity comes easily to me.

I put my ear to the door, naturally, to find out what was going on. I recognized the voices of Mitchell Du Bois and Larry Rhinebeck. They were accusing Alan of changing the script behind their back. It was an argument full of egos, ambition, suspicion, and jockeying for meaningless protocols of power. It went on and on, seeming to go nowhere. My headache grew worse. There were two other doors in the bedroom. I opened one, looking for the bathroom, planning to splash cold water on my face. But it opened out to the hall. No, the argument didn't seem to be winding down. I closed the hall door behind me, took the elevator down, and, not quite sure why, I went home.

11

I didn't hear from Alan the next day.

I called Elissa. I asked her if Stephen had ever mentioned a twin. There definitely was one. What Sonny and Cowboy had observed was backed up by office research. There was a Harold, same last name, same birth date, same birthplace, same parents.

Elissa said that no, he never had. I told her that we had not been able to tell them apart. But then we had not gotten up close and personal as she presumably had. I didn't know if it was possible that they were so identical that they could pass for one another in intimate circumstances. Perhaps she might check and see if there was some particular distinguishing mark that appeared and disappeared.

I didn't hear from Alan the day after that. I began to seriously mope. I visited Willie. She was deranged, or something close to it, about the beverage commission, the IRS, some large legal fees, and whether or not the saloon would survive. Either her problems were very complex and I was incapable of understanding them or she had been driven to the point of incoherence. Next to that my mope was as a breeze in a hurricane.

I went to visit my friend Joanna. She'd been working on a script for a made-for-TV movie for six years. It was going to get its network premiere in a week. She had just been informed that the producer had removed her name as the writer and put in his own. While I was there, she was on the phone to the Writer's Guild. Yes, she could appeal. But, it would take six to nine months to schedule said appeal. No, she could not get a ruling between today and the premiere next week. Yes, even though the producer was a double-dealing, lying, sneaky snake, this was a successful *fait accompli*. Next to credits, romance seemed trivial.

So I went home. I studied my lines. Tried to think of bits of business that were true to the character. I examined myself in the mirror to see if I was the fairest one of all and worthy of the love of the prince/film director. Could he see, staring in my eyes, how lovely my soul was, or did he see, staring in my eyes, how lines were beginning to form and that I would need cosmetic surgery very soon?

I watched my telephone. It never moved. Not once.

I took a long bath. My telephone has a long cord. I keep it beside me while I bathe. He had to call. Our moments together had been moments, real moments. We were artists, our souls touched, we respected each other, we had talked and laughed, he made my work better, and I made his work better. He had to call. He would be mad not to call. Why didn't he call?

When he called I said, "I'm sorry about the other night."

He said, "I'm sorry about the other night."

"I shouldn't have left."

"I shouldn't have let them interrupt."

"Then you're not angry?"

"Then you're not upset?"

"No, not at all," I said.

"No, not at all," he said.

"I'm so glad."

"I am too."

"Oh."

"Well."

"Yes?"

"My schedule," he sighed.

"You are directing a major motion picture," I said. Understanding his schedule.

"John Huston went off big-game hunting in the middle of *African Queen*, I'd just like to do lunch. And I can't seem to figure out when."

"Oh," I said. Disappointed in a big way.

"Look . . ."

"Yes?"

"Could you . . . would you?"

"What?"

"Come out here. To the studio."

"Yes," I said.

"I have to warn you, we'll only have . . . there's something I do want to talk to you about, but we won't have a lot of time."

"I'll be there," I said.

"Thanks, Annie," he said. "There's something special about you."

"About you too, Alan," I said.

They were shooting when I arrived.

It was a scene with Choice Wardell and Gwendolyn Ript. Gwen was young, about eighteen or nineteen, and without ever having seen the script, without knowing anything about the film, it was obvious that she was the Other Woman. Whether or not the body was all natural didn't matter, it would have had Duke or Sonny firing their gun and knocking over furniture to get at her. Choice was doing a fair job at emoting a similar sort of lust, given that he was a tofu eater.

She had a face almost as emphatic as her body. Had her lower lip been surgically enhanced? Or did she simply maintain a permanent pout? Personally, I thought women had stopped looking at men in that simpering way along about the time we realized it wasn't romantic when John Wayne threw one of his babes over his knee and gave her a spanking.

If Alan was working with this teen sex wonder, no wonder he hadn't had to rush to call me. No wonder Glenda had trouble hanging on to her man, he was a shallow, mindless cretin that responded to the most obvious, tawdry, plastic sort of allure.

Shortly after I arrived, they stopped for lunch.

Everyone wanted to talk to either Gwen or Alan. All the men around Gwen sort of rose up on their toes and craned their necks as if by getting high enough they could see down into all that was covered. She headed for the dressing room. Larry Rhinebeck, looking both sad and lecherous, tried to follow her, but she said something that froze him. He looked around to see if anyone had seen him be shut down. Nobody was watching him, and if they were they didn't care.

He spotted me and started coming my way.

I looked to see if Lazlo and Amy and Mitzi and Ms. Ript's hairdresser and Ms. Ript's body makeup artisan were done with Alan, but they were all conferencing away. I had nowhere to run from Larry. He was upon me.

"Hiya there, Annie."

"Hello."

"Hey, did you hear the one about Mother Teresa?"

"Yes. Mitzi told it to me."

"She stole it from me," he said.

"Actually," I said, "I don't get jokes."

"Did you hear the one about the Polish starlet who went to Hollywood?"

"Really, I just don't understand them."

"She slept with the writer."

"Oh."

"You don't get it. See, she was so dumb . . ."

"I understand it. I guess."

"You just didn't find it funny, huh? It's . . ."

"It's not personal. I just don't laugh at jokes."

". . . a writer's joke. Writers and Rodney Dangerfield, we don't get no respect."

"Oh, I'm sure that's not true. There must be someone who respects you," I said.

Alan smiled at me like he was truly glad that I was there. I had watched how he'd watched Gwen and it had been totally professional. I was glad he wasn't one of the shallow ones. Mitzi said, "Hello," and looked as if she had something more to say, but didn't say it. Amy looked at me and back at Alan and it seemed to me that something territorial passed through her mind. I didn't know if it was the loyal, secretly loving secretary syndrome or if there was, or more likely, had been, a little certain something between Alan and his continuity person.

Alan came to me, and the two witches seemed to know enough without anything being said, to let us walk off together. We didn't touch but moved close beside each other, close enough that I seemed to feel his aura brush against mine. His aura had blue and white highlights, mine, red and gold. Or so I imagined they would be.

We went into his private office. I expected him to take me in his arms. Would he want to have sex there and then? I rather dreaded that. It was barren and harsh. There were so many others—not in view or earshot—but still surrounding us, somehow able to know. This would be so very wrong. As a way to start. Of course, once we'd had that first time in romantic circumstances with candlelight and sweet privacy in a special place, we might, madly in love, dash into his office and spend our lunches together in any way he might want. But not now.

He took my hands in his.

"What I'd like to do," he said.

"Yes?"

"There's sort of one break in the schedule. If all goes well and nothing screws up between now and the end of the week. . . . Look, this is just an idea and I may be presumptuous . . ."

"What is the idea, Alan?"

"We're doing your scenes upstate at this resort called Mohonk Mountain House. It's large but rustic, in the mountains, and there's a big nature preserve. As it stands, I have a day to rescout before we shoot and I could even go up a day, half a day before that. And I thought . . ."

"Yes," I said, squeezing his hands, gazing into those tan, tawny, mystery eyes.

". . . I was hoping, that if I invited you, you could come up with me."

"Yes."

"We might even be . . ."

"What?"

"Alone."

Mohonk Mountain House is in the Shawangunk Mountains about an hour and a half to two hours north of New York City. The Shawangunks, shaped like ocean waves, long rising slopes that end abruptly in crashing cliffs, are dramatic and romantic. Mohonk, itself, was a peculiar structure, or rather series of structures that had expanded out of itself in a set of not quite related styles. There probably was a time that it looked foolish, even tasteless, but time and the far greater tastelessness of postwar motel and apartment and institutional architecture had rendered the mistakes of the past infinitely charming in comparison.

The building sort of rambled around one corner of a gem of a lake. It was filled with casual antiques and fireplaces. Carriage roads, walking paths, and hiking trails ambled through hundreds and hundreds of acres of grounds. There was no bar. There were no televisions in the rooms. Men were required to wear jackets and ties to dinner. It was as old-fashioned as I fear that I am.

For the record, Alan and I had separate rooms.

It was spring. I was on the fifth floor. I had a balcony that overlooked the lake. I opened the doors and went outside. It was late afternoon, not yet evening, the cinematographers' favorite time to shoot. The light was gold, the lake was blue, the scent of new growth and wild azaleas and fresh water was in the air.

I think I was genuinely in love.

I took a long slow bath—of course—then put on my best dress for dinner. It was from China, I bought it when I was in China, embroidered, blue silk, slit up the side, and truthfully, about one woman in five hundred is slender enough to fit into it. I wondered if it was too dramatic. Then, if it wasn't dramatic enough. It seemed to cry out for a flower, a white flower in my red hair.

There was a bouquet in the room, thoughtfully ordered by Alan. I clipped a gardenia from it and pinned it in my hair. Then I went down to the dining room. I knew I would barely be able to nibble at my food. Getting fed isn't the point of eating together. Courtship, ritual, anticipation, that's the point.

Alan told me he had arranged a table for two with a lake view for us.

When I got to the dining room, a huge area with a domed ceiling, I looked along the lakeside wall for him. I didn't see a man seated alone at a table for two.

But I thought I saw the back of his head at a table with several people. I hadn't seen the back of his head that often, but when I'd seen it I'd looked at it with loving attention and I was quite certain that was his head that I was seeing the back of. Except that there were two women and two children seated with him.

In spite of whatever it was that the mâitre d' was saying to me, I hurried past him in the very tight Chinese dress that made me make very small Chinese steps to see if that was indeed Alan. It couldn't be. It had to be one of those horrid mistakes where someone else was traveling around with the back of his head.

Just as I arrived at the table, the head turned toward me and revealed itself. It was indeed Alan DeLucca. Certainly there would be an explanation. And he would give it to me.

"Annie," Alan said, and he explained: "This is my wife, Angelique della Verona, my son, Gavin, my daughter, Chelsea, and"—he indicated the blond woman who had pasty skin and slate gray eyes—"this is Brigette."

12

Of course that was the end of my romance-to-be with Alan DeLucca, motion picture director. I was willing to fool myself, foolish woman that I was willing to be, when his wife and his children were an abstraction that was referred to in terms of *his lawyer* and *her lawyer*, which made them seem like cousins thrice removed.

I retreated from the dining room as fast as tiny little Chinese steps would permit me. I did not dine that evening. I spent a sad and melancholy night accompanied by a woman's truest companions, heartbreak and a sense of betrayal. Thank God for my balcony. I stood out there in the chill night air, almost shivering, shawl around my shoulders, gazing at the stars. Their light glittered in the tears that watered my eyes. The tears themselves fell silently to the lake below. I tasted each moment of pain, knowing that it would help me with Glenda the wimp.

When the day, at last, dawned, the sense of loss of what never was had not yet left me. After I did my makeup, I put on a casual but flowing dress and set out to wander through the gentle woodlands. I am not one of those people who think a woman ought to dress like a lumberjack, in lumpy boots and presoiled jeans, just because she is not in an urban environment. The dress I was wearing, a pale peach color, was washable silk. It's easy to care for, practical as well as pretty, they're importing quite a lot of it lately, reasonably priced, especially since I'd bought it at the Sunday street market at Eightieth Street and Columbus Avenue.

When Alan at last found me, I was in a gazebo atop one of the many picturesque cliffs that overlook the scenic lake.

He was not alone. The two witches, Amy and Mitzi, flanked him. They wore jeans and very official-looking hiking boots. They both had notepads and pens. Mitzi had, in addition, an instant camera. At a sign from him, like two well-trained bitches —of course I mean that in the very literal sense of canines—they heeled, or whatever it is that doggies do, and stayed behind when he came forward to speak with me. I was backlit and aware of it. There was a breeze that molded the soft and flowing fabric against my body and drew attention to my red hair. Frankly, I don't think that Lazlo Viktorska with his gaffer and their HMI lights and a wind machine could have set me up much better.

"Let me explain," he said, as men do.

"There is no point," I said.

"But there is," he said. "You're a very special person."

I looked away. I turned my back into the wind. I looked at a hawk circling high over the cliffs on the other side of the lake. It felt like a scene that should be played with someone named Heathcliff. It was a bit much, I admit it, but I enjoyed it, and was hardly about to stop. I said nothing.

"Please," he said. "Won't you talk to me."

I looked at him now. Directly into his eyes. Searching for truth. Willing to accept nothing less.

"I can explain," he said.

Part of me—that part that knew that he was an extraordinary

creator, a great director, who could relate to me, artist to art-ist—was all there. But there were other parts as well. One was the detective, member of the SAD squad, special antiadultery division, who'd seen it all and heard it all, and wondered if these were the exact same lines that my partner Sonny Gandolfo, or our boss, Duke DeNobili, would use when they got caught with the right woman in the wrong place. Another was the actress, who realized that I was playing this out more as Glenda than as Annie. Annie would have lost her temper and called him some very definite names and possibly struck him. As he deserved.

Mitzi coughed and looked at her watch. I flicked her out of my consciousness like lint off of a cuff. But Alan took heed.

"I have to pick final locations for the shot tomorrow."

I didn't answer. I had all day.

"I feel like I'm in some dreadful soap opera, where you just happened to walk in at the wrong moment, when things looked like something they were not. Did I ever tell you that I actually wrote for 'General Hospital' for a year? Under an assumed name, of course. We always had to work very hard at keeping characters from hearing the very simple explanation that would straighten things out and end the story line. Misunderstandings are a way of life in soap operas. That's because they can't deal with real conflicts in real ways. That's part of why I quit, even though, at the time, the money seemed good. Also because, at the beginning, I could do a week's work in about four hours; after a year, it took me a week to do a week's work."

We heard the sound of horse's hooves coming toward us, galloping up the old carriage road. Suddenly a horse appeared coming around the curve. It came rushing right at Amy and Mitzi. They jumped back, off the road, into the protection of the trees.

The rider, Angelique della Verona, Allan's wife, came to within five feet of us. She pulled back on the reins. The horse, glossy and shining with sweat, reared quite dramatically, before settling to a stop. Angelique wore jodhpurs, a riding jacket, and a helmet.

She held a riding crop in her hand. She tapped it against her high black riding boots as if she were auditioning to be the Odd Sexual Practices Poster Girl. She stared at us, long and hard.

I hated her. She had upstaged me. Of course, she had to use props to do it.

Raising one eyebrow at Alan, she abruptly lashed the horse's rump with her crop. The horse leapt forward and she galloped off.

"I can get away," Alan said, "for a little while, tonight."

I said nothing. What did he expect, a quick romp in the woods? Not with me.

"All I ask is a little time, for me to explain. And to talk to you. God, you look beautiful here, in this place, the fresh green of spring around you and the good, clean sunlight, and the spring breeze. I will carry this moment with me for the rest of my life, no matter what happens, whether you give me a chance to make you understand or not."

I looked upon him with a little more sympathy.

"I'm supposed to go to dinner at seven," he said. "There's a little waiting room, right next to the dining room, it's kind of a reading room. I'll go to dinner. I just have to spend five minutes there with Mitch. Dan Ginzburg, from the studio, is supposed to be with him. Then I'll make my excuses. By 7:05, 7:10, at the latest, I'm out of there. You'll see me go. Follow me. I'll have the car waiting. There are lots of nice restaurants around here. We'll go somewhere away from this movie and that bitch and we'll talk.

"Please," he said.

I let the wind caress my hair. I stared at the high cliffs, from which a girl could throw herself in despair. If she wanted to. Which I was hardly about to do. I wasn't that heartbroken. But still, one must entertain the possibilities.

When I looked back at him, regally I thought, he said, "I'll be there. I'll look for you. I can't insist. But I can hope. Until then."

I didn't say anything. Let him wait and wonder.

*　　*　　*

117

On the way back to the hotel I passed a man in a tight tank T-shirt with great bulging muscles. He was headed in the same direction that Alan, Amy, and Mitzi had gone. I waved pleasantly to him. In this rural paradise everyone seemed to greet each other. He did wave back, but it was as if I didn't really exist for him and he was preoccupied with his own special drama.

I proceeded down the carriage road.

Then I heard a scream. It was a howl of horrendous pain and rage. Something between a death yowl and a cat fight. It came from off to the side, through the woods. I plunged into the trees, looking for some way through the underbrush. The whole area was honeycombed with trails and eventually I found one that seemed to go in the direction from which the sound had come. It was meandering and narrow, growing narrower. It abruptly came up against some towering rocks, then tacked beneath them. Just past their looming, and seemingly precarious, presence, the path split, uphill to the left, down to the right. Then I heard yelling. It was from the downhill side and that was the direction I went. The path led to a stream, where the hardwoods changed to evergreens and the pines grew large. As soon as I plunged in among them I felt a change. It was cooler and darker and damper, more primeval. The air itself, rich with ozone, smelled different and even looked different.

The trail merged with another of the carriage roads. That seemed like it would take me closer to the sounds. I followed it. Then one side of the road was open, where it ran along the side of the cliff. The wind was stronger, blowing quite hard from this angle; it whipped my hair around and chilled me.

I kept going and then I saw a man dressed like a park ranger. He was speaking, or trying to speak, to Gavin, Alan DeLucca's son. The strange-looking woman, Brigette, stood by, appearing both angry and distressed. The ranger-type person held a small rifle in his hands. Gavin was screaming at him and stamping his feet. He was having a tantrum, the way I would expect it in a very small child, a two- or three-year-old. Gavin was not small.

He was nearly as tall as me and had to be eleven or twelve, at the beginning of puberty or quite near to it.

The rifle, I began to understand, through all the ranting, belonged to Gavin. It was actually an air rifle or BB gun. But that didn't matter to the ranger person, who had taken it away because Gavin had fired it and because he had fired it at a hawk. There were no firearms permitted on the preserve, and this particular hawk, or all hawks, I wasn't sure which, was a protected species anyway.

Gavin had gone quite over the edge about it. He was saying things like, "I like to hunt. I like to kill little animals. You can't take my gun away, I'm a member of the NRA."

"I'm trying to be polite about this because you are a guest at the hotel, but I'm perfectly willing to call the police and have you arrested," the ranger said.

"I've killed lots of little animals, squirrels and rats and birds, and how about if I killed a big one, like you, you big pig," the boy screamed, spitting and snarling.

"That's it," the ranger person said and reached for his walkie-talkie.

Brigette stepped up to Gavin and slapped him across the face. "Stop, you must stop," she commanded with a Teutonic accent.

Gavin seemed to come out of whatever place he had gone to. And he didn't seem to resent the slap. It seemed as if he were . . . what? . . . used to it?

"That will be all, *Herr* Park Officer," Brigette said.

"Well," Herr Park Officer said, dragging the syllable out, like he no longer wanted it to be all.

"Der young man will be good now. There will be no more discharging of firearms during our presence here, I can assure you."

"I'm gonna keep this," the ranger said, holding the gun. "I'll keep this until you check out and then, if the hotel management wants, they'll give it back to you."

"Be quiet, Gavin," Brigette said, before Gavin had a chance to speak. "That will be very good, sir," she said to Herr Park Officer.

They stood there as the ranger walked away, toward a four-wheel-drive vehicle. When the truck started up, Brigette put her arm around the boy. She fondled him and murmured in his ear. Though I couldn't hear the actual words, it seemed she was speaking endearments, sweet nothings. Then, leading Gavin, she headed my way. I thought for a moment that I ought to retreat before they saw me. I didn't suppose they would want a witness to such a scene. But before I could move, Brigette spotted me. She fixed her strange gray eyes on me and marched very purposefully toward me.

"Do you believe in the family?" she barked at me.

"Huh?" I said.

"The sacredness of the family. The foundation of all that is civilization and goodness."

"What?"

"The family, the family, the family," she said.

"Oh."

"We are not animals. We are not savages. It is wrong to mate and then run off and around and do more mating and rutting elsewhere. Do you understand me?"

"Huh?"

"Of course, you understand me."

"Who are you?"

"I am going to protect this family. That is what is important. That is what is necessary. I will do anything to protect this family. I am believing of the nuclear family. The building block, the foundation stone."

"Fine," I said. Who could argue with that.

"I am Brigette, the nanny," she announced.

"Oh," I said, as if that explained things.

"I am Swiss," she said. "Swiss."

Nonetheless, I was there in the little room off to the side, come dinnertime. Actually, I was early, ten or fifteen minutes before the hour. I brought Larry Rhinebeck's second book. I still hadn't been able to get a copy of the first one. I sat behind it and pretended to read as I kept an eye out for Alan.

After I'd been there at least twenty minutes, cursing myself for coming early, I spotted Amy coming in. She was with the man with very, very large muscles. They both seemed full of fury. Marital fury to be precise. Loudly not speaking to each other. Mitzi came in with one of the gaffers, younger than her and quite good-looking. Mitch Du Bois showed up, with some people I didn't know, but not with Alan. It must have been 7:30 when the DeLucca family showed up—without Mr. DeLucca—but with Brigette.

By then I was starving. I hadn't eaten dinner the night before. I had only had tea and a dry biscuit for breakfast—one doesn't eat when one is in the Camille mode. Though I hate to admit it, I didn't eat lunch after my encounter with Alan because, well, because I hoped he would be able to explain things and I was full of anticipation and confused romantic musings.

By 7:45 I said to hell with Alan, put down Larry Rhinebeck's stupid second book and marched into the dining room. "A table for one," I said.

Who would walk in, right at that moment? Larry Rhinebeck. "Make that for two," he said in a manner that he must have imagined was suave.

"How's that for suave?" he said.

"I am dining alone," I said. "I need solitude."

"Too bad," he said, " 'cause I think you're one hell of a dish."

A dish?

"Well, see you round the campus, babe," he said. The odd thing was that he could write pretty good dialogue. Sometimes the discrepancy between creator and creation is disconcerting.

I sat. I ordered. I waited. Several other members of the crew arrived and were seated around the dining room. Then I got the shock of my life. In the door walked Lucy Kohl. The actress who was supposed to be in rehab—again—as a condition of her parole, who had been originally scheduled to play Glenda. Who was on her arm: Fernando "Fern" Howard. Looking as deadly as only a casting director can. They were avidly avid about something. Probably about getting rid of me and giving the part back to Lucy, she of the cauterized nostrils and producer parents.

To make me feel even more threatened, then Choice Wardell walked in and went right to their table. He greeted both of them like old friends. Or more. Lucy squealed with excitement to see him. She rose from her chair. She kissed his cheek, she squeezed his bicep, she fondled his buttocks. Was there anything this woman wouldn't do to get her part back?

Watching them, it was only pride that made me stay at my lonely table through dessert and eat my chocolate *mousse* with chocolate sauce. When I'd eaten every bite—after all it was chocolate—I arose calmly and with great dignity left the dining room. I had been trifled with. Lied to. Stood up. Is this why women get involved with men? Is this fun?

When I opened the door to my room, Alan DeLucca was lying on the floor. Blood puddled around his head. He was dead. I screamed.

13

I am a professional detective. Or at least I had been for a few years. I have worked on a large number and a fair variety of cases. Some of them notorious and more familiar to tabloid readers than certain members of their own immediate families: the Preppie Murder, the Subway Avenger, the Divorced Mobster, the Crazy Tycoon.

Nothing worked as it ought to have in film or fiction.

First of all, this was my first dead body. I did not react with calm or aplomb. I got hysterical.

Second of all, I never once thought that I would be the chief suspect. Until the real detective, from the Ulster County Sheriff's department, a man with a long, sad face and lugubrious eyes, arrested me.

Third, in terms of "solving a case" like Columbo or Angela Lansbury, I had never done that. Moreover, I had no idea how someone does that. Normally we—Sonny and me, and even

Duke, our boss—sort of do what we're told. Follow someone. Watch a place. Deliver a subpoena. Talk to witnesses. Canvas for witnesses. Then we make a deposition and later, if necessary, testify to what we'd seen and heard. Someone else puts it together. The lawyers, mostly, or a judge and a jury. Or the police. But not us. Yet how was I going to prove I was innocent unless I figured out—God help me—who done it?

I had been crying and answering questions for two hours when it suddenly occurred to me that I was allowed to make a phone call. Or at least on television suspects were allowed phone calls. I had no idea, never having been arrested before, what the relationship between television and reality was.

"I want to make a phone call," I said to the Real Detective. He'd introduced himself but in the hysteria of the moment I'd promptly forgotten his real name.

"Let's talk a little more first," he said. "There's plenty of time to make a phone call."

"Now," I said, "I want to make my phone call now."

"You know, you look like you could use a cup of tea or coffee, what do you say?"

"I want to make a phone call," I cried. "And . . ."

"And?"

"And I want to fix my makeup."

"Which do you want to do first?"

He led me to a bathroom. My makeup really was a mess. I was a mess. There is no question that being a murder suspect ages one. It's stress, and stress is almost as bad for the skin as cigarettes and should be avoided. "Do you have to watch?" I said to the Real Detective.

"Sorry, ma'am," he said politely, but he stayed.

When I was done he said, "Would you like a quarter?"

"A quarter?"

"For the phone."

"Who can I call for a quarter?"

"Anyone local," he said.

"Why would I call anyone local? I need help."

"I can't let you make a long distance call."

"I have a calling card. I will pay for the call."

He put his quarter away and led me to the phone. Duke had always said, *If you're evuh in a jam, kid, you call me first.* So I did. He wasn't in the office. No surprise. He wasn't at the bar in the Hotel Rensselaer. That began to worry me.

"One call," the Real Detective said.

"It's all part of the same call," I said.

I tried the car phone. I gave it four rings, and as soon as the Real Detective looked away, I tried—this was really desperate—Duke at home.

His wife, Anita, answered the phone. She said, "Hello."

I said, "Is Duke there?"

She didn't recognize my voice and she reacted as she usually does when a woman whose voice she doesn't recognize calls the house late at night: "Which bitch are you? Don't you ever call this house again. Keep your filthy business in the street where it belongs."

"Wait a minute, Anita . . ."

"Who the hell are you calling Anita, bitch. . . ."

". . . it's me. Annie."

"Who?"

"Annie. Annie McGrogan."

She's met me. She's seen for herself that I'm small breasted and I have straight hair. "I thought you were that other bitch," she said.

"Which one?"

"Ahh, I don' know her name. I just know what's she doin' with my Kenny. And I don' like it." Kenny is Duke's real name. No one calls him Kenny except his wife and his mother.

"Anita, I'm in big trouble. I need Duke."

"He ain't here."

"Do you know where he is?"

"He better not be with that other bitch. Not if he wants to come home again, ever."

"He didn't say where he was going? Or leave a number?"

125

"I think he's off bodyguarding them Saudi princes again. In Texas or somewheres."

"Thanks, Anita," I said, full of despair.

"Hey, Annie, if you find him, you tell him somethin' for me."

"What's that, Anita?"

"You tell him, he better watch his ass, or he's gonna be paying alimony like nobody in Queens ever paid alimony before. You tell 'im for me."

"You're only supposed to get one phone call," the Real Detective said.

I frantically tried another number. Sonny always said to me, *If you're evuh in a jam, kid, you call me first.* So I was calling him. There was no answer at his apartment. There was no point in calling him at home, insofar as home meant the place where his wife and his children lived. He hadn't been there overnight for years. Were the horses running at Hialeah? If they were, he'd be in Florida with Caren. I hoped he wasn't. But I could call Caren. She knew about me and didn't consider me a threat. "No," she said. "He's not here. But if you talk to him, tell him to come and see me." I said I would. Now, did I dare call Mercedes? According to Sonny, he couldn't tell Mercedes that he had a female partner because she wouldn't be able to conceive that we weren't sleeping together.

"Hello," I said. "I'm looking for Sonny Gandolfo?"

"Who are you?"

"Uh, I work for Duke DeNobili . . ."

"Bullshit, you do. I know everybody works for Duke DeNobili. They're a bunch of old cops. You are a woman, you're not an old cop. So what you want with my Sonny? Huh?"

"I work . . ."

"Lissen, I don' know why he give you my number, but if you call here again, you gonna be in big trouble. You got a lotta nerve callin' him up right in my face. . . ."

"Mercedes, does that mean he's not there?"

"You bet. And he better not come here. Not without some good explanation about who you are and why you—"

I hung up on her even though I consider that a rude thing to do. I then called the person I should have called in the first place, the one person who always knows where Sonny is, more or less, who can always be counted on to give him a message, and who doesn't find me threatening—his mother.

"Hello, Mrs. Gandolfo," I said.

"Annie, honey, is that you?"

"Yes, Mrs. Gandolfo, how are you?"

"It's pretty late. Whatcha doin' callin' so late? You in the neighborhood?"

"No, Mrs. Gandolfo . . ."

"Oh, Jeeze, what am I thinkin' of. You callin' this late, you must be in some kinda trouble or on the job. Lemme get him for you . . ."

I said, "God bless you, Mrs. Gandolfo, may you live forever." Not that she heard me. She'd already put down the phone and was yelling, "Son-ny. Son-ny. Get yer ass in here. It's Annie. She's in trouble."

"Annie, that you?" said the wonderfully familiar voice.

"Sonny, you have to help me."

"Yeah, sure, anything, wha's the problem?"

"Do you remember Alan DeLucca? The director?"

"Of course."

"He's dead."

"Oh, does that mean I'm not gonna be in the picture?"

"Sonny, I'm arrested for murdering him."

"Ahh, whaddya go and do that for? He seemed like an OK guy."

"Sonny, I didn't do it."

"Oh. Sorry about that. Then why'd they arrest you . . ."

"Because he was in my room, I guess."

"I was a cop a long time and practically never arrested the wrong person."

"Dammit, Sonny, I didn't do it. Think about it, can you imagine me killing anybody?"

"Of course she didn't do it," Mrs. Gandolfo yelled. "What are you stupid? A nice girl like that? Gimme the phone. . . . Hello, Annie . . . Yes. Gimme the address. . . . Get your pants on and get going," she said to Sonny. "He's getting dressed now," she told me. "Are you all right?"

"Not really," I said.

"Well, just hang on. Don't let 'em upset you or nothin'. . . . Sonny," she yelled, "and bring a lawyer with you. That Jew shyster. You know the one I mean, the guy who gets everybody off." She repeated that into the phone for me. "Don't worry, we got this shyster lawyer, gets everybody off, all the time. . . . Sonny, you ready?"

"Ma, stop yelling," he yelled. "Where are my cigarettes?"

"Here, here on the table where you left 'em."

"OK. Tell her I'm on my way."

"He's on his way," Mrs. Gandolfo said. "And lissen to me, don' say nothin' to nobody until your lawyer gets there."

I did as Sonny's mother advised me. I spoke no more. The Real Detective put me in a tiny room with no windows.

About two hours later the door popped open. There was Sonny, twice as big as life. There was another man with him, about twice as small. Not as small as Danny DeVito, but close, with a mustache. I ran to Sonny and hugged him. He seemed embarrassed by that. It was confusing. I was one of the guys to him. But guys don't hug. So if I wasn't a guy, then he would have to come on to me. Which he probably didn't want to do because I was the first, and still the only, female he knew that he didn't have to come on to. When I thought about it that way, I realized that it must be very relaxing for him, being my friend. It must put tremendous pressure on men, thinking they have to hit on every single woman they meet.

"Hiya," the other man said. "I'm Sammy Spiegal. They call me Sammy 'My Guy Don't Do No Time' Spiegal. I'm gonna help you out here. Though God knows, you done everything you could do to screw things up. Didn't nobody ever tell you, don't talk to the cops, let your lawyer do the talking."

"I'm sorry," I said. "I was . . . there was Alan . . . I didn't think
. . . I was . . . I was hysterical."

"Ahh, forget about it. It's prob'bly first time you killed anybody, how were you to know, a nice girl like you."

"I didn't kill him," I cried.

"It don' matter to me, you did or you didn't."

"I didn't."

"Fine. You didn't. Whatever. Now let's talk about something
serious. My retainer. This here's the middle of the night and all,
that's on the one hand, the other hand, you're a friend o' Sonny's,
on the one hand this here's a capital case, on the other hand, you
are clearly a damsel in distress, I tell you what I'm gonna do, two
thousand dollars down, against my regular retainer which is five
large, normally, for something like this. If we get you outta this
quick or you wanna cop a plea, that could be all it's gonna cost
you. If it looks like it's gonna get serious and I gotta start comin'
back and forth to God's country or wherever the hell we are,
then I gotta have the five."

"I can't afford that," I wailed.

"Let me tell you something, lady, and this is free advice, being
a criminal is expensive."

"I'm not a criminal. Sonny, please, tell him. I didn't do it."

"She didn't do it," Sonny said.

"Lissen to me, you two. You better understand what they got
already. Half of what they got off of your big mouth. They got
motive. You and him was . . ." Sammy the shyster made an
obscene gesture.

"We were not. We never did," I said.

"OK. You was contemplating doin' the do. You wanna be
girlie-girlie, you're a virgin about it, fine. We say you had a crush
on him. Same difference. Motive. You had the opportunity."

"He was killed while I was at dinner. There were, there
must've been, fifty people there that can swear to that."

"Excuse me. You think I don't know what I'm talking about?
They figure, from lividity, temperature of the corpse, onset of
rigor and all that, your amorata or whatever he was to you, this

DeLucca director, he bought into immortality just about seven P.M. Give or take ten minutes. You, you di'n't show up the dining room 'til almost eight."

"I was in the little room off of the dining room."

"Sez you. And I believe you, sister, I really do. But there are no witnesses to that. Only to you being in the dining room, which, according to your own statement which you were so conveniently blabbing about to Detective Moser in there, didn't take place until a significant time after the corpse was a corpse on the floor by your bed."

I sat down and began to sob. "I don't have that much money. I don't have that much money."

"You're getting paid for this here movie, ain't you?"

"Sammy," Sonny said. "She's a friend of my mother's. You gotta help her out. You wanna talk to my mother about it?"

"Jeez. You gotta bring your mother into it?"

"Do what you can," Sonny said.

"Lissen t' me," Sammy said, kneeling down beside me. "Hey, lady, lissen."

"What?"

"You wanna get outta here? Go back to the hotel, clean up. Or you wanna stay here?"

"I want to get out of here. Of course."

"All right. Lissen up. A grand. A measly little grand, I'll get you outta here. You'll be outta here in ten minutes. Then we'll take it from there. We got a deal, girlie?"

"Fine," I said. "But I don't have it on me."

"I know that. You're a friend of Sonny's. And his mother. It's OK."

Sammy left.

"You want a cigarette, somethin'?" Sonny asked me.

"Sure," I said.

He gave me one of his Trues. I rarely smoke, but when I do, I like Luckies. The old-fashioned short kind, without a filter or flavoring. I broke the filter off and lit up. It immediately made me feel a lot tougher. I wiped the tears away. I still had my handbag. I took out my compact and examined myself in the mirror. Good thing I wasn't shooting in the morning. I repaired the damage as best I could.

Sammy came back with Detective Moser. "Here's what I worked with the detective here. You go back to the hotel. You are not yet formally charged. You are not to leave the grounds. It's what you call an informal agreement. We're gonna see what transpires with the evidence and the forensics and such."

"You understand?" Moser said to me.

"Yes."

Sammy led Sonny and me out of the building to the parking area. The Silver Bullet, Sonny's old Cadillac, was parked next to Sammy's new one.

"OK," Sammy said, "here's what I think. They don't want to be too precipitous here. Thank God you stopped short of a confession. These upstate clowns, sort of a confession and six eyewitnesses, they're not gonna get no murder conviction. With what they got, I could prob'bly get you sprung at a prelim. So they wanna hold off, till they find somethin' more. Also I think they're waiting for the final coroner's report and forensics. It's not like they got their own lab here. They use BCI, up in Albany.

"What I think is, I mostly bought you some time. It would behoove you, the best thing in the world, would be you find somethin' that says someone else done it. The reason I say that is this. You don't have enough money to enjoy being charged with murder. First off, you would then have to make bail. Which from your weepin' and pleadin' in there, it is my understanding you won't be able to do. You being from out of town and an actress, which to these folks is pretty flaky, you are not going to get no ROR. Then you have a choice: copy a plea, or go to trial. If you go to trial and I'm your lawyer, and nothing too much new shows up, unless it's two witnesses seen you do the deed with a blunt instrument, I'm prob'bly gonna get you off. Reasonable doubt and all a that. Except. Except that it's gonna be six months at least before you go to trial. All that time you're in the Ulster County Jail. Which is not bad as jails go, but hardly what I expect you're used to.

"Except, also, that it's gonna cost you, rough guess here, forty large. If I do it *pro bono*, which I ain't gonna do, twen'y large. Which is my way of saying, it's twenty out of pocket, travel, overhead, paperwork, experts, all of that, for the attorney.

"Which, as I understand it, you ain't got. Maybe, if you're poor enough, which you may not be, you get a public defender. I been up here from time to time. The public defender is pretty good. But what you don't know, that I know, is that the judge, he used to be the DA. When he was the DA he had two assistants. His first assistant became the new DA, his second assistant, that's the head public defender. This is not to say he'll give you a bad defense. It's just to say that they're three peas from the same pod. Also, and this is more important, is they won't be spending no twenty grand out of pocket on your defense. Remember, in the American system of jurisprudence, rich people walk, poor people talk.

"So the best thing would be," Sammy said, "is you do just like a TV show or somethin.' You find the killer yourself. Find him or her quick, before the cops decide they should charge their very favorite suspect."

"Thank you," Sonny said.

"Thanks," I said. "For getting me out of there."

"No problem," Sammy said. "My pleasure. And a pleasure to meet you. You're a very attractive person and, Sonny assures me, a fine actress."

"Thanks," I said.

He got in his car and slammed the door. The window slid down and he looked out. "It's a good thing I work for a lot of drug dealers. They can pay. It's their money that subsidizes people like you. Murderers never have any money."

14

It was nearly dawn when we returned to the hotel. As we drove up the mountain I made Sonny stop. I got out of the car. I felt the fresh breeze of freedom. I smelt the aroma of growing green things. I listened to the sounds of the early morning birds chirping and making other bird noises in the forest. I watched the sky acquire color in the east and the last of the stars vanish without notice or noise. Wow. It was too heavy to be true. They could actually take all of that away from me. And more. It was hard to grasp just how serious it was.

I got back in the car.

"What we do?" I asked Sonny.

"I thought maybe I'd stick around, get a room, get some breakfast, you know."

"You know what I mean," I said. "What do we do?"

"I don't know."

"What you mean you don't know?"

"That's pretty clear, I thought. I don't know."

"Come on, Sonny, you're the detective."

"You gotta understand," Sonny said, lighting another True. "I'm not much more of a detective than you."

"What do you mean? You were on the force twenty years!"

"Yeah, but I never made detective. Annie, I'm an under-achiever, you know that. I done detective stuff and I worked plainclothes, but I never actually, you know, solved a case, like Columbo or Angela Lansbury or something."

"Oh God, Sonny, what are we gonna do? I can't do time. Not hard time. Not me, Sonny, I couldn't take it." What was I talking about? Why was my mouth spouting noises from movies whose titles I couldn't remember that I hadn't even liked when I'd seen them?

"Well, I got a call in to Duke."

"Great. And where's Duke?"

"You want another cigarette?"

"Sure," I said. I went through the same ritual, tearing off the filter and lighting up. This time it didn't make me feel tough. Or better.

When we got to Mohonk, Sonny checked in and the hotel gave me a new room. That was fine with me. I believe in spirits and that bad memories of evil events can linger in physical places.

My old room had been sealed by the police. All my clothes, my toothbrush, my script, and my notes were in there. Did my script and my notes matter anymore? If I proved that I wasn't a mur-deress, would the film ever be finished? And if it was finished, would it be with me or that vulture, Lucy Kohl?

I called Detective Moser and asked him if I could get my things out of my room. Moser sounded like a German name. I said, "I need clean clothes. And my toothbrush."

"I understand," he said. "I'll come over. I can't let you in there alone."

*   *   *

134

The door was locked and discretely sealed with tape over the lock. Not so much that it would pop out at guests like a traffic light, but enough that a hardworking maid wouldn't open the door and clean up whatever evidence was left.

The room still held odors of death. And of stale tobacco smoke. That, I realized later, was from the cops who must've spent several hours in the room. The outline of the corpse that had been removed—of Alan DeLucca, who, I had thought as recently as the night before, might love me—was drawn on the floor in white chalk. I realized now that he had been lying with his feet near the bed and his head in the fireplace, right on the metal grate that cradled the logs. If it had been cooler that night, I might have had a fire going. Would that have mattered in any way?

"Come on," Moser said. "I've been up all night with this thing. I'd like to get home to breakfast."

I got my suitcase from the bottom of the closet, placed it on the bed, opened it, and opened the dresser drawer. I had left it neat. Now it was messy. Police had obviously been pawing through my skirts and blouses, my stockings and underwear. It was an unpleasant feeling. The thought of being a prisoner, of my possessions, however few or many, subject at all times to someone else's inspection, to someone else's control, passed across my mind in a manner that was so distinct it had a physical dimension. Like a cold wet draft from a blown-open window.

I looked at the Real Detective. "Do you really think I killed him?"

"Don't cry," he said. "I hate it when women cry."

"I'm not crying," I said.

"The strange thing is it makes me angry. I should be sympathetic, but it makes me angry."

He watched my hands and he looked at each object as I put it in my suitcase. When I was done, he locked the door, put the key in his pocket, and put new tape over the lock.

"Look at me," I said. "Do you really think I did that?"

"Somebody did."

*   *   *

By the time I unpacked in my new room and bathed, the sun was up and they were serving breakfast downstairs. I put on clean clothes and fresh makeup, paying special attention to the dark and puffy area under my eyes.

I didn't realize it until it happened, but I was about to make a major entrance.

All the film folk were in one section of the huge dining area, to the right as I entered, the lake side. There was a buzz and hum of anxious chatter. Everyone was talking about what had happened and what would happen to the film. The family, Angelique, Gavin, Chelsea, and Brigette, the Swiss nanny, were at one table. Mitzi, Mitch Du Bois, and Dan Ginzburg, the man from Quad-Star, were at the next table. Amy, red-eyed and puffy, sniffling, sat with the muscular man. I took him, by his attitude, to be her husband, which, I later found out, he was. His name was Derek and he was a stuntman. Lucy Kohl, wearing a blouse that was awfully low cut for breakfast, sat with Choice Wardell, heaving and simpering at him as if she thought she could make him cry out, *Her, her, I want to act with her.*

Breakfast had both waiter service and a huge buffet table. Larry Rhinebeck had his own buffet spread out on his table in front of him as if, with someone else footing the bill for the first time in his life, there was nothing he could pass up. Lazlo Viktorska was impassive as if he had breakfasted with tragedy far too often to be bothered by it. He sat with his camera operator and the gaffer. Then, thank God, there was Rain. It lifted my heart to see him. A truly friendly face. Probably the only one in the place, with the exception of Sonny, asleep upstairs, that I could totally trust. He was seated with his mother.

Smiling, at Rain, for Rain, I crossed the silent and hostile room.

"What is wrong with the authorities in this country? She should be in jail," Brigette said, loud enough for me to hear. She sounded very strict. I was glad she wasn't my nanny.

Angelique put her coffee cup down on the saucer with a clatter. She rose—I must say she had a flair for the dramatic, in the old operatic manner or like a silent movie actress, every gesture broad enough to be understood without spoken words. One, two, three, Brigette, Gavin, and Chelsea, each popped up after her, as if they'd choreographed it. Flinging her napkin to the table, Angelique marched from the dining room. It had been befouled by my presence. One, two, three, Brigette, Gavin, and Chelsea, like two little ducklings and one large duckling, wad-dled off behind her. The only thing that marred the production was that Chelsea carried a piece of toast larded with butter and jam in her hand, traces of it on her lips and cheeks.

A cellular phone rang at one of the tables. I looked toward the sound. Both Mitch and Mitzi were reaching for their phones. The call was for Mitzi. Mitch looked me over in a speculative way, then returned to hustling Ginzburg.

"You, you, you," Amy said at me, a muttered, mumbled ac-cusation.

Derek put a hand as big as a ham, powered by an arm as big as a thigh, on her shoulder and shoved her down in her seat. "Control yourself," he said. In his other hand he held a cup of herbal tea. It was full. Shoving his wife down took so little effort that not a drop sloshed over the rim of the cup.

I kept going, eyes kept staring. I would pass through the gaunt-let. That dear and innocent little boy, Rain, would bring some love and comfort to my soul, then I would sit and face them all down, knowing in my heart I was innocent.

"Rain," I said.

The woman who sat beside him had high, surgically enhanced cheekbones. The skin of her face had been pulled a little too tight. She pointed a finger at me. Her nail was long, red, and glittering. "You have ruined the start of a brilliant career."

"Mom," Rain sighed.

"My son was on his way to stardom. And in one act of de-praved lust you have ruined it. Have you no shame?"

I sat alone. The one thing to be said for an old-fashioned Catholic upbringing is that it inculcates a taste for martyrdom. I remembered a thousand images of gaunt men with spears piercing their sides, blood dripping down a washboard of emaciated ribs, eyes cast heavenward; hands and feet nailed and spiked; martyrs flayed with knives; true virgins tied to stakes, flaming faggots piled beneath them; nuns with bloody palms, giddy with stigmata. *Mea culpa, mea culpa, mea mossima culpa!* What was my suffering compared to theirs?

This was heavy stuff. To show that I was not afraid I ordered a fruit cup, two poached eggs on toast, and black coffee.

I ate slowly. Let them leave first. Would no one, no one at all, stand up for me?

Finally, someone did. Larry Rhinebeck arose from behind the formidable wall of food with which he had ensconced himself at his table. He came across the room to my table. I could more or less tell what he'd eaten by the traces scattered here and there on his shirt and the front of his pants. "Hiya, doll," he said. The last thing he'd eaten had been kippers. It came over with the *H* in *Hi.* "I'm one ginkgo here that knows the diff between a bum rap and the bum's rush. And I'm betting the pot that whoever fingered you is dealing seconds, drawing to an inside straight right from up his, or her, sleeve. It could be writ in neon on Times Square. They can blow smoke up some copper's ass, but they can't blow it up mine. My butt's too wise for that jive. Nobody plays me for a sap. . . . What I'm saying is I'm wit cha, girl."

"Thanks, Larry," I said, wishing that someone a little more prepossessing were saying this to me. Someone with a little less food on their shirt.

"I know what you're thinking. . . ."

I hoped he didn't. He was trying to be nice. "Oh, no, no . . ."

"You're thinkin' *He's just the writer.* But I'm gonna square this caper. We're gonna put the right cat, or kitty, in the cube. Then you're gonna know I'm more than just a cheap scribbler and it'll be you and me, babe, hand and hand into the sunset, down Hollywood and the Vine."

How could he possibly speak that way? Maybe he couldn't

138

hear himself in real life and needed to see his words on a page in order to have some idea of what they sounded like. I tried to think of something polite to say. What I came up with was, "I'm glad someone is on my side."

He stood up. He got ready to go. But he had a parting message. It was, "You and me, babe: Marilyn and Arthur."

By the time he was gone, the only ones left were myself, Choice Wardell, and Lucy Kohl. Lucy looked me square in the eye and she smiled. Like the cat that stole the cream, or a coke whore just back from the powder room.

Now it was Choice's turn to come to my table. He turned the unoccupied chair across from me around and sat on it facing the wrong way. His arms hung over the backrest and his jacket hung open so that I could see that he was wearing a gun in a shoulder holster. He chewed, for a moment, on a nonexistent piece of gum.

"What I figure," he said, "is let the chips fall where they may."

"Sure."

"Someone nailed Alan. And someone's got to take the fall. If it's someone else, then it's someone else. If it's you, sweetheart, well, that's OK with me too."

"Did you ever," I asked, "study with the Actor's Studio?"

"See, Alan might've had his faults, but he was a *paesano*. And someone's got to see that . . . justice is done."

I'd seen this happen before. It primarily affects very driven but truly shallow actors. The instruction to "be real" and the concept that reality is the goal of performance affects their credulity control, and it turns into a craving to be really real; and then, when they fall into some certain role, all that psychobabble from the Actor's Studio hits like a full-fledged acid flashback and, having schooled themselves to believe that it is a great good to actually be the character they are playing, they do it. Depending on the part, there are worse things that can happen to a person. Choice had been lucky that it happened to him on a fairly mainstream action picture, not when he was playing, for example, a cockroach in *Naked Lunch*.

When I got back upstairs to my room I found all my underwear cut into little pieces and scattered like a confetti obscenity. There was a knife plunged into the middle of my bed. A Swiss Army knife. The knife blade was stuck in, the fork part pointed up.

15

I cleaned up the bits and pieces of material scattered around the room. I called room service and asked them for a new mattress. Then I got the hotel livery to drive me into town, where I bought new underwear. I got the plainest, least erotic, lowest priced ones I could find so that if it happened again it would cost me as little as possible and give whoever it was as little pleasure as possible.

When I returned it was almost lunchtime. Sonny was awake. I didn't feel like going back to the dining room. The hotel routinely packs lunch for hikers, so Sonny got two packed lunches and brought them up to my room. I didn't feel like eating.

"What are we going to do?" I asked him.

"Why don't we call Duke. Duke really was a detective. He solved cases and everythin'."

Sonny called Duke at all the numbers we had for him. He was still not around. It was up to us, just us, again.

"I guess what we should do, I mean the regular thing to do, is question everybody. Where were you? Where was everyone else? What was your relation to the deceased and alla that. It's prob-'bly not that hard. Duke done it all the time and we both know, he's not a rocket scientist. The only reason I never done it, I never had the motivation. And you're real smart about this stuff, just cause you're a woman, that don't matter."

"Thanks."

"So we make a list. You take half. I take half. We see how it goes, meet up, consult and revise as required."

I took out a pen and a notepad and did as he suggested. He got Angelique, Lucy, Gavin, Brigette, Choice, and Larry Rhinebeck. I took Amy, Derek, Mitzi, Mitch, Fern, and Lazlo Viktorska.

I found Mitzi on the phone in the room on the second floor that had been set up as the production office. In the midst of the spring green woods, fresh air, and sunshine, she had created a little dark corner of production hell for herself, surrounded by full ashtrays and half-empty cups of coffee.

I heard her on the phone before she saw me. "I know everything he planned to do. Every shot, every setup. Of course the film can be finished. And finished almost exactly the way that Alan would have done it himself. Let's face facts. There's no question that Alan was a genius, with an incredible track record, but if you'd ever been on set with us, you'd realize that it was me carrying the ball very, very often. . . .

"It's not a question of visual sense. Not in reality. Everything is boarded out and Lazlo really sets up the shots visual-sense-wise. . . . Hold on." She'd seen me. She pushed the hold button. "What are you doing here?"

"I wanted to talk. A little. About Alan."

"Sorry. I just don't have the time now. There's a crisis and it's got to be handled."

"Oh, I know, but . . ."

"A lot of money may be lost. Or saved. Jobs, too. Now, if you'll excuse me . . ."

"Maybe later."

"I doubt it. Don't slam the door on your way out."

As I left without slamming, she tucked the earpiece into her shoulder pad and resumed her conversation.

I tried to call Mitchell Du Bois's suite. The line was busy so I knew he was in. I consulted our call sheet and found his room number. He was on the third floor, facing the lake. I knocked.

"Bring it in. Just set it up on the table," he yelled from somewhere inside.

Obviously he wasn't talking to me, but I accepted the invitation. I walked into a combination living room and office. Mitch was in the bedroom, like Mitzi, with a phone stuck between his shoulder and his ear. His shoulders were more natural than hers. As I looked in, he looked out. As soon as he saw me panic flashed across his face, as if I'd caught him at something. He slammed the bedroom door shut as quickly as he could reach it. I had the impression that I'd seen things laid out on the bed. But what?

A few moments later the bedroom door opened, but only eight or ten inches, just enough for him to slither out, not enough for me to see past him. "What do you want?"

"I'm sorry," I said. "I didn't mean to intrude. I knocked."

"I was expecting room service."

"Can I talk to you for a couple of minutes?"

"I thought you were arrested?"

"Well, they wanted to talk to me. I mean it happened in my room. But they don't think I did it, not really. And they didn't arrest me."

"Oh. Oh-oh."

The phone rang. He picked it up. "Du Bois," he said. "Mikey, baby. How are you. . . . A tragedy. A tragedy of the first order. . . . Absolutely, he was a love. And he will be missed. . . . No, no. no. There is no reason. . . . No, no reason for the picture and eighteen million dollars to go down the tubes. . . . Hey, Mikey, who loves you, baby. . . . When it happened, my first thought, after sorrow and grief, of course, my first thought was of you. . . .

I mean that. Sincerely. . . . Yours is the first interest that has to be protected here. All the way. I mean all the way down the line.

"Shut down? . . . We're running the numbers now. And as we're doing it, they're speaking to me. You know what they're saying? . . . Very funny, very funny. Mikey, baby, what they're saying is *completion, completion.*

"No. Absolutely not. It's your interests I'm concerned with here. Me? At this point, I gotta work myself into an early grave trying to pull it off. Jesus Christ, what a mess, you know what I mean? The only reason I'm even considering it is because of you and me, our relationship. Our past. Our future. . . .

"I'll meet you at the airport. . . . No. I'm not gonna send a limo. Whatever you do, don't fly commercial. Grab a G, they got an airport right near here. I'll pick you up myself. I wouldn't dream of doing it any other way, Mikey, baby." Mitch hung up. "What do you want?"

"I cared for Alan," I said.

"We all did. Great guy. Great talent. Be sorely missed. No question. Whaddaya want?"

"I didn't . . . do it."

"Of course not. . . ." The phone rang. He looked at it longingly. "What I'm trying to do, I'm trying to save the picture. Not for me. For all you kids, you actors and the crew that worked so hard." It rang again. His whole body vibrated in response. "What you shouldn't do, is stir the pot, mess things up, cause more concern." It rang. He twitched. "You need help with lawyers or something, maybe we could arrange that. . . ." The phone rang. He couldn't stop himself, he grabbed it. "Du Bois. . . . Donnie, baby, how are you. . . . A tragedy. A tragedy of the first order. . . . Absolutely, he was a love. And he will be missed. . . . No, no, no. There is no reason. . . . Donnie, I wanna talk to you more than anybody on the planet. But I got someone in here. . . . Nah, just an actress, so hold on one second.

"You'll excuse me, don't mean to be rude," he said to me, gesturing at the door. "Long distance. Gotta take it."

"OK, thanks," I said, backing out of his suite. Somehow I

would have to get into that bedroom to see what he was hiding. As I closed the door, I thought I heard a noise. I felt like someone was watching me. But as I turned around, the hall was empty.

Across the lake from the motel, the land rises in that typical Shawangunk way, sloping slowly and steadily upward, and then, at the highest point, it becomes a cliff, one side facing the lake, which curves around to the left like the blunt prow of a ship. Upon this point there is a stone tower. It looks like a lighthouse but it has no purpose except to rise above the trees and provide hikers and hotel guests with an even better view. At the top, his dramatic hair pushed back by the wind, I found Lazlo Viktorska.

"Picking out a shot?" I asked him.

"No."

"Oh," I said.

He pointed to the east. "You see the flats there. The Indians grew corn there. Just like in the history books. They buried fish to fertilize the corn. There were lots of fish in the river once, and easy to catch. Then it was settled by the Dutch and the Huguenots. They built houses of stone. There are a lot of them left. Very picturesque."

"What do you think, will they cancel the movie without Alan?"

"A place like this, the panorama, it actually does not make for a good shot."

"Then why did you come up here?"

"Here," he said, "I'll show you." He was wearing a light jacket with a lot of pockets like a fisherman's vest. A lot of camera-people wear them. He took out a director's finder. It's sort of a small zoom lens designed for the purpose of viewing things as they would be seen through a camera and setting up shots. He handed it to me. I looked through it. He was right. The landscape actually diminished in some way through the lens. "For the wind," he said.

"What?"

"The wind is strong up here. I like the wind in my face."

I pointed the finder at the hotel and twisted it to its longest focal length. I saw Lucy Kohl. She was calling and waving. I followed her with the lens as she jogged over to someone. It was a girlish jog, everything bouncing and adorable. It was Dan Ginzburg, the man from Quad-Star. She simpered at him. Little Lucy would just love to go for a walk in the woods with Dan.

"Did you know Alan well?"

"I like to get out of the studio. Wind, rain, snow. Sometimes it's hard, you know, because we stand around so much. Still, it's good to get out of the studio."

"How were my dailies?"

"Very good."

"Do you think I killed Alan?"

"A nice girl like you, dedicated to Art, fragile and sensitive, how could you be a killer? Is that what you are asking me?"

"I guess so."

"Once upon a time . . . but having done so many movies, I see gouts of blood all the time. People shooting, all the time. Stabbing and drowning. Are these dreams? Visions? Or reportage? So you ask me, do I believe in innocence? Do I believe in fairies?"

"Lazlo, are you always this noncommunicative?"

"Ask me about the camera. Ask me about the shots. Look at my footage, communication is what I am about."

"You knew Alan a long time. Who had reason to kill him? I didn't. I really didn't, you know. He was giving me the biggest break I've ever had."

"Are you familiar with Bertolt Brecht?"

"With his plays? Yes. Very much."

"With the man?"

"Not really."

"He was the consummate Middle European of the middle of our century. You must read sometime his testimony before the House Un-American Activities Committee. Brecht was a Communist, yes, a committed Marxist. The rest of these people from Hollywood, they defied the committee, or they wept and had breakdowns. Brecht, he said his English was weak and he used a translator, which slowed everything down and made for much confusion. When they asked him if he had written these poems that called for violent revolution, he said no, no, no, that translation is all wrong. When they asked him if he was a Marxist, he said no, but admitted he had studied Marx for his views of history. When he was done the committee thanked him as a friendly witness. The next day he left the country. To Switzerland, then to East Germany, where they gave him his own theater, the Berliner Ensemble. He was their prize, their showcase intellectual. But in his pocket he kept an Austrian passport."

"I don't know what you're talking about," I said.

"Yes, well, you see."

He took the director's finder back and started down the concrete stairs inside the tower. I followed him. At the base he took out a small map, provided by the hotel, of the trails and carriage roads. He considered the various routes from the tower, made a decision, folded the map, placed it in one of his many pockets, and began walking. I walked along beside him.

"Once you would have believed me?" I asked. "Believed in my innocence?"

"No," he said. "I did not say that."

"Oh."

"Would you like to know my family secrets?"

"Sure."

"My grandfather, he was a scholar and a writer and fascist. Hated the Jews with a passion. A famous anti-Semite. Hated Communists. My father, who hated his father, became a Communist. He informed on my grandfather, so I am told, to the Russians, who sent him off to a camp somewhere from which he never returned. My father was successful, as a Communist, for a time, so I got a pretty good education. Then it turned out he was the wrong kind of Communist and he was put on trial. He was sent away and we became very poor. My grandmother hoarded gold. My mother stole it and with that gold got us both out of the country.

"So," he said, "everybody is capable of anything. Good story, huh?"

"Yes," I said.

"My family secrets are not very secret. I tell everybody. You can read it in more detail in *American Cinematographer*. It makes people take me seriously."

I arrived back at the hotel at teatime. They served coffee and tea and little cookies in a large lakeside room. There is a row of rocking chairs on the veranda, occupied, mostly, by old people with throws over their laps. I saw Sonny. He had a brown paper bag with what looked like a bottle in it.

I asked him what he'd found out. He asked me if I'd seen Angelique.

"She's on *your* list," I said.

"I know that," he said. "She's not exactly what you would call a grieving widow."

"Does that mean you talked to her?"

"Yeah."

"What did you find out?"

"I found her down in the stable. She got that outfit that they wear, those pants that are real tight and then they come out at the sides—jodhpurs—and riding boots. So I says, you know, to make contact, I says, 'Hey, good-looking horse.'

"'You ride?' she asks me.

"I says, 'Nah. But I spend a lot of the time at the track. You go to the track?'

"She says something like, 'Watching does not interest me. I like to be on top.'"

"Did she really say that?"

"Yeah, you think I'm making this up?"

"No," I said.

"She's got some kinda accent I can't exactly place it. It's not exactly Italian, not exactly French. I know it's not Spanish. I don't know. Do you know?"

"No."

"Then she swings herself up in the saddle, you know how they do. There's something about women and horses. This Angelique, she's really into that woman and horse thing."

"What do you mean?"

"Well, you know . . ."

"What?"

"She moved around, kind of fittin' herself to the saddle, if you can visualize what I'm sayin'."

"Yes," I said. I could, but I didn't.

"I says, 'If I was to get a horse, maybe you could teach me a little.' That didn't work."

"No?"

"Nah. She says, 'I don't enjoy teaching. I usually want someone who already knows.' With that accent, it was, uh, provocative."

"Yes," I said. "Provocative."

"So I decide to try something else. 'This is the first time I ever stayed somewhere they don't have a bar,' I said. 'If they did, I'd say come and have a drink with me when you get done.' She says, 'Then maybe you shouldn't be here.' But her eyes are saying something different. So I says, 'What do you drink?' She says, 'Russian vodka. Iced. With pepper.' " He held up the paper bag.

"She say anything else?"

"She rode away. I start back to the hotel, I hear a kid, calling 'Mama, Mama.' Maybe Angelique could hear it, maybe not, but if she did she ignored it. Then I saw the nanny with the two kids. What's their names again?"

"Chelsea and Gavin. The nanny is Brigette."

"Right. Cute little girl, she's wearing a white dress with a big red bow at the waist and a straw hat. Like a paintin'. She starts to run after the horse. The nanny, who's wearing these tweedy clothes, grabbed her. 'Don't run,' she says. 'You will trip and dirty your dress.'

"That ain't right," Sonny said. "OK, Sunday mornin', you dress the kids up for church, but otherwise, little kid like that, you let 'em run and get dirty. Of course her brother yells, 'Run, run.' I got a feeling this is not a nice kid. Then the little girl says she wants Mama and throws herself on the ground, where she's getting dirty, so the nanny is uptight. The brother picks up a handful of pebbles and begins to drop them on his sister. Not a nice kid. The nanny picks up the little girl. The little girl starts to yell, 'I hate you, I hate you,' like that. Bangin' at her with her little fists. 'You must stop this now,' the nanny says. She talks funny. What is she, German?"

"Swiss. She is Swiss."

"So I go over, figuring this is a good time to be of service, a helpful stranger and all that, make friends. I mean the nanny looked like she was ready to employ corporal punishment. So I smile at her and I say, 'They all get like this from time to time. Especially at this age. I got two of my own and I remember.'

"The nanny gets real snotty: 'That your children had tantrums is no reason for Chelsea to have a tantrum.' So I try the little girl. I kneel down, kids like it, you go down to their height. 'Hey, little girl,' I say, 'that's a nice dress. You like wearing dresses?' Little girls, they don't change, they grow up, they still like it when you tell them that they're wearing nice dresses. She starts to say she wants her daddy. The nanny says her daddy is in heaven. I pretend not to know anything. I say, 'Poor kid, her father's dead?' Like a question, you know."

" 'My daddy's not dead,' she says. 'He's in heaven.' "

" 'Yeah, with Santy Claus,' Gavin says."

" 'Do you know what heaven is?' I ask her."

"Little girl says that heaven is where her daddy went, but her nanny won't let her go there and join him. So I pick her up and hold her. Little kids, they like hugs.

"This nanny, she's somethin' else. She says, 'It is not good for the girl to be handled by strangers. You must give her to me. You will give her to me. I am the nanny.'

"So I didn't do so good with the kiddies or their keeper. But I'm communicatin' with their mother."

"I hope you remember," I said, rather testily, "that we're try-ing to keep me out of jail. I hope you remember that."

"Sure, Annie, sure. Don't worry about it. I wonder where she is?"

"Try her room."

"Good idea."

Larry Rhinebeck was at the cookie table. He was very carefully looking over the cookies and little baked goods to determine how many he had to eat to satisfy his food sampling compulsion. Before I could flee, he saw me. He came at me as fast as he could while still balancing a cookie collection in his right hand and a cup of coffee in his left. He did pretty well. He only lost one cookie and—while there was a trail of coffee drips from where he started all the way to me—there was still some coffee left in his cup.

I shouldn't, I decided, be so negative about him. I had yet to discover anything, and Sonny certainly hadn't discovered any-thing; maybe Larry had. "Have you discovered anything?" I asked.

"We're stumbling through a nest of vipers here," he said. "But they're silent as clams. Somebody's keeping the lid on and mum's the word."

"OK, Larry. Call me when you find something out."

"Would you like a cookie, Annie? I got lots."

Fern was in the library. He had a cup of tea in front of him but when I entered I saw him fill it with the contents of a pocket flask. I pulled up a chair and sat beside him. He was soused enough that I could smell the alcohol coming through his pores. The odor of tobacco smoke and ash was strong as well. He looked me over with an expression of hatred and disdain that made him seem particularly feminine.

"Well, I guess that taught Alan DeLucca never to cast anyone over the recommendations of the casting director."

"Oh," I said, getting my back up, "you were opposed to my being cast as Glenda. Did you happen to hear the crew applaud? How often does the crew applaud? Did you speak to Lazlo Viktorska? Did you happen to see the dailies?"

"I did indeed see the dailies, and I saw the corpse as well."

"Do you really think I killed him?"

"You heterosexuals. Your passions are so out of control. As if not one of you had ever heard of sex before."

"I didn't kill him."

"Really."

"Really."

"Well, you certainly screwed up my schedule." He reached into his pocket and took out a silver art deco cigarette case. He opened it but was annoyed to find it empty. He snapped it shut. "I have two MOWs I should be casting right at this very minute and a very prestigious feature."

"Did you know Alan a long time?"

"Do you think, if he came back from the dead, he would listen to me this time? You bet your life he wouldn't. Never underestimate a casting director. We are an underappreciated species. Frankly, compared to being a casting director, having an alternate gender orientation is a day at the beach."

I was looking for Amy. I found her, unfortunately, with Derek. "Don't say nothing," Derek said to her. She sniffled back her tears and didn't say anything.

"I spoke to a lawyer friend of mine," he said to me. "And he told me we don't have to say anything to nobody and we ain't." He stared at me and flexed all over.

I was very depressed.

It was soon to get worse. When I went down to dinner, Bob Moser, the Real Detective, was waiting for me.

"I spoke to the district attorney," he said. "He put his first assistant, Tom Costello, on this case. Costello is, well, pretty ferocious. He wants an arrest. I advised him to wait for the full lab reports and forensics and all of that. He agreed. He got on the phone with them and pushed for priority. So, what we're looking at here, is about noon tomorrow. Maybe, if you're lucky, after lunch. But I don't think so. I thought, as a courtesy, I would let you know."

That killed my appetite. Rather than eat, I decided to go up to my room and cry. Or take a bath. Or both. And where was Sonny? Was he off with that woman? Doing perverse things that involved riding crops and the exchange of jodhpurs? As I went upstairs, Mitchell Du Bois passed me going downstairs, to dinner. It was, I realized, the perfect time to break into his room and see what he had been hiding.

But how? I know that on television detectives break into rooms all the time. With credit cards or picklocks or through windows. But I don't know how to do that. Maybe Sonny did. But where was Sonny?

I would have to think of a ruse. I was better at ruses than break-ins. I decided to rush up to the desk in disguise, loaded down with bag and packages, announce myself as Mrs. Du Bois, and demand the key to his room.

I pinned my hair up. I picked out a hat that would hide most of my distinctive red hair and I put on a pair of large Gloria Steinhem glasses. As I watched my disguise growing in the mirror, I rehearsed in my mind what would happen at the desk. I realized that the desk would just call a bell man for bags, then call the room, and not finding Mitchell there, would look for him, logically, in the dining room, which, of course, was exactly where he was.

That wouldn't work.

If it were earlier in the day and the maids were working I could walk right in. If the maid came when Mitchell was out. If he had not disposed of whatever he'd been hiding by then. If he did not take it with him.

I went down to Mitchell's room and stared at the door as if that would inspire me. I tried it, just in case, but it was locked. I paced. I bit my lip. Neither one helped. Someone was coming down the hall. I sensed the person before I saw him. It was a room service waiter. Would he be suspicious of me? Loitering about? More to the point, would he have a passkey and what would I have to do to get him to use it?

When he came close I did what I had to do. "Help me, help me, please," I whined. I sniffled.

"What's wrong?"

"Oh God, oh God, this is so embarrassing. You have to let me into that room for a minute. Please."

"Well, ma'am, is it your room?"

"I'll pay you, please help me."

"If it's not your room . . ."

"How can I tell you . . ."

"Perhaps if you went to the front desk . . ."

"No!" I clutched his arm. I held him there. I was a damsel in distress. Deep distress. Why was I in distress? Why did I have to get into the room? "If I tell you," I said, "will you promise not to tell anyone?"

"No, ma'am. I mean yes, ma'am . . ." He couldn't have been more than nineteen and he had acne. Not a lot, but what he had was large and juicy. "But, it doesn't matter because . . ."

"Oh God, oh God," I cried again. "I'll have to tell you."

"It's not necessary."

"Only then will you understand." He tried to get out of my grasp. I held him tight. What would I tell him? "My panties," I said. "Are in that room."

"Is that your room?"

"No. Don't you see. That's the point. It's a man's room!"

"Yes, ma'am."

"My lover," I said.

"Why don't you, uh, ask him for the key."

Why not? "Because . . ." Why not?

"Because?"

"Because, he is, right now, in the dining room with . . . his wife." Who else? "Who just arrived. And he and I . . . one last time . . . before she came . . . and I rushed out and he rushed out

. . . and he's down there . . . and my underwear is in there . . . and when they've dined he, and she, will come up here. And the evidence will be—there!"

"Oh."

"You must help me. Let me in. Let me find them. Let me leave."

"My job . . ." He was wavering.

"It's worse than that. She's . . . unstable. Just released from the asylum. She grows violent. She attacked him. Not long ago. With a knife. It was at dinner. Fortunately it was just a butter knife. But he still has bruises from it. This could . . . over the edge . . . you must, I beg you."

"I . . ."

"*I beg you.*"

"I'll tell you what I'll do. I'll go in and look and if I see any . . . you know . . . underwear. I'll bring it out to you."

"But, but how would you recognize my underwear? You don't know what my underwear looks like. I'd recognize it and it would be much simpler. Just let me. You could wait right here and be sure I didn't steal anything. I just want my underwear. To prevent a tragedy."

"I'll go," he said. Nodding his head up and down in rapid, determined little nods.

And he did. He opened the door. He went in. I followed.

"No," he cried, blocking my entrance. "You must stay out."

"I'll help."

He pushed the door shut in my face. He locked it from inside. I heard him shuffle around. He came back, opened the door. "I didn't find anything. At least not out in plain sight. Your friend must have hidden them." He came out, closed the door behind him, and double-locked it. "Or, maybe, you lost them somewhere else."

He left me standing there. When he was gone, and there was no one there to see me, I sank down to the floor and sat there. Rather stupidly, I thought. I was alone. Abandoned. Helpless. Incompetent. There was only one sensible thing to do. I cried.

Drowning in my own tears, I missed the arrival of the next person to enter the hallway until I glimpsed his boots within the periphery of my downcast vision. I stood up, wiping my eyes. There was Choice Wardell, until two days ago a good and popular actor, now, in his own mind, a *P.I.*, a *gumshoe*, a *dick*.

"Hiya, sweetheart. Who put those raindrops on your pretty face?"

"Mitch Du Bois is hiding something."

"What?"

"I don't know. It's hidden."

"Evidence, you mean?"

"I hope so."

"A clue at least."

"At least."

"We better get in there and find it."

"The door's locked."

"Stand back, babe," he said. He pushed his jacket back with a flourish. He sort of wiggled his piece at me the way large-breasted women sometimes throw their bosoms around. But he didn't reach for his gun. He reached for his wallet. He took out his credit cards. He had about twenty of them. He gave a lot of thought to which one he used the least for buying things. Once he'd decided, he removed it from the rest. He put his wallet away and then sidled up to the door. He slid the card into the gap between the door and the frame. He felt for the lock with it, then jerked the card against the lock. It was a really cool move.

Nothing happened.

So he tried pulling the card toward him. That didn't work. Then he pulled the card out and tried coming up from underneath. I always knew there was more to this than there appeared to be when they did it on TV. He began to sweat, more frustration than from heat. He pushed the card up, down, forward, back. It began to buckle and shred at the edges. The less it worked, the harder Choice worked at it.

Then it slipped out of his wet fingers. More in the gap than out. When he tried to grasp it, he only succeeded in pushing it farther in. Biting his lip in anger and concentration, he tried to get a fingernail under it to pry it back far enough to grip. Now it went all the way and fell inside the room.

He looked at me. He looked at the door. Life is tough when you don't have it scripted and prepped and propped for you. He squared his shoulders and gave the door a hard look, hard as Cagney ever looked.

Then he picked up his foot and kicked the door open. The wood was fifty or sixty or a hundred years old and snapped and splintered easily. I had the distinct sense that I would be blamed for this and would go to prison for breaking and entering and malicious mischief and vandalism as well as murder. But, as long as the door was open, I might as well look and discover what it was that Mitch Du Bois had been hiding. As I started to enter, Choice held me back. He drew his gun. He held it pointing up alongside his ear. Pressing his back against the door frame and pursing his lips, he whirled into the room. It seemed a bit much, since the one thing we knew was that the room was empty. But who was I to tell him how to live his movie?

I followed him in.

I went directly through the living room to the bedroom. There it was. Mitchell Du Bois's secret, laid out on the bed. From bottom to top: cowboy boots—Tony Lamas from Fred Segals; $590 linen pants by Yukio Kobayashi for Matsuda from Maxfield in Los Angeles; Navaho belt; a $450 floral print shirt from the Gianni Versace Boutique; and sunglasses from Robert Mark Opticians. Where a left hand would've been, there was a stopwatch, and ready for the right hand, a director's finder just like Lazlo Viktorska's that I'd looked through earlier in the afternoon.

Du Bois wanted to direct. And this was his costume, ready to be worn, should the mantle fall on him. He had not, I was certain, left the hotel after Alan died. He'd certainly not gone far enough or been gone long enough to acquire all of this. Which meant that he'd had it with him when he'd come to Mohonk. Could he have been certain even before he'd left New York that the opportunity to wear it would soon arise?

"Is that what you were looking for?" Choice asked.

"Yes," I said.

He reached for me and pulled me to him.

I said, "Uh, buh, buh . . ."

"There's something about you, babe."

"Choice, Mitch could be coming back at any second."

"Something dangerous."

"We should get out of here."

"It turns me on, in a powerful way."

"We should get out of here, now."

"I know you feel it too. Dangerous, and powerful, that attraction."

"Actually, no I don't. Not at all. Now let me go."

"Aww, come on."

I pushed away from him. I ran out into the hall. He followed me.

"Annie." He grabbed me again. He made love eyes at me. I recognized them. It was one of Rowdy's best routines. Rowdy'd busted up my marriage with that limpid stare. If he could have packaged it and bottled it, he could have peddled it at discount department stores for Valentine's Day. It didn't do a damn thing for me, not anymore.

"What's the matter?" I asked. "Don't you have anyone else to have sex with up here on location?"

"It's not like that."

"What happened? Lucy Kohl dumped you for the producer?"

"So what if she did?"

"That's what I thought. Now let me go."

He did. He was bitterly disappointed. He was a creature of the movies. In the movies when a dick did something for a doll, she was supposed to show her gratitude in a big way. He didn't quite know what to do about it when I showed no inclination to do so. Confusion became anger. "You better watch out," he said. "Lucy's after your job, and the bitch can suck the chrome off a 'fifty-seven Buick."

I hate it when men speak like that. I really do. And I don't understand where they think it will get them.

I went downstairs and called Sonny's room from a hall phone. There was no answer. I checked the desk for messages. I couldn't believe he had abandoned me for a widow with a riding crop.

I had one clue and about eighteen hours of freedom left.

Dinner was still being served, but I didn't have enough spirit left to put on a defiant face and a straight spine and stare them all down. Not after what happened yesterday with Rain.

At the snack bar I bought a cup of tea and a chocolate bar, a large imported one with nuts for $3.00, and took it across the hall into the library. Someone who had been working on the crossword puzzle had left a pen behind. I went back to the snack bar and got a couple of napkins, then went back to the library and sat down and made a list.

> Mitchell Du Bois: Brought director's costume with him. Kill to Direct?
>
> Mitzi: ?
>
> Amy & Derek: Why so adamant about not talking? Why had they already called a lawyer?
>
> Angelique: No grieving widow she. Did she kill Alan *because he was in love with me?*
>
> Gavin: Strange. But strange enough for patricide?
>
> Brigette: Motive? None that I understood, but she might well be disturbed. And was she really Swiss?
>
> Lucy Kohl: Wanted her part. She would have gotten nowhere with Alan because *Alan loved me.* So, kill two birds with one stone by killing Alan in my room. Move in on whichever influential male she could. If the movie was not continued without Alan—she had nothing to

lose, almost the only one with nothing to lose, because she was already off the picture.

Larry Rhinebeck: Not likely. He would have left crumbs at the crime scene.

Choice Wardell: ?

Lazlo Viktorska: Too busy being Lazlo Viktorska. Not likely.

Fern: A casting director—capable of anything.

In other words, almost anyone could have done it. Except me. I checked Sonny's room again and the desk for messages. No luck. So, having finished my chocolate bar, I bought another and went upstairs to lie in bed sleepless with worry.

When I walked in, there was a dead, decapitated squirrel on my pillow.

16

Murdered squirrels leave bad vibes behind. Not as bad as murdered directors, but bad enough. I insisted on another room. But I scarcely felt better after I moved. I felt terribly, and increasingly, vulnerable. I got in bed and tried to sleep, but one tormenting vision followed another.

I was at the lowest point of my life.

Lower than the day when I auditioned for the part of an actress-detective and was told that I was simply not the type. Lower than the day when I checked into a Buddhist retreat in Sri Lanka and, when I discovered there was no toilet paper, was told that I was expected to use my hand. Lower than the day when I returned from my trip around the world, ready to decide who I would choose to return to, my husband or my lover, and found that in my absence they had each of them found new girlfriends, both of them aerobics instructors.

Strangely, what made it so awful was not that I was under

suspicion for murder. I was still, I guess, in denial about that. Since I was innocent, I believed that somehow, some way, the truth would out and the truth would save me. This was America, land of the Happy End. It was not even that I had finally had my Big Break and because the director was dead, the movie might never be completed. I believe in my talent and I look upon acting as an art. Big Breaks are not what it's about. I hope.

What depressed me was the thought that *Alan had loved me.*

Looking back over my life, this seemed increasingly important. While I did love my husband, we were fourteen when we started dating—we were children—and somehow our relationship got stuck there. We were together seventeen years and I feel like I was a girl, not a woman, with him. My fling with Rowdy, however violent and destructive our passions were, turned out, in the end, to have been just that, a fling. And the pitifully few others that passed in review in my memory meant even less. Normally, I don't think about all of that. I am not one of those women who is always searching for a man, who gets frantic whenever she has to eat dinner alone, who subordinates her life to finding a relationship and, when she succeeds, almost immediately begins to wallow in the angst of the inadequacy of that relationship. Normally, I don't care.

Now I did. I hadn't been looking, but in Alan I had found something special. He was intelligent, incredibly talented, and had a spiritual dimension. He cared about the same sort of things I did and we could communicate. He had been slim, good-looking, well groomed, well dressed, and a fastidious eater. All the shallow things that are of vital importance to me. And he had loved me.

I was going to get another part a lot faster than I would find another Alan.

Sonny finally showed up in my room, the new new room, at two in the morning. He had had a great deal to drink. However, he knew how to hold his liquor and it barely showed.

"Annie, we gotta talk," Sonny said.

"You were my partner. I counted on you," I said, sitting up in bed. I was wearing my flannel pajamas. They are not provocative. I was too angry to be concerned that Sonny was seeing me completely without makeup. "Where have you been?"

"I told you where I was going."

"Not that you were going to disappear into her arms."

"Do you know who Angelique is?"

"Yes, yes," I said. Ten years ago it had been hard to miss her. Her face and all but the most clinical parts of her body had been everywhere. "She's a retired and very rapidly aging supermodel. I bet she has collagen lips."

"Ah, ahh . . ."

"I have never once been critical of your, your compulsion with women. Mercedes and Caren and your wife and who knows who else. But when you can't resist hitting on some boot-wearing, whip-bearing slut, while my entire life is at stake, that's pathological behavior. That shows that something is really wrong with you."

"Hey, Annie, gimme a break here."

"Where've you been?"

"First I went to the front desk. I asked for Alan DeLucca's room number. I went upstairs to the room they gave me. I knocked. No answer. I tried the door, it was open. I went in. There was no one there, I started lookin' around, I mean what the hell. Only one person was livin' there and there was nothing there didn't belong to a guy. So I figured Angelique, she had separate accommodations. . . ."

"Are you sure?" Separate accommodations. Somehow that made me feel better.

"Yeah, I'm sure. I can tell the difference between a man's stuff and a woman's. I'm a detective. I went back to the desk and asked if there was another DeLucca registered. The guy said no, so I asked for della Verona. He found it under *V*."

"And where have you been since then?"

"With Angie."

"Oh, Angie, is it?"

"Yeah."

"I rest my case," I said. An unfortunate choice of words.

"I was investigating."

"What? Her . . ." I wanted to use a coarse expression, but I did not. I said, ". . . sex organs. Were they different than the usual ones?"

"Ya got ya'self all in uproar ovuh nothin'."

"I do?"

"Yeah. Calm yourself. You wan' a cigarette?"

"All right."

He gave me one of his Trues. I tore off the filter and lit up. I would have preferred a chocolate bar. Or a brownie.

"Like I said, I discovered her true identity. She's really a nice person."

"Of course she is. That's why she walks around in a costume left over from *Ilsa, She-Wolf of the SS. Vould you like some kinky sex, I vear lots of leather and I vant to hurt someone.*"

"She's not like that, that's Alan's thing."

"What? What utter bullshit."

"Are you gonna lissen to me, or are you gonna rant and rave? Huh? 'Cause I got no patience for rantin' and ravin'. You notice I don't live with my wife."

"OK, so you investigated Angelique della Verona and found out that deep inside she's a nice girl who went to Catholic school, wears clean white underwear, and goes to confession every Saturday, where she has to make up things to tell the Father."

"You think you're being sarcastic but you're closer than you think."

"I am?"

"Yeah. Her real name, it's Angie Getzevitch. She's from Staten Island. She's half Lit'uanian and half Italian. I thought I recognized her from somewheres. She used to go out with my cousin Paulie, long time ago. I met her, Paulie's sister's weddin'. She was Paulie's date."

"And the continental accent and the della Verona?"

"Verona was her mother's maiden name. And the accent, she

developed that for her modeling thing. It worked, people go for that image stuff, you unnerstand that."

"Yeah, well, what about the riding crop and the attitude?"

"It was that kinky German photographer, first made her famous. That's what made her a super-model. Though she does like horses. If it was up to Angie, she'd wear reg'lar clothes and cook some pasta and get fat. Maybe even go back to Staten Island."

"You're out of your mind. She brainwashed you. Nobody wants to go back to Staten Island."

"I'm telling you what she says. I'm not here to argue with you about it."

"So what you're saying is that she's been forced, against her will, to wear glamorous clothes, stay thin and beautiful, indulge in cosmetic surgery—if I don't miss my guess—live in a major ten-room, view-of-the-park condo with a house in the Hamptons and a place in Malibu and a nanny for the kiddies, when what she really wants is to be a fat Italian mamma in a hot, stuffy little kitchen, stirring spaghetti sauce and changing diapers? Is that what you're saying, or did I miss something?"

"I got a lot of information from her."

"Like what?"

"Like her husband liked to jump on anything that moved."

"That's a lie," I cried.

"You know the ones that everyone calls the Two Witches, which Angie calls the Two Bitches?"

"She's the bitch," I said, "slandering Alan. Now that he's dead and can't defend himself."

"If he didn't have anyone else, he'd boff them."

"Mitzi, with the shoulder pads? You have to be kidding."

"Convenience, you can't discount convenience."

"Hogwash. I bet your friend *Angie* is the killer. And she's spreading dirt to cover her tracks."

"There was others. Angie, she was thinking of divorce. She had dicks on him. Someone else's SAD squad was watchin' him. Not now, but awhile ago."

"She's, she's just jealous of me and can't stand that Alan loved me," I blurted out, "and maybe she killed him before he divorced her."

"Annie," Sonny said, "lissen to me."

"What?"

"I gotta ask you somethin'."

"What?"

"I know how you feel about your private life being private and such . . ."

"Yeah?"

"I gotta ask you."

"What? Ask me already."

"Alan and you, did you?"

"What?"

"Did you do it with Alan?"

"No," I said. "We did not."

"Did you mess around, you know, did you do . . . this or that?"

"We barely even kissed. Why?"

"See, when I went looking for Angie, when I went to the wrong room first, DeLucca's room . . ."

"So?"

"So I looked around. I looked through his stuff. He had a lotta drugs. Prescription drugs. One of them was AZT."

"No," I said.

"There's only one thing you take AZT for. So Alan, he was HIV-positive, and he knew it."

17

I had to see for myself. Sonny took me to Alan's room. It was
true. Inside the left-hand top drawer of the bureau there was a
bottle of AZT with a prescription number and Alan's name on
it. There were several other prescriptions of drugs whose
names meant nothing to me. One of them, Sonny said, was a
painkiller, and another, a mood elevator. I was tempted to take
one of each.

"And I thought . . ."

"What?"

". . . that I meant something to him."

"Men," Sonny said. "They think with their dicks. You can't
trust 'em."

I began to look around the room. The room was mostly picked
up and the bed made. But it should have been if he'd come in
from location scouting at—when? about five, six in the evening,
certainly after the maid had done the room—and gone to my

room in time to die at seven. The room key was on top of a table, which helped explain why the door was open. There was a cigarette butt in an ashtray. No filter, brown paper.

"This isn't yours, is it?" I asked Sonny, knowing he smoked True Blues and already sure it wasn't.

"No. I figured it was Alan's."

"No," I said. "He doesn't smoke. And he eats very fastidiously. . . . Didn't," I corrected myself. "Ate."

I picked up the butt. It seemed like the thing to do. This was *evidence.* I vaguely remembered seeing Sherlock Holmes in a film. He had picked up a cigarette butt, sniffed it, touched the ash, mentioned in an offhand way that he had written a monograph on the 427 varieties of tobacco ash for the Royal Academy of Sciences and he could deduce that the smoker had been five feet ten inches, two hundred pounds, about fifty years old, in the habit of wearing brown tweeds, born in Wales, and recently returned from India. I hoped the brand name would be written on the butt. It wasn't. "Do you know what kind of cigarette that is?" I asked Sonny.

He looked it over, then touched his tongue to the paper.

"Yuchh," I said. "How can you do that?"

"Sherman's," he said.

"What?"

"It's a Sherman's."

"How can you tell?"

"It's a fancy tobacco store, Manhattan, makes it's own brand of cigarette. Very expensive, half again or twice as much as regular cigarettes. Mercedes, she got them for me one time. Waste o' money but it's the thought that counts, you know. The paper, it's sweet, brown and sweet, I remember that."

"So sometime between when the maid cleaned the room and when he . . . left the room, Alan left the room, someone who smoked Sherman's was here. Should be easy to find out who smokes Sherman's. Alan was out location scouting. He would have been doing that until pretty late, five or six or later even. We can find out by talking to the two witches. So that would mean, probably, that whoever smoked these was here, after that, pretty close to . . ."

"To seven," Sonny said.

"Yes."

I went into the bathroom. A bath towel and a washcloth had been used. A toothbrush was out on the sink. Alan had taken a shower and brushed his teeth before he went to my room. I recalled how he'd looked on the floor. He was dressed differently than the way I'd seen him on the mountain. He'd changed his clothes too. That was nice.

I went back into the bedroom. I went through his closets and his drawers. They were virtually empty. That wasn't right. I didn't know Alan terribly well—obviously I knew him a lot less than I'd imagined—but I was still certain that he would have traveled with a lot of clothing. There was a suitcase set on the small folding table designed for that purpose. It was almost full. But it still didn't contain as much as it ought to have and what there was had been thrown in, the way someone like Larry Rhinebeck would pack, not folded and set in neatly by a man who valued his clothes in the way that Alan DeLucca had.

"Where's his script?" I said. "And his notes."

"What?"

"I don't think they were in my room, when I went in to get my clothes. I would've noticed the script, if only because I still haven't read it," I said. "And I don't see them here."

"They weren't here when I came earlier," Sonny said. "I tossed the place pretty good, just like you done, and it wasn't here."

"He wasn't staying here," I said. "Not really."

"No. I guess not," Sonny said.

"What do you think, Sonny? Did Alan get this room just to . . ."

"What?"

"Just to fuck me."

Light was visible, a small spill into the hall, from the crack between the door and the jamb. Sonny knocked. "Yess, who is there?" Angelique della Verona said in her Eurotrash accent.

"It's me."

"Oh, Sonny," Angie said, sounds of Staten Island coming through. "I'll be there in a secon'." She came to the door wearing a thin, scoop-necked T-shirt and a pair of very expensive sweat pants.

"We gotta talk to you," Sonny said, moving into the room.

He initially blocked me from sight. When she saw me, she said, "What are you doing with her? What is she doing here?"

"Take it easy," Sonny said.

"No," Angie said. Now she was all Staten Island. "I am not gonna take it easy. You bring this bimbo who killed my Alan heah and I am not gonna take it easy. Read my lips, get the bimbo outta heah."

"She didn't do it, Angie." Sonny said.

"How the hell you know what she did or di'n't do?"

"We found a witness," Sonny said. "Who seen her some-wheres else at the time of the crime." Only cops and psychopaths can lie with such total and casual sincerity on the spur of the moment.

"Well, I don't care," Angie said. "She was gonna do it *with my husband*. Any woman does it with another woman's husband, you know what she is. You know what you are," she said pointing at me.

I flushed. Yes, I was. I should've known better too. "I'm sorry," I said. "I really am. He told me that . . ." I couldn't even complete the sentence. Of course he told me one thing or another. All the husbands do and women are supposed to know better, they're supposed to look for a ring and to know that if there is a mark of a ring where there is no ring, it means he's not just a cheating son of a bitch, he's a lying, scheming, deceitful, cheating son of a bitch.

"Don't be mad at her," Sonny said. "She's OK. She never made it with him or nothing. I know her real well. . . ."

"You didn't tell me you knew her."

"I di'n't tell you I was born in New York Hospital neither. We di'n't get to my whole life biography. Angie, come on, we need to talk to you. Angie"—he paused, switched gears—"we know about Alan."

"What do you mean?"

"We just been to the other room. We seen the drugs and everything. So . . ." He looked infinitely sympathetic. He does that very well. ". . . we know."

She looked at him. "You think that I . . . ?"

Sonny shrugged.

She gave a short, harsh laugh. "Good thing my husband gave up making love to me after Chelsea was born. I lucked out. I'm not infected."

"I'm glad to hear that," Sonny said. His attitude toward her changed from the easygoing friendliness he used to get along with everyone, and to get witnesses to talk, to something a little more animal.

"Are you?" she asked. Glad, she meant.

"Yeah," Sonny said. "When I seen the AZT, I was worried about you. Nice kid like you, from Staten Island."

"So now you know the truth about Alan DeLucca. The great man. You gonna spread it around?"

"Not me," Sonny said. "Though I imagine it'll come out, in the autopsy and all."

"Yeah," she sighed.

"The rest of his stuff still here?" Sonny asked.

"Yeah," Angie said.

"What time did he come back from looking at locations?"

"You wanna pour me another glass of the vodka?"

I saw where the bottle was, two fingers short of empty. I looked around for a glass. I found the one with her lipstick on it beside the bed.

"On the rocks, will ya, hon," Angie said to me without hostility.

Most of the ice was melted, a few quarter cubes floated around. What the hell, the alcohol would kill the germs and the pepper would cut the taste of stale water. I made her the drink.

"About five, a few minutes later maybe," she said.

171

"Alone?"

"No. He had the two bitches with him. Do you know how long he's been sleeping with them? The both of them? He's been screwing them so long that when he started, they looked young. He went over his notes with them, and then they left. They left in a hurry with me staring at them."

"Do they know?"

"I don't know."

"Oh," Sonny said.

"I shoulda told them. But I didn't. Not because I hate 'em. Because I figured if he was still doing it with them, the damage, it was already done, you know. It wasn't so long ago that I found out myself, you gotta understand that. Alan didn't exactly come home and say, *Guess what I got, hon.* I found out like how you found out. I found the medicine."

"What's the other room?" Sonny asked. "The one that's registered in his name. Got one suitcase, a toothbrush, and some prescription bottles in it, looks like he just moved in."

"When the bitches left we had a fight. Nasty fight."

"Yeah, well," Sonny said, sounding very understanding, "you're married."

"Yeah," she said.

"What you fighting about?"

"Her," Angie said, pointing at me with her glass, vodka sloshing just to the rim but not quite over.

"What about her?"

"I told him if he went with any other women, I would kill him. I said he was evil. He said I shouldn't worry about it, it was none of my business. I said he was killing people. He said, and I think he actually believed this, that he just was HIV-positive, that he wasn't actually sick, and before he got sick they would find a way to cure it. Look at me, he says, I'm fit, I'm strong, I'm healthy. I said that if he went with her I was gonna tell the whole world what was wrong with him and no one would think of him as the Great Director anymore, just as evil. Everyone in the whole world would know cause it would be on all those TV shows and in the *Post* and *Newsday* and everything.

"He grabbed a suitcase and threw some clothes in it, and his pills, and he left."

I thought I heard someone outside the door. I moved as quietly as I could across the room. At the same time I asked Angie, "His script? His notes?"

"What about them?"

"Did he take them?"

"Yes," Angie said. "Of course."

I opened the door. There was no one in the hall. It was time to leave. I think Sonny wanted to stay, now that Angie had told him she had not been sleeping with her husband and was not infected. I didn't believe her about that much more than I believed her about the rest, so I made sure he got out of there with me. I don't think Sonny has anything to fear from men with knives and guns, but he does need someone to protect him from women and his own nature.

Our next stop was the front desk to confirm part of Angie's story. We walked down the main staircase.

"Who smokes?" Sonny asked me.

"Mitzi. She's the assistant director. Fern, the casting director. Lazlo—he's the DP—occasionally, like when we're done shooting and he gets the camera assistant's last report."

"DP?"

"Director of photography."

"Everybody's got director in their name, huh?"

"And Lucy Kohl. When she's doing coke, she smokes too. At least she used to, in L.A."

"Is she doing coke now?"

"She was a couple of weeks ago. She was busted on her way to LAX. That's how I got this part. There's gotta be some karma involved here."

"Anyone else?"

"I don't think so."

"Sherman's? Any of 'em smoke Sherman's?"

"Not so I noticed. And you'd think I would. They're pretty distinctive."

When we reached the next landing, Sonny stopped and took out one of his own cigarettes. We were next to the main public room, and the doors to it were open. The far end of the room, lined with windows, had French doors that led out onto the veranda, lined with rocking chairs, where the old folks sat and watched the lake. It was the time before sunrise when the stars disappear and there's a thin bleak light in the sky. There was someone out there. A dark silhouette on a field of gray. I wouldn't have noticed him except that he was smoking and when he inhaled, the lit tip glowed bright red. I put my hand on Sonny's arm and stopped him.

Whoever it was, was restless and agitated. He paced. I figured out by his size and shape who it was. "It's Derek," I whispered to Sonny. "The stuntman."

Sonny didn't light up. "He wasn't on your list," he said.

"Well, so, I missed him. Or maybe he's nervous."

"He's smoking a jay," Sonny said. "Watch."

Sonny was right. Derek was holding the smoke for a long time before he exhaled and then working much harder at inhaling than a tobacco smoker usually does.

"Let's go talk to him," I said.

"I got a better idea," Sonny said. "He's Amy's husband, right?"

"Yes."

"Amy wouldn't talk to you with Derek there, right?"

"Yes."

"Let's go talk to Amy."

Amy was awake. She was frightened that someone was knocking at her door at that hour of the morning.

I said, "It's me." Figuring a woman's voice would be less threatening.

"Go away," she said.

"Amy, I know."

"Know what?"

"Amy, you don't want me to yell about it through the door. I'll wake people up and everyone will hear your business. You don't want that."

She opened the door. At first she was startled by seeing Sonny, then she recognized him from his day on set. The door was only open a crack and we weren't exactly welcome, but when I pushed my way in, she didn't really resist. She looked gray and weary, a portrait of sustained stress. She wore a cream-colored nightgown that buttoned to the neck. It had pink and yellow butterflies, small, faded ones.

"What do you want?"

"I'm sorry," I said. "You must be going through hell."

She didn't say anything.

"I can sympathize."

She looked away.

"Derek must've been pretty mad when he found out."

"Derek didn't do it," Amy blurted out.

"Do what?" Sonny asked.

"Anything," she said. Her lower lip trembled. She backed away until she reached a chair. She sat down in it and drew her legs up, so she was sitting almost in a fetal position. She tugged the hem of the nightgown down so that she was covered.

"He didn't do anything?"

"No, he didn't, nothing." She was on the verge of tears.

"Did he hurt you?" I asked her.

"No. No, he didn't. He never hit me. He just looks ... he's gentle. He's really gentle and sweet." She hugged herself tighter and I was certain she was black and blue under that childlike nightgown.

"He must've been pretty mad at Alan," Sonny said.

"No. He wasn't."

Sonny looked around for a spot to sit down, so he wouldn't loom over her. He sat on the bed. "Amy, come on, you say that,

175

it makes you sound untruthful. Of course he was mad at Alan. He's human, he's got to be mad."

"OK. Maybe he got mad. But he didn't do anything. He was with me when, when it happened. I'm a witness. He was with me all that evening."

"After you got done location scouting, you mean?"

"Yes."

"After you got done being with Alan all day."

"We were working."

"I know that," Sonny said. "I wasn't suggestin' nothin' else."

"Good."

"Just it had to be hard on Derek. Knowing you were out there with the Other Man the whole time."

"I'm not crazy. Do you think I'd do it with him after, after I found out?"

"Well, it depends, I guess, on what your condition is. I mean if you're both . . ."

"I don't know yet," she cried.

"You don't know yet? You haven't been tested?"

"We're waiting, for the results. OK. Now you know. We're waiting. We should know tomorrow. I mean today." She buried her head, surrounding her face with arms and knees and soft old fabric. "By the end of the day, today, they said. Oh God."

"Both of you, waiting for test results?"

She picked her head up. There were tears. "Yes. Both of us."

"Was this when you had to tell Derek, about you and Alan?"

We all heard the key in the lock. The husband coming home. The three of us turned and watched the door. The door opened.

When Derek saw Sonny, and then me, his face went white and then red. He was built like Rambo and though he did all sorts of stunts, his specialty was staging fights.

"You're tough, but you can't stop a .38," Sonny said. There was a gun in his hand. I knew he wore one on his ankle, but I hadn't seen him take it out. Also, Sonny handled most things with words and with his easygoing, everybody's friend way of talking. "Now, put your hands on your head."

Derek did as he was told. He glared at Sonny. "Get out of my room," he said. "Get away from my wife."

"I didn't tell them anything. I told them you were here with me," Amy said.

"Shut up," Derek said to her.

"You," Sonny said. "Turn around. Face the wall." He pulled the hammer back. I think that's what what he did is called. In any case it made a noise. An audio-graphic exclamation point. "Now."

Derek turned, slowly, looking back over his shoulder as he did so.

"OK," Sonny said. "Assume the position."

The stuntman very reluctantly put his palms against the wall.

"Spread your legs," Sonny said. He moved toward Derek, his gun pointing out in front of him. "Listen to me. I used to give out beatin's on 125th Street. To bad boys make you look like a punk on your best day. So don't even think tough thoughts, you'll get in worse trouble than you're already in." He kicked Derek in the ankle, making him spread wider.

"You got some kind of warrant or something?" Derek said.

"We just came for a friendly conversation," Sonny said.

"Then get outta here."

"We were just saying good night," Sonny said. "We'll be happy to go now." He gestured for me to leave first. Which I did. When I was in the hall, Sonny backed out.

"Wow," I said.

"What you gotta do," Sonny said, "is take control of the situation right away. Not let it get out of hand."

Our next stop was the front desk. I asked the night manager if he could tell me when Alan DeLucca had checked into his room.

"About five-thirty," he said.

"Were you on then?"

"No. That probably would have been Howard Gluck. He works four to midnight usually."

"Do you have a phone number for him?"

"I couldn't give you that."

"It's really important."

"I'm sorry. You can ask the manager. He comes in around eight-thirty, nine."

"Right, I'll do that."

"Is there anything else?"

"Is there some place we can get a cup of coffee and a pack o' cigarettes?" Sonny asked.

"Nothing's open now. Not 'til six. But if you go down to the dining room, and take the stairs just before you enter, you can get down to the kitchen and there's a little cafeteria set up for the hotel workers. You can get coffee, tea, juice, rolls, and that sort of thing. That's strictly unofficial and you didn't hear it here."

"Thanks, thanks a lot," Sonny said.

"We call him Howard the Duck," the night manager said. "But he doesn't think it's funny."

We found our way to the basement. The room was behind swinging steel doors. It was industrial but clean. As the night manager had promised, a cold buffet breakfast was laid out. "I'm not hungry," I said.

"You never are," Sonny said, "or hardly ever. But you should eat somethin'." We helped ourselves to juice, coffee, tea for me, bread and muffins, butter and jam. "There you go. That's better," he said when we sat down.

"Do you think he did it? Derek?"

"Could be," he said. "Prob'bly get off if he did."

"But what about the cigarette and the missing script and notes?"

"Not everythin' has to do with everythin'. Life ain't 'Columbo' with clues and such."

I suddenly started to shake. Like shivering. But I wasn't cold. I was just shaking and I wanted to cry. I tried to hide it. I held on to the table to keep it from showing. Sonny pushed a glass of orange juice into my hands. "Drink this," he said.

"I don't want it."

"Drink it. You need it."

I needed two hands to get it to my mouth without spilling it. I swallowed it down and it did make me feel better.

"You ain't slept in a while. You're just tired," he said.

"It's not that," I said.

"Well, it coulda been you, but it wasn't you." He shrugged. "When your time is up, it's up. When it ain't, it ain't." He put down his cigarette and picked up a knife. While the smoke rose in curls from the ashtray, he spread a thick wad of cholesterol on a muffin made mostly of white flour and sugar. He put jam on top of that. Then he poured at least two tablespoons of sugar into his coffee.

It looked like the thing to do. I did the same. It tasted good.

Then came the sound of tramping feet and chattering voices from down the hall. Some in English, some in a foreign language. A stocky woman in her seventies wearing hiking boots marched into the cafeteria, five hotel guests with her. One of them was Lazlo Viktorska, who was speaking to her in German. He smiled at me and waved. He came over to our table. "We have just been on the sunrise hike," he said. He gestured at the older woman. "That's Ilsa. She's the masseuse here and she leads a sunrise hike every day. And goes for a swim when there's no ice on the lake. The hike was quite wonderful. Up the mountain, through the woods, in the dark. Then, on a ledge, facing east, you see the sun come up. And the world is lit.

"The light comes creeping, spreading, glowing. To capture moments like that, that is what God gave me a camera for. Were you out for the sunrise too?"

"Nah, we missed it," Sonny said. "Wandering around in the dark."

"Too bad," Lazlo said.

"I regret it already," Sonny said.

"Excuse me," he said, "I'm going to rejoin the group."

He went to the food table, filled a tray, than sat with his hiking friends. They ate. We ate. We finished first. We got up to go. As we were leaving, they all waved at us. "You must come with us tomorrow," Ilsa said. "To greet the day."

Lazlo, having finished his food, sat back and reached into his pocket for a cigarette. Though sunrise hikers are unlikely to be cigarette smokers, he politely offered to share with the group. He held in his hand a distinctive flat, wide, dark red box—Sherman's.

18

"**W**here were you two nights ago, around seven?" I asked Lazlo Viktorska.

He inhaled, then exhaled before he spoke. "Why are you asking that?"

"Were you with Alan?"

"No, I wasn't."

"He was out all day location scouting. He didn't want to discuss the shots with you?"

"I was with him earlier."

"Not when I saw him."

"You know less about the business than you should. Do you think that a director would pick a location, especially one like this, without his DP? Especially Alan. You know Alan was a genius in many ways. But his primary genius was in using others. I do not intend to diminish him in any way. This was a great talent. Do you know why he cast you? He thought he

saw in you someone who could contribute something unexpected. Alan had quite a common mind. But Alan knew it. So
always he brought great contributors around him. He was terrified of Choice Wardell. Bad choice, Choice. Because Choice
goes for the obvious. Choice needs a director to push him,
something that Alan cannot do. That is why Alan got you. Plus
Gwendolyn Ript. Who, we all must admit, is of great sexuality.
Maybe even more in person than on the screen, and for Choice,
this is good, because—pardon me," he said to Ilsa and the rest
of the hikers, "his brains are below his waist and it shows,
which is also right for the part. I have seen nobody so stunned
on camera in many years, since Emil Jannings and Marlene,
since Bogie and Bacall.

"Two women, both powerful in different ways, one of the
spirit, one of the carnal. And he lets you loose. To fight over
possession of the meat.

"Not bad, not bad at all. And Larry Rhinebeck, with the
crumbs all over his shirt, he comes up with unexpected things.
And the little boy, Rain, very good. I heard you were impressed
that Alan sent you to rehearse with Rain, that it was the key to
the part. This impressed you that Alan was a genius.

"Have you ever been to see the gypsy? A professional psychic
person? This is the way Alan worked. The gypsy says this and
that and then the other, until she sees the flicker in your eye—she
has hit. Then she follows that line, dada dada da." He gestured
rhythmically with the hand that held the cigarette, leaving a
smoke pattern in the air. He smoked in a very European style
and used his cigarette in very theatrical ways. "And when she is
done, you think she has told you much, when actually, it is you
who have told her everything. So: did Alan sit and think through
your nature and the key to Glenda? No.

"You were demanding attention. Rehearsal. So, the only person he had for you to rehearse with, without disrupting everyone else, was this little boy. So he throws you the little boy, and
your own energy, *your* creativity, it finds in this little boy great

meaning and depth, something to key off the role with. *Brava, brava, brava* for you.

"*Bravo* for all of us," he added. "You and me and Mitzi. . . ."

"Mitzi?"

"One of Alan's great tools. Yes. Some day, a little academic fellow, a cinema historian, he will make a chart of the films that Mitzi has worked on. Each time she works on a film in between Alan DeLucca films, the next Alan DeLucca film, it is using all of the other director's tricks. She is like a kitchen thing—a sponge. She absorbs and retains all that she touches and after you can squeeze all out."

"Does she mind, being used like that?"

"How curious, this concern with being used. Mitzi makes a lot of money. Seven hundred a day, a thousand a day, when we are shooting. Where else can someone with nothing much but their wits make so much? It's a good thing to be used. I am used. Thank God, the day that I am not used, how will I be able to spend, spend several hundred thousand dollars a year? It is a terrible thing to be unused."

"So Mitzi is, was, happy, forever being the assistant?"

"This I don't know. Maybe she is like a volcano, full of repressed ambition, great force building up underneath. Maybe. And Fern. Alan owed a lot to Fern."

"Fern?"

"You don't like Fern, because he is a casting director and because he is fat and nasty. In this, too, you are too American. Because someone is fat, you think they are, what? not smart? not capable? not good? And nasty, you think this is a problem too."

"Hey, you don't happen to have seen Alan's notes?" Sonny said.

"His notes?"

"Yeah, you know, about the movie, his notes."

"Well, of course I have seen them in the normal order of things when we are working."

"Since."

"Since he died?"

"Yeah, since he died."

"They're missing?" Lazlo asked and for the first time he seemed genuine, not busy doing his Lazlo Viktorska act.

"And his script too."

"Are you sure they're missing?"

"Unless you got 'em."

"No. No. I do not."

"Or someone else got 'em."

"I wouldn't know," Lazlo said.

"You think they're important?"

"No, no," he said. "Unless . . ."

"Unless what?"

"Unless they are what you call a clue to his murder. They are missing, whoever saw him last took them, and whoever saw them last, *ipso facto*, is the person who killed him."

"What did you and Alan talk about," I asked Lazlo, "just before he died?"

"Excuse me?"

"It's the cigarette, Lazlo. Someone who smokes Sherman's was one of the last people to see Alan alive."

"The Sherman's?" he said. He looked at the cigarette between his fingers, took a long slow drag on it. After he exhaled he said, "Everyone smokes Sherman's."

"I doubt it," I said.

"You check." He held out the box. "Have one," he said. "Then you come back to me after and if I am the only who smokes Sherman's I will confess."

"I will," I said. "I'll be back."

Detective Bob Moser had been to my room looking for me. The night manager told him he'd sent some people down to the kitchen. He headed toward that end of the building and we ran into him just as we emerged from the stairs.

"Have you found anything out yet?" he asked.

"A lot," I said. "How come you didn't search Alan DeLucca's

room? And shouldn't you have sealed it too? Have you been looking for the notes and the script? And what about the Sherman's?"

"That's a lot of stuff," he said lugubriously. "What room are you talking about?"

I told him. He wanted us to show him, so we took him upstairs. I pointed out the prescription bottles, the key, the cigarette butt, the lack of clothes, and the absence of Alan's script and script notes.

"I guess," the Real Detective said, "this is an oversight."

"I guess so," I said, feeling vindicated.

"We better track this down," he said. "And see where it leads."

"You better do that," I said.

"I wouldn't get carried away," he said. "I like you and on a personal basis I would not pick you for this murder, but, if I had to make the arrest right now, you would still be the one."

"I don't smoke," I cried out.

He looked at me as if he'd seen me light up in the parking lot.

". . . except sometimes," I said.

"Um," he said. He put on a pair of half-lens reading glasses and peered at the prescription bottles. He moved them around, using his pen, until he could read the labels. He reached into his jacket pocket and pulled out a small notebook. The same kind I learned to carry when I became a detective. Then he carefully wrote down the names, the dosages, the doctor's name, and the prescription numbers.

"What about the AZT," I said. "And the key and the script and the notes?"

"Annie, you seem like a nice kid. But you folks from the big city, you just don't understand. We have real law and order in this county. We got a judge who believes in hard time for hard crimes. We got a DA interested in higher office. That means the first assistant, Tom Costello, wants to make sure that everyone knows who he is when it comes time for him to run for DA. Besides, Costello believes that no one is innocent.

"The way Costello would read this is the AZT is evidence

against you. That's motive. The key? You probably took that off of the deceased and did something with the script and the notes that you say are so important, just to confuse the motive and mess up the crime scene. Costello asks for the death penalty in capital cases, and in spite of the fact that there is no death penalty in New York State, two times he's gotten a jury in this county to vote for the electric chair.

"You should hang out at the courthouse sometime. They get some downstate dingo, got a list of ten, fifteen priors and has never done more than a hundred and eighty days at Rikers, and now he's here, in our county with a couple of crack sales, five or ten dollars each, or on a robbery. What they like, is to see the expression on the perp's face, when the guy finds out that Judge Thomas don't plea-bargain and he is going to do three to nine in a real penitentiary. They think that's real knee-slapping funny. I do too, for that matter.

"Just because we like to put folks away for the longest possible time," Moser went on. "That doesn't mean we're a bunch of hicks, neither. We don't like to lose 'em on technicalities, so we're pretty damn careful about following the rules. Nobody's gonna forget to read you your rights or fail to provide the proper amount of disclosure to your attorney. So don't count on the hicks blowing the case, for you staying out of the slammer. We've had lots of nationally known big city lawyers up here. Mostly they lose.

"The bottom line, the sum of it all, is that what you want is for me not to arrest you. Once that happens the Jaws of Justice crunch down real inexorably. It's something awesome. So what you want is for me to arrest someone else in the first place and let Costello and the judge go to work trying to fry this other him or her. It would make those two so happy if the governor would just stop vetoing the death penalty. I bet if Judge Thomas could actually sentence people to death, he would never retire."

I stamped my little foot. "Is that an excuse for screwing up? How come you didn't find this room, search this room, and secure the evidence?"

"I don't know," he said. He leafed through his notebook, going backward until he found it. "The desk gave me a different room as Alan DeLucca's room. The one his wife is in. No one mentioned this room. We'll try to figure out what happened. I'll lock this room now, get forensics to come over, take a look at this cigarette butt, get fingerprints . . ."

"Well, my fingerprints and Sonny's are all over the room now."

"Darn it, Annie," he sighed, like he was really on my side. "Tom Costello's gonna think you're his Christmas present."

The three of us walked down to the front desk. The night manager was still on. He was willing to give Howard Gluck's phone number to Moser and let him use a hotel phone. There was no answer.

"I'll try to track him down," Moser said. "This could look really bad, us pulling a boner like this."

"Why don't you stay here and talk to Derek and Amy. They have motive. They have twice the motive that I have. They've been up all night scared to death waiting for their test results to come back. Why don't you arrest Lazlo Viktorska and threaten to deport him. I bet he won't be able to spend hundreds of thousands of dollars a year if he's deported and can't shoot major motion pictures. Why don't you arrest Angela della Verona for impersonating a European. She's a phony from Staten Island and besides, most people are killed by those nearest and dearest to them. What kind of detective are you?"

"I'm a real detective," he said. "The regular kind. I tell you, Annie, I did question most of these people and they're all very savvy, very rich—by my standards—kind of people and every single one of them, they don't want to talk to a cop without a lawyer. Which is their right and which is why rich people get away with a lot more than poor people. Ah, the old days, when we could drag him into the back room and scare 'em shitless. You must remember them days, huh, Sonny?"

"Yeah," Sonny. "Those were the good old days."

"But even then"—he shook his head ruefully—"you couldn't beat a confession outta rich people. Not real rich ones, anyway."

"We hardly ever arrested rich people. Except dope dealers," Sonny said. "But they didn't have that many rich people, up the two-five."

"Hey, I got an idea," Moser said. "Why don't you tell people that you found a witness, alibi witness, seen you elsewheres the time of the murder. Maybe somebody'll panic. It could work."

"Do you have a witness that saw me?" I asked. "Did you look for one?"

"Listen," Moser said, "I'm trying to do you a favor here. I'm not gonna cut you loose because you went to Catholic school and you got cops for friends. I will cut you loose if you give me something better'n you. So how about it?"

"What you're sayin'," Sonny said, "is you want us to do your job for ya."

"What I'm sayin' is, I'm gonna arrest somebody for this here crime. I don't care who, just so long as I clears it. You are one person who should understand that. And you do. You," Moser said to me, "you have what we in the profession call *motivation*. So go use that motivation and go save yourself if you wanna. Or don't. But I think you oughta get right on it, seeing as how you got about six hours to save your neck. Now me, I'm going into the breakfast lounge, which should be open about now, and I'm going to have a coffee and a Danish. Just like a big city cop. Then I am going to find this Howard Gluck or Howard the Duck and find out how this room business got screwed up and clear it up so I don't end up looking like a horse's ass in the newspapers."

Announcing that there was a witness that would clear me and that therefore someone else had to have done it, was, Sonny and I agreed, not a bad idea. The time and place to drop the bomb, for maximum impact and consternation, would be breakfast. I had a feeling that if we could get all these people in one place and somehow get just enough leverage to make any single one of them start ratting on one of the others, the outpouring of truth, accusation, and venom would be sufficiently sustained to create a complete third act. Or fifth act, if we were thinking Shakespearean. In any case, a denouement that would be the metaphorical equivalent of Hamlet—slain and dying reputations all over the stage, some garish from wounds that spouted heart's blood, others writhing with the agony of treacherous poison. Although normally a mild-mannered person, wishing no ill to anyone— except perhaps casting directors as a class—I had begun to yearn for such an apocalyptic bloodletting. Not a single one of these people had spoken up in my defense, had rallied to my cause, had even doubted for a moment that I was the murderer. With the coffee-stained and crumb-laden exception of Larry Rhinebeck. And possibly Choice Wardell, who, while not on my side, at least purported neutrality. On the other hand, Choice seemed to me the male equivalent of a bimbo, a beautiful but mindless block of careening testosterone and self-adoration.

I went up to my room for a bath and a change. At the door I told Sonny that he had to ring me in fifteen minutes to be certain I didn't fall asleep and drown in the tub. He said, "Don' worry about nothing, Annie. We're gonna crack this one." I stood up on my tippy-toes, which made me feel very girlish, and kissed his cheek. I opened the door and went in.

When Sonny heard me screaming, "Goddammit! No! No! No! Nooooo more!" he rushed in. He dropped to one knee, grabbing for his gun again. There was no one in the room, but there was a large, slimy, green dissected frog pinned to my pillow.

Sonny gestured me to silence. Leading with his gun he crossed the room and made his way to the balcony. He kicked the door open, then moved outside in the wake of its motion. I saw him rush to the side of the balcony.

I ran out just in time to see him grabbing Gavin, who had been trying to climb down the balcony and do what? Jump to the one below? We were five floors up, above jagged rocks. Sonny had probably saved his life. Or was saving his life. It wasn't done yet. The eleven-year-old was struggling violently as if he'd rather die than be caught. Sonny got angry, cursed the boy, and yanked him up on the balcony.

Sonny was panting and winded. Two or three packs a day for

thirty years, steady and happy drinking, and a love of hamburg-
ers, steak, and junk food have got to take some kind of toll
eventually. Gavin took advantage of that gasping moment and
broke free. He ran into the room and tried to dodge around me.
But there wasn't enough space and I grabbed his shirt as he went
by. I hung on tight. He was a vicious little killer of small animals
and he grabbed my arm, holding it like a shank of lamb and
started to bite. Sonny, somewhat recovered, stumbled up to us
and gave the kid a huge openhanded swipe on the back of his
head.

Yowling, Gavin let go of my arm. Sonny grabbed him by the
shirt front and slapped him across his face. Normally I am ap-
palled at adults who hit children. It's a terribly destructive, un-
justifiable thing to do. Except with Gavin.

"You can't do that to me," he sniveled.

Without letting go of Gavin, Sonny sat down on the bed. "This
is too much work," he said.

"Let go of me," Gavin screamed.

"Shut up, punk," Sonny said. "Uh, Annie, I dropped my piece
on the porch there when I was grabbing the kid, you wanna get
it for me?"

"Sure," I said, talking the way Sonny talks. "Watcha gonna do,
shoot him a couple of times?"

"I don' know," Sonny said. "If he don' talk we could just toss
him off the balcony. Say he fell, trying to escape. He woulda
anyway, so I wouldn't have no compunction about it. I feel like
his life belongs to me. You know what I mean?"

"Yeah," I said, sounding tough and hard-hearted. Not at all
the kind of girl who screeches at dead frogs and squirrels and
slashed underwear.

"You're running pretty wild, aren't you kid," Sonny said to
Gavin.

"Screw you, copper," Gavin said. His father had been a director. Most directors spend most of their lives watching movies.
Gavin had probably been listening to forties' gangster films since
the womb.

190

"You seein' a shrink?" Sonny asked him.

Gavin looked at Sonny with wary eyes.

"What I figure," Sonny said, "is some judge, he's already set you free under care of some shrink. 'Cause you're too damn dumb not to get caught." Gavin squirmed at that. But it was obviously true. "So, if we go back, and tell the judge, psychiatrist don't seem to be working with this little punk, I think we can talk the judge into institutionalizing you. Put you into reform school with the real tough kids. There's plenty of eleven- and twelve- and thirteen-year-old killers and rapists and gangsters in this state. Plenty of 'em. And a pampered little punk who's never gone up against nothing bigger than a squirrel, they're gonna make dog food out of you. They're gonna beat you and kick you and stomp you and rape you and use you every single day. And you know what, I feel good about it, 'cause I don't like you."

"Wait, Sonny," I cried.

"For what?" he said.

"Maybe, maybe if he helped us . . ."

"Nah. Why bother. He's a little sadist. Kills small animals. Gonna grow up to be a psychopath, kill defenseless old ladies, stuff like that. Time to crush him is now."

"Can I talk to him?" I asked.

"You can, but it's useless."

"Why did you do this?" I asked Gavin. Meaning the frog.

"Because you're a bimbo, and you were gonna do it with my father. Then you killed him."

Actually those sounded like very good reasons. How had I been such a fool? How had I been so blind? "Did you do anything else? In my room?"

"Yeah."

"What?"

"I did the squirrel. I notice you didn't like that and switched rooms. And I chopped up your stinky underwear."

"Gavin, I didn't kill your father."

"Crap," he said.

"Talkin' to him is a waste of time," Sonny said. "I'm gonna

drag him down to juvie hall. And all his mother's money and shrinks and alla that, ain't gonna get him out. Or I'm gonna toss him over the side, for havin' a fresh mouth. Whichever is less work."

"Wait, please, Sonny. Let my try one more time."

"Waste o' time. But go ahead. You know what the kid needs is a beatin'. A real serious beatin'."

"Maybe I'm a fool," I said, "but I believe there's some hope for you, Gavin." I wondered if I did. "But now, it's up to you. You have to give me something." I knelt down so that we were both more or less the same height. "Information, so that I can convince Sonny not to hurt you."

Sonny smiled at him and gave him two solid pats on the cheek with his big hand. Not hard enough to hurt, but enough to announce how much he could hurt.

"The night your father died, where were you?"

"Here and there, around and about."

"OK. Your mother and father had a fight. Did you hear it?"

"Yes."

"Was it a bad fight?"

"Yes."

"What did they fight about?"

"I don't remember."

"Did they fight about you?"

"No."

"All right, did they fight about me?"

"Yes."

"Was the fight all about me?"

"No. It was about a bunch of stuff."

"What stuff?"

"I don't remember."

"Was it about your father staying with your mother?"

"Yeah."

"OK. What about it?"

"He wanted to stay. He did. For me and my sister. But she wanted to kick him out. For being bad. For being . . ."

"What?"

". . . I don't know."

"He wanted to stay and she wanted him to go?" That was not the way his mother had told the story.

"Yes."

"Where were you, when you were listening?"

"I don't know."

Sonny raised his hand to slap Gavin across the top of his head. I held up my hand to stop him.

"Come on, Gavin," I said. "I know, you know, and Sonny knows, that's not true. You know where you were when you overheard the fight."

"No, I don't," he said. "It's a displaced memory," he announced, smugly parroting someone. "I am blocking out trauma." He thought it was working so he tried to milk it. "I do that a lot because I have so much trauma. Like I wouldn't remember dissecting the frog on your bed, except you just mentioned it and reminded me and restored the memory. I've had a very difficult childhood."

"Gavin, where were you when you overheard the fight?"

"You see, children should never experience trauma. It can produce lifelong scars. . . ."

I shook my head sadly. I stood up. I said to Sonny, "I tried. He's all yours," and I headed for the door.

I didn't know what Sonny was doing to him, if anything. My back was turned and I was on my way out of the room. I just heard, "Hey, the hell with you. You touch me and I'll have your job. Get your hands off me. . . ." And then, "Hey, hey, lady, please, get him off me, I'll talk. I'll talk. I promise."

I turned around. Sonny was holding Gavin's hand in some peculiar way. "Where were you?"

"Outside. Outside the door."

"Did you stay there and hear the whole fight?"

"No."

"What did you do?"

"I went to see Brigette. Brigette cares about me. She takes care of things. She wanted my parents to stay together. Brigette says America is sick and decadent because the family unit is falling apart. We're all turning into animals like the lower races."

"What happened when you went to see Brigette?"

"She hugged me tight and held me."

"Did that make you feel better?"

"Sure. You bet. Read my lips."

"After that, what happened?"

"Brigette said she would take care of it."

"Take care of it?"

"Yes."

"Take care of it how? What does that mean?"

"It means take care of it. Take care of it," he cried out in frustration.

"Was she going to go make them kiss and make up?"

"I don't know. Take care of it."

"Was she going to pull out a gun and say, 'Stay together or else?' "

"I don't know. She was going to take care of it."

"Did she leave the room?"

"Yes."

"With you or without you?"

"Without me."

"When? When did she go?"

"I don't know. After a while."

"Then what happened?"

"Then I hung out, you know."

"In Brigette's room?"

"Yeah."

"Where was your little sister?"

"Taking a nap. She naps a whole lot. In our mother's room."

"How long did you stay there?"

"Until Brigette came back and said we had to get dressed for dinner and go eat. I didn't want to. I hate the stinky dining room here. But Brigette said I could have two desserts and lay down with her after if I was good. That sounded like an OK deal."

"Did she say she 'took care of it' while she was gone?"

"No."

"No? She just went away and came back?"

"Not exactly."

"What exactly did she say?"

"She said something like, Daddy would never cheat on Mommy again and don't worry, she would never leave us."

"Who would never leave you?"

"Brigette," he said.

"Do you realize that's unlikely to be true? She's a hired person. Hired to look after small children. When you and Chelsea are grown she's going to go work for another family."

"No. No, she wont. And you won't make her."

"I won't make her," I said softly. "Did she say why Daddy would never cheat on Mommy again?"

"No. Just it was taken care of."

"Did she say she did something to Daddy, to make him never do it again?"

"No."

"Did she explain why Daddy wasn't coming to dinner?"

"Oh, she didn't have to explain that. Daddy always has work and meetings and shoots and stuff. He lets me come lots of times. Or he used to."

"Is it possible Brigette did something to your father?"

"Can I go now? I want to go now."

"Were you following us around, earlier this morning or during the night?"

"No. I just got up. And Brigette made me go to bed early. Because of the trauma."

I couldn't think of anything else to ask. I looked at Sonny. He nodded. I said, "OK." Gavin ran to the door.

"Wait a minute," Sonny said.

To my surprise, Gavin stopped. Sonny got up, picked up the pillow that had the dissected amphibian on it and said, "Here, kid. Take your frog with you."

19

I called Duke at the office. He wasn't there. Sonny called him at home. I didn't want his wife to suffer all that agitation again. He wasn't there and she didn't know when he was going to return.

Angie Getzevitch, aka Angelique della Verona, aka Angelique DeLucca, sat with her two children, Gavin and Chelsea, and their Swiss nanny, Brigette. Angie looked little worse for the wear of a late, late night and a lot of vodka. It was mostly the gifted application of makeup. I imagined that if I scrubbed her down with cold cream, a washcloth, and strong soap, bags would appear under her eyes and her cheekbones would begin to fade away. Gavin appeared to have recovered from being caught. The next small animal that crossed his path would have to beware. Brigette looked as she always did, weirdly self-possessed, stern, and Teutonic. It was difficult for me to conceive of how anyone could derive comfort from her, but then, men are not known for being discriminating. Chelsea, sniffling, red-eyed, and cranky, was the only one who seemed genuinely afflicted with grief and sorrow.

Derek and Amy sat together, alone.

But the center of the action was Dan Ginzburg, the man from the studio, who would decide if the picture would go forward or not. And if it went forward, who it would go forward with.

Judging by her proximity and the air of intimacy between them, Lucy Kohl was racing to the inside. She looked at him with simpering eyes, laughed at every witticism, and touched him, frequently, below the table line.

Mitchell Du Bois and Mitzi also sat at his table. I thought it would make a marvelous scene to hear their words and then hear their real thoughts, Mitchell with his director's outfit in the closet upstairs, as secret a fetish as if he wore satin French underthings with British schoolgirl frocks, Mitzi with her shoulder pads, her tape recorder, and her notes, all very efficient and more conversant with what a director does than most working directors, a pair of carrion birds waiting for the lion to let them at the carcass.

Lazlo Viktorska, his chair set so he could watch Ginzburg, sat with his crew people. Larry Rhinebeck was also at that table. He was asking camera questions and Lazlo was answering them in ways that made it sound like the director was the third wheel between cameraman and writer.

Fern sat alone, morose or hung over or possibly grief stricken. A black cloud hovered over him, his own dreary, drizzly consort. He wore black, but it hung badly on his heavy, sodden frame.

When Choice walked in, he looked around. The regular guests seemed to live up to Mohonk's reputation as a place for the newly wed and the nearly dead. Among the film people, since he'd been rejected by me and by Lucy, the only women available were the newly widowed Angelique and Mitzi, the first AD. Perhaps he hesitated to approach Angie, surrounded as she was with the baggage of her life; in any case, he decided on Mitzi.

Who could blame him? It had probably been at least three days since he'd been with a woman.

Fierce and confused, Rain's mother had pushed her tiny table closer to Dan Ginzburg's table. She was quarreling with a waiter who wanted the table back at its station. Rain looked mortified, as children so often are by the behavior of their parents.

When they were all there, I walked in, Sonny by my side. It had been a long time since I'd slept. I hoped I'd done as good a job with my makeup as Angie had done. Once again, my entrance upstaged everyone else. That's what happens when you're a celebrity-killer.

We went to the widow's table first and said, "Good morning." She returned the greeting politely, although the Swiss nanny snorted and Gavin quailed, ever so slightly, and the room took on a new buzz.

Next we strolled over to the table where Dan Ginzburg held court. I hadn't actually met him yet. "Let me introduce myself," I said since no one leapt up to do it. "I'm Annie McGrogan. I play Glenda. I hope you've seen the dailies. I was suspected of having killed Alan DeLucca. I didn't do it. Last night we fortunately found a witness who saw me in the waiting room, right over there"—I pointed—"at the same time of Alan's death. You can imagine my relief."

"I'm very glad to meet you," Ginzburg said. He didn't stand up. I didn't know if it was because he was rude or he couldn't untangle his lap from Lucy Kohl's hands.

"This is Sonny Gandolfo, he's a detective, my ex-partner. Mitch and Mitzi and Choice you met, and that's Lucy Kohl."

"Hey, everybody," Sonny said. "Please to meetcha." He patted his pockets and looking straight at Lucy he said, "Anybody got a cigarette?"

Lucy looked in her pocketbook and came up empty. Mitzi said, "I do. Which would you like better, Carltons..."—she rooted through her shoulder bag, pulling out a notebook, a small tape recorder— "... or Sherman's?"

"The Sherman's," Sonny said.

Mitzi found the red box and offered it to Sonny.

"I hope you're not going to smoke, uh, in this area of the dining room," Ginzburg said.

"No, I would never do that," Sonny said.

"That means that someone else must have done it," Choice blurted out. It sounded like a non sequitur, but it was just that the information that I had an alibi witness had taken a long time to percolate through his brain and it was only now that the obvious deduction had boiled to the surface.

"Yeah, I guess so," Sonny said.

"All right then," Choice said, a New York accent suddenly appearing in his voice. "I'm gonna check this out. This is a big case. I crack this, I'm made as a dick. Then I can dump this phony acting racket." He stood up, he put both hands flat on the table, he looked at each of us in turn, making good eye contact. "I'll tell you what I'm up for, I'm up for a double dose of reality. I'm tired of stunts, I want action. When I pull my gun, I don't want some FX man blowing squibs—lead's gonna fly from here on out. Now I don't know which one of you did this, but I'm betting my rep that it was someone right here in this room. Whoever you are, better watch your back, Choice Wardell is on the job."

"Wow, with acting like that," Mitch said to Dan, "you can't let the picture go down the tubes. Guy is giving the performance of a lifetime here. Whoever does it, me or someone else, can't miss with Choice in the picture."

"You don't get it, do you, dwerp?" Choice said. "Performance time is over. There's just so much playacting a man can do in a lifetime."

"Oh, Choice," Mitzi said. Mitch had just demonstrated that he did not know how to handle talent. Mitzi was about to show Dan who could. "You are so right. Particularly a guy like you who's a real man, not some Hollywood phony. I don't blame you. And I tell you what, if this picture does go ahead and shoot, the fact that you're a real detective, who really knows the streets, knows action, knows what it means to put it on the line, that'll bring so much to it, like the fact that McQueen really rode a motorcycle, that Doug Fairbanks did his own stunts. People know the difference between real and fake and I love the fact that you're real."

She wasn't bad.

"Thanks, babe," Choice said, and he hitched his shoulder to feel his shoulder holster tug around his chest.

"See you all later," I said. "Good luck, Choice." Sonny and I started to walk away.

"Choice, why don't you sit down and finish your breakfast," Mitch said, trying to recover the ground he'd lost. "It's not every day we have Dan Ginzburg out here from the studio. It's quite an honor."

"That's what's so great about being my own man, Mitch. Being a dick may be just a two-bit, penny-ante racket, but it's my racket. Mine, see. And I don't have to suck up to some jerk, just 'cause he's from the studio."

Sonny and I were announcing our news to Larry and Lazlo, but we could still hear the other conversation. Lazlo said, "*Brava, brava, brava.* I am so cheerful for you, brave girl. Your innocence shines forth from your eyes and vindication is good stuff."

"I knew a doll like you would have to be the straight goods," Larry Rhinebeck said. Maybe he regarded living speech as sort of an out-of-town tryout for what he wrote, reality as the time and place where he got to say things the wrong way so he could cut the bad lines or change them before they got stuck on the page. "A straight shooter and true blue."

Choice came over and sidled up to Sonny. "Hey, uh, Sonny, could I, uh, talk to you for a second here, could I?"

"Sure, whatcha want?"

In a half whisper, Choice said, "You got any clues? Like extra clues that you wouldn't mind sharing?"

"Well, I don't know . . ."

"See, it's just that it's my first time and, well, usually I have a script. Or something."

"I guess I could share one or two. Can you wait a minute, we sit down, get a cuppa coffee."

"Sure, Sonny, sure. Take as long as you want and, uh, Sonny . . ."

"Wha?"

"Thanks, man."

"Annie," Lazlo said, "you smoke sometimes, yes?"

"Yes."

"Why don't you ask Fern for a cigarette. Trust me. It would be a good idea."

So I went over to Fern's table, while Sonny sat down with Choice.

"I heard," Fern said, sounding hardly at all pleased.

"Well," I said.

"Goody-goody for you."

"What did I ever do to you?" I asked him.

"Does anybody but me care about Alan?"

"What?"

"Look around. Look for the tears. Look for the sorrow. I see one widow, looks relieved, frankly. I see the man who produced him for years, lived off of Alan's talent, he certainly has none of his own, and he hasn't wasted a minute for . . . regret or whatever. He's pitching the man from the studio. And the man from the studio . . . well, I don't have to speak the obvious, we both know why he looks a bit glazed and dazed this morning. Little Mitzi, who Alan raised from the groveling masses of the DGA to her present lucrative status, are her cheeks tear-stained, has she torn her hair and rent her clothing? Maggots on the carcass. Let us dine on the flesh of the dead. Did you want something from me?"

"I'm sorry, I didn't know . . ."

". . . that fat, old casting directors have feelings?"

"I didn't say . . ."

"Oh, but we do. Deep and pure ones. Deep and pure as yours. Maybe deeper and purer. Is that inconceivable to you? I bet it is. You are awfully shallow for all your dedication to Art with a capital *A*. I don't like you."

"Why? Why don't you like me?"

"I don't know," he said. "And if I did, I probably wouldn't tell you, because then you might be able to fix it and I'd have to find someone else."

"Do you like anyone?"

"I used to like Alan, quite a lot, if it's any of your business."

"Oh," I said. I didn't feel like I could now ask him for a cigarette.

"Are you going to go or are you going to stand there, unwelcome and gawking?"

"I'll go. I'm sorry for your pain."

He raised his eyebrows and rolled his eyes. He belched. Took a sad slurp of coffee, and as I left he pulled a pack of cigarettes from his pockets. A thin, wide, red box of Sherman's. I couldn't help but look over at Lazlo. He smirked.

I went over to Rain's table.

"I heard," Rain said. "I'm so happy for you, Annie."

"Never mind," his mother said severely. "We don't take sides."

"We haven't had the pleasure of actually talking to each other," I said. "I have the pleasure of playing Rain's mom and you're his real mom...."

"And that makes all the difference, doesn't it. You play it. I am a real mother. Do you mind if we eat without all this excitement. It's better for Raymond's digestion."

"Certainly. Excuse me," I said. Sometimes it's easier to see how hard it is to have a mother than it is to see how hard it must be to be one.

20

Choice and Sonny were having a real guy-to-guy communication. I could tell by their postures and attitudes. And moment by moment, gesture by gesture, Choice was turning into a junior Sonny.

As I arrived at the table, Sonny said, "Pump her."

"You think I should, uh, pump her?" Choice said.

"Yeah," Sonny said. "Pump her."

"Yeah," Choice said. "Pump her."

This is what men think conversation is. The same grunted, faintly suggestive, monosyllables repeated over and over, each time with a slightly different intonation. It is how they bond and, probably, why women and men cannot bond.

"Pump who?" I asked.

"Thanks," Choice said, rising.

"Hey," Sonny said.

"Uh, yeah," I said, just to fit in.

"See ya, doll face," Choice said, leaving. Which was part of the difference between an imitation Sonny and the real Sonny, who, if he said something like that, would've said it to someone who wouldn't think he was ridiculous saying it.

So I asked Sonny, "Pump who?"

But he didn't have to answer, Choice returned to Mitzi.

Still, some questions remained. "Pump how?" I asked. "Pump why?"

"Ah, he'll improvise. Play it as it lays."

"But, uh . . . ," I asked, meaning did he think it could be Mitzi?

"Ah . . . ," he said, meaning it might be a long shot, but it could be.

"But, uh . . . ," I asked, meaning if she's a serious suspect, do you think we should let Choice pump her?

"Ah . . . ," he said, meaning, Choice probably couldn't screw it up worse than anyone else and who knows, maybe he'd come up with something.

"Yeah," I said, agreeing.

"Yeah," Sonny said, meaning he'd just tried to think of something the kid could do 'cause the kid wanted to do something so badly.

"Pump her," I said, meaning that was indeed a thing that Choice could do.

"Pump her," he said, meaning that's what we do, we probe and probe and hope we get a response.

"Pump her," I asked, meaning I do hope you mean interrogate.

"Pump her," he said, meaning of course that's what I meant, I'm on the case.

After breakfast we called Duke again. He wasn't at the office. He wasn't at home. "Hey," his wife said, "you think I wouldn't give him the message? Of course, I woulda give him the message if he ever came home to get his messages." Maybe the cavalry wasn't going to ride to the rescue.

Then we looked for Moser and the night desk clerk. We

couldn't find either. We went into the commissary. Sonny bought a pack of True Blues. He asked the clerk if she had Sherman's.

"Sure," she said. She turned around to look for them, but didn't find them on the shelf behind her. Then she looked under the counter. "I was sure . . . we had a whole carton."

"Too bad," Sonny said.

"Wait one second," she said, looking through some papers. "Well, I guess we are out, here's a note to reorder."

"So you didn't sell them?"

"No. Greg, he works evenings, he sold them. Or at least he put in the reorder. That's his handwriting. I recognize it."

"Could I reach Greg someplace? To ask him who bought the Sherman's." Sonny reached into his pocket and took out his wallet. He flipped it open the way TV cops have been doing since "Dragnet." Since Sonny does it, I guess real ones do it that way too, but maybe they learned it from television. Cops are supposed to turn in their badges when they retire. I don't know what Sonny has in his wallet. I never thought to ask, but everyone reacts like he's Joe Friday. "It's actually part of the murder investigation."

"Oh, oh well, of course," she said. "I have his number here somewhere. He's a student at the university. He might be in class there. But you could trace him through the registrar and then have him paged in class. That's what you would do, isn't it?"

"We might," Sonny said.

I looked at the clock on the wall. The distance between breakfast and lunch had never seemed so short. And I'd never seen a clock tick quite so fast.

"There's something about a celebrity murder," she said, still looking through her interminable scraps of paper. "That's just so, so something. I bet they make it a miniseries."

"Could be."

"Here it is," she said and read it off. Sonny copied it down. "Who do you think will play me?"

"I don't know," Sonny said. "But there's a casting director here at the hotel. You could ask him about it."

"Could I really?"

"He'd probably enjoy the attention."

When we called, Greg was not in.

"Should we go over to the school and track him down?"

"Nah, they look at badges real close and make you fill out forms. Dealing with universities and such, that's a pain in the ass. Moser could do it."

"What do we do now? We have to do something," I said.

"Let's go over the list of suspects and see what we got," Sonny said.

"And then what?"

"And then maybe that'll make us think of somethin'."

> *Gavin:* Clearly disturbed, but small. Big enough to strike his father?
>
> *Brigette:* Said she would take care of things. Went out, came back, told Gavin not to worry, his father would cheat no more, and that she would never leave Gavin.
>
> *Amy:* Rage over Alan's criminally irresponsible acts.
>
> *Derek:* Same, plus being a cuckold.
>
> *Lucy:* My favorite. Motive—to get the part, unfortunately no evidence, possible Sherman's.
>
> *Angie:* The wife, always motive enough, plus had lied to us.
>
> *Mitch:* Wants to direct, clearly not mourning, ready and waiting to jump in. Nonsmoker.
>
> *Lazlo:* Wants to direct, too smooth, Sherman's.
>
> *Mitzi:* Sherman's. Wants to direct, long shot, Choice was pumping.
>
> *Fern:* Was his grief really remorse? Sherman's.

"It seems to me you got a couple names missing," Sonny said.

"Who?"

"Choice Wardell and Larry Rhinebeck."

"But . . . ," I said, meaning they were the only ones remotely on my side.

"Yeah?" he said, meaning that don't mean nothin'.

"Oh," I said, acknowledging that the world is a cruel and treacherous place, but intimating that I, for one, thought it should be better than that.

"So?" he said.

"OK," I said, writing down Larry's name. Regretfully. He did want to direct. I guess it was motive enough. One successful film—even an unsuccessful film—could mean a lifetime of fame, fortune, and fun. Which is a lot better than poverty, obscurity, and frustration. "Choice?" I asked. The idea of putting Choice on the list didn't disturb me one bit, which made me realize that I must have had some emotional resonance with Larry Rhinebeck. But Choice didn't appear to want to direct or have any motive whatsoever.

"Could he be crazy enough to kill somebody so he could be the detective that solved the crime? Would that be like the Method?" Sonny asked.

"Acting is not that weird," I said. "And the Actor's Studio may be a little twisted but it's not that twisted."

"Well some of the things I've heard. . . . But you know better, about actors."

"I'll put his name down, but it's a waste of time. Of which we have little."

"So let's go back and talk to everybody again."

"You take half and I'll take half," I said.

We split them up. I walked upstairs past the maids working their way through the halls with their wheeled carts, dispensing linens and collecting trash. I knocked on Larry's door.

"Am I glad to see you, sweetheart," he said. "You're like sunshine for flowers and you make me one happy daisy. Wow, that's one stinking metaphor that I'll never use. At least I didn't say pansy. Anyway, drive it in and park it, sister. Kick back and tell me why your heart is achin'."

"Larry, could you direct this picture, now, with Alan dead?"

"In reality or in reality?"

"What does that mean?"

"We got a couple o' alternate realities here. As a writer I recognize that. You always got at least two, usually three, four realities happening. But you don't want metaphysical jive, you want the straight dope, the real skinny. All right, sister, I'll give it to you. In reality, my script is director-proof. With the actors we got, and I include you in, and Lucy Kohl out, yes. As a matter of reality, no. Nobody would let me do it. Now, if this movie gets made and it breaks out in megabucks, then I can direct the next one or the one after that, using my own scripts as leverage, capisce? The third reality operating in the sphere of there and now is you are asking if I have a motive for the offin' of Alan DeLucca. As a matter of my career, the answer is no. With Alan directing, the picture gets finished and makes some money, judging by the track record. That means I have written a successful picture. That means some of the glamour rubs off and I get to be a glittery personality. If, say, Mitch or Mitzi or Lazlo or someone else from the outside finishes the picture, it could be dog meat and then I'm a dog-meat dispenser, which is not something I look forward to."

"I thought you said the script was director-proof."

"If the director follows it. Most directors got to prove that they are more important than the writer, that they're not just traffic cops. So that's what a director-proof script is worth. Now there's a fourth reality."

"What's that?"

"My passion for you, doll. For me, yours is the face that will launch a thousand scripts. That makes my pen run wild. I could gaze upon you 'til the moon turns blue, and never get enough of your smile. But you had the hots for Alan DeLucca. Slim, overdressed, neat, overpressed, and the director to boot. Would a humble little scribe even stand a chance with him around? I don't think so. Is that motive, motive enough to kill? . . . In one of my books it would be."

"That's very flattering, Larry," I said. "But I have to go now. I have a lot of investigating to do."

"Let me help you, doll. Let me be your Walter Raleigh and throw my coat across the mud puddles of your world."

"That's a great offer," I said, backing out of the room.

"Wait, don't go," he cried. But he moved too quickly and banged his shin against a protruding piece of chair.

"Sorry," I said. "I'll see you later."

I rushed down the hall. I noticed the maids again. Of course, it was the perfect time to get into someone's room. It was a matter of checking the room numbers with the pattern of the cleaners and then devising some strategy to distract the maid, or talk my way in.

Angie's room had a Do Not Disturb sign on it. I presumed that meant that she was in. I found Lazlo's room next. It was at the far end of the corridor from where the maids were working. It would be anywhere from an hour to three hours until they got to it.

Then I found Lucy Kohl's room. The door was open. The maid was in the room across the hall. That was how they seemed to work, two rooms at a time, the cart in the hall. So I just walked in. The maid hadn't even dumped the ashtrays yet. I looked. Sure enough, there was a Sherman's. I ripped a sheet out of my notebook and dumped the butt in it, then folded it and put it in my pocket.

I heard a noise behind me.

Startled, I turned.

"Oh," the maid said, "I'm sorry."

"No problem," I said. "Go ahead."

"I can come back later," she said.

"Well, if you could give me five minutes," I said. "I just wanted to get a couple of things."

"Sure," she said. "I'll do the next room first."

She closed the door behind her. I searched. Yes, it looked to me like Lucy was tooting again. There was no stash—she probably had that with her—but there was makeshift paraphernalia: a stripped Bic pen, a small makeup mirror that had been licked clean. Could the drugs have made her crazy enough to kill?

It was a thought, but by no means an answer.

When I left, I stuck my head in the next room, thanked the maid, and said she could do the room now.

This was a great idea. And easy. On the same floor, but in the next wing, the maid was almost at Mitch Du Bois's room. I bided my time and waited until she opened his room up, then I strolled toward the door like I belonged there.

"Excuse me," the maid said, "is this your room?"

"Yes," I said, and recited the number.

"May I see your key?"

"My key, my key," I said, patting my pockets. "Oh dear, I left them down at breakfast."

"I'm sorry," she said, "I must not let you in."

"Are you going to make me run all the way downstairs and back upstairs? I just need to go in for a minute."

"I am sorry. I must not do it. Imagine if someone else were trying to go into your room, I am sure you would want me to tell them to show me the key. That is what we are told to do and I must do it."

"Go ahead, make my life difficult," I said, walking away, scheming.

I needed someone to distract her. I needed them soon, before she was done with the room and locked it. I raced through the halls, but couldn't find Sonny. In desperation I checked Choice's room. Then I checked Mitzi's room, looking for Choice. There was a Do Not Disturb sign on the door. I knocked nonetheless. I could hear noises from within but no one responded to me. I knocked again. "Can't you read," Mitzi yelled. "Go away, you illiterate, go away."

Even more desperate, I went back to Larry Rhinebeck's room.

"You're back," he said.

"I need your help."

"Sure," he said. "Whatever I can do."

"I need you to distract the maid, while I sneak into Mitch Du Bois's room."

"I'll do the best I can," he said. "I'm not that quick on my feet. I'm a better writer than I am a person."

"Come on, let's go, before she's done."

He grabbed his room key, then a pen and notebook, and came out in the hall.

"What's that for?" I asked.

"I'll pretend to be a reporter. Doing a story about hotel maids and life in the mountains. Or better yet, a movie about a hotel. Background research."

"That's pretty good," I said.

"I do it all the time. I'm afraid to talk to people. Not afraid so much as not good at it, because I don't care about the things most people care about and when I try to make small talk I go blank. So I pretend to be a reporter, or researcher, just so people will talk to me."

"You're speaking like a normal person," I said in sudden realization.

"I always speak like this."

"No, you don't. You always say things like Gimme a cup o' Java, I just rubbed out your sister, sister, with my heater rod."

"Oh, that," he said. "I have a contract to finish the last unfinished novel of a famous fifties hard-boiled detective writer. Very Raymond Chandler. So I've been trying out the patter and the argot of the milieu."

"Hold it," I said, grabbing his arm. "There she is."

"Here goes nothing," Larry said and walked down the hall without me.

I stood back in the stairwell, peaking out as he walked up to her. He spoke to her and it seemed clear by his attitude and gestures that he was introducing himself and giving her his rap. He maneuvered around so that when she faced him her back was to me.

I slunk down the hallway, skittering from doorway to doorway, on silent sneakers. When I got near to my goal I took a deep breath and, letting it out slowly and evenly, moved as smoothly and quietly as I could into Mitch Du Bois's suite. The bedroom door was closed. When I opened it I saw that the bed had been made and the room straightened. Now that I was on the other side of it, I closed it again. Clearly she was done with this part of the suite and if I were quiet there was no reason for her to come back in. I began to search.

I went through the bureau first. There was no reason for him to have hidden the script in some elaborate place. His director's outfit was still there, including the lens and the stopwatch. But underneath I found a piece of women's underwear. It was a shimmering silver silk, French-cut with a loose leg. This was something I had not suspected in Mitchell.

They looked too small for Mitchell, so it probably wasn't evidence of cross-dressing. There was a monogram: *ADB*.

I continued my search, still looking for Alan's notes and his missing script. I heard a noise. I froze. I listened intently and tried to decipher the sound. It was the maid, cleaning up the living room. Larry had followed her in and was still interviewing her. She was, I overheard, a Jehovah's Witness and had been for twenty-eight years. She sounded a very happy person. At last she was done. I heard the door close behind her and the click of the key in the lock, carefully double-locking it.

I went out into the living room part of the suite. In the desk I found a copy of the script, but, as far as I could tell, it was Mitchell's own. I was still dying to read it. I was tempted to borrow it, strictly out of curiosity. But I felt that somehow, now, knowing would be a terrible disappointment. As I started going through the closet, I heard a hand on the knob and the rattle of the key. I grabbed the silk underwear and dashed into the bedroom looking for a hiding place.

I slithered under the bed. I watched his shoes pass by me, forward and back. Then he sat down on the bed. With enthusiasm. The spring sprang down, touching my hair and my back. He took his shoes off. They dropped in front of my eyes. Then came socks and shirt and pants. Now he leapt to his feet. The bed rose away from me.

Now what?

To my horror, Mitchell lay down on the floor. Fortunately, for the moment, he had his head turned away from me.

The bit of evidence, the lush bit of silk that I held in my hand, spoke of a secret passion. And being secret, repressed and compacted with the potential for violence.

He began to do push-ups. All he had to do was peer slightly to his left and he would see the bulging whites of my terrified eyes staring at him from the darkness beneath the mattress, exactly level with him and not more than three feet away. He exercised with intensity, as if the push-up were the pressure valve on a steam boiler, each movement the release of an energy that would otherwise cause an explosion. How many was he going to do, popping up and down past me. One, two, three . . . eight, nine, ten . . . how could he miss me . . . fourteen, fifteen . . . who trained him to look straight ahead . . . eighteen, nineteen . . . what if on the last one, he put his head down flat, looking to the side . . . twenty.

He bounded up.

Next, toe touches. When he was done with those, some twisting things. Everything was done with breath control and directed concentration that I would expect with a karate workout, not mere calisthenics. Come on, Mitch, I said silently, that's enough, go jump in the shower. But it wasn't enough. There were still deep knee bends and sit-ups. The sit-ups were almost as frightening as the push-ups. But he was a man who only looked straight ahead, never to the sides. I decided he would make a lousy director.

At last, he headed for the bathroom. But he didn't close the door. I heard the shower go on and I could tell by the alteration in the sound of the spray against porcelain that he'd stepped in. It was my chance. I scrambled out from underneath and made for the front door. I was so intent on getting away that I stepped out without looking first.

Derek and Amy were in the hall. Right in front of me. They

were startled to see me. I just said, "Hi," like I belonged where I'd just been.

Derek looked at me with a jaundiced eye but Amy smiled. They looked very different. I realized what it was, they looked happy. Every time I'd seen them, until this moment, they'd looked miserable. What a profound alteration that can make in the countenance. To do that at will—not a mere change of expression, the full transformation, including posture and bearing, adding vibrancy to the skin and brightness to the eye, erasing wrinkles and firming the skin under the jaw, polishing the aura and greeting the world with an air of receptivity—that would be great acting.

"You got the test results," I guessed. "And they were negative."

Derek drew himself up. He wanted to pretend that I didn't know. And by the rules of normal social intercourse, he was right, it was none of my business. Amy, however, nodded and smiled. She put a happy and proprietary hand on her husband's oversized arm. He seemed happy with that. I wondered if, when the sense of relief wore off, the memory of infidelity would return to poison what they'd regained.

Downstairs there was a message for me. Detective Bob Moser was looking for me and he would be waiting in the coffee shop. I found him there with a coffee and pastry. He looked very pleased with himself. "Hiya, Annie," he said, and waved me over. When I got to the table he announced, "Good news."

"You found out who really killed Alan?"

"No, no. Not that. But I cleared up why we missed his room."

"That's wonderful."

"You see they work an eight to four shift, then four to midnight. The night of Alan's death, the computer was down. It went down around five P.M. DeLucca got his new room at around five-thirty, five-forty-five at the latest. Howard at the reservations desk makes a note of it, intending to enter it in the computer as soon as it was up, that 508 is now della Verona, DeLucca is now 437. So from five-forty-five, anyone who asks for DeLucca gets sent to 437. Until seven-thirty that night. When Howard gets an emergency call. His mother has been rushed to the hospital—we verified that—and he leaves to go to her side. The assistant manager takes over. The computer comes on line around eight. The police arrive a little after eight. When I ask for De-Lucca's room the assistant manager punches the computer, because that's what he's in the habit of doing. He doesn't see the handwritten entry that Howard made. You follow this?"

"Yes."

"So that night we get DeLucca's room number as 508. Next day, Howard is working again at four P.M. He notices that his note is still there, so he checks to see if it was entered into the computer record. He sees that it was not. He corrects it. When Sonny asks for DeLucca, after that, he gets the correct room, 437, which is open, with the key on the dresser.

"So," he concluded, "we didn't screw up. It was just one of those things. I'm much relieved." He took a big bite of pastry.

"I don't give a damn," I said.

"What did you say?" Moser asked, hunks and chunks of pastry visible in his stunned open mouth.

"Did you ask Howard who made the room change?"

"Huh?"

"Who requested the room change? Did you ask?"

"Uh, no," he said, trying to swallow or at least tuck enough of the flour and filling into the side of his cheek so he could talk without spewing. "Is it important?"

"Yes. Can we talk to him again?" I looked at the clock on the wall. "Immediately."

"Well," he swallowed. "I can try."

"And we need the clerk from the commissary. They sold out of Sherman's. They had a whole carton and they just sold out. Who bought them and when?"

"You want me to do that too?"

"Yes," I said. "You can and I can't."

"Sure," he said. "OK."

"How much longer do I have?"

"Jeez, I dunno, about half an hour, forty-five minutes."

"Then what?"

"When Tom Costello gets here, I'm gonna make an arrest. Who's it gonna be?"

"Could we get everybody in one room?"

"All the suspects together? Just like on a TV show or something?"

"Yes. It's my best shot."

"Sounds like fun and what do I care. Whether it works or not, I still do the same thing. Sure. I'll do that."

21

An hour later, I finally met Tom Costello. He wore a suit and a tie. He had plump, bowed lips, which he kept pressed tightly together as a symbol of rectitude and repression. He looked at me like he was measuring me for a cell. But then, he looked at everyone that way. Just as Moser had said he did.

He had a man from the BCI lab in Albany with him. His name was Dick Davenport. His smell brought back dim and faint memories of high school chemistry labs, flaming bunson burners and reagents. He wore a civil-service-salary suit and a faded tie, but he had a flinty and skeptical look in his eye.

All of us—cast, crew, suspects, witnesses, and representatives of law enforcement—were assembled on the third floor at the far end of a large room overlooking the lake. It was a perfect day and the windows had been thrown open. The air was full of spring, the room was full of hostility.

Everybody grumbled about it, but everyone had their own

motive for being there: to defend themselves, to appear cooperative with the police, to make sure the matter was finally wrapped up so that they could go on with their lives or get back to their hustle. The one exception was Rain—I now assumed his real name was Raymond—and his mother. "My son and I have no reason to be here, no need to be here, no need to hear what will be said here," his mother said to Detective Moser.

Moser looked at me. It was his authority but my show. Rain looked at me with pleading eyes. This was where the action was and clearly he wanted to be there. But to say that he had to be there as a participant or witness I would have had to lie and I didn't want to do that. Reluctantly I admitted his mother was right and Moser said they could go. Mrs. Popko dragged her son away.

Everyone else stayed.

Brigette was there with Gavin and Chelsea. Mitzi, looking glowy and a bit flummoxed, sat possessively by Choice. Fern sat with Lucy. Angie sat alone, but near her children. Mitch sat across from her. Larry Rhinebeck sat next to her, looking straight at me. Lazlo perched on the edge of a table in position to watch everyone, or look past them out to the mountains and the water, his back almost to me and Sonny.

Sonny and I sat with Bob Moser, Tom Costello the first assistant DA, and Dick Davenport down from the BCI lab in Albany. I was in charge, until I failed to prove that someone else had killed Alan; then I guess Moser or Costello would be in charge and take me away. As a detective I had always been able to trust my instincts. Just as I had been able to as an actress. Yet about Alan DeLucca they had deserted me. Deserted me quite completely. How had I so misjudged him? Because he was the director? Because buried deep inside I wanted love more than I could admit to myself?

Now that I needed instincts to save my life—were they in working order? Or was I still as foolish as I had been about Alan?

"We don't have a lot of time for this foolishness," Tom Costello said to Bob Moser.

"OK," I said. "We'll start." I'd made notes, putting together the bits and pieces I knew, trying to place everybody from about five in the evening until just after seven, just after the murder. "Let's start at about five. Alan, and Lazlo, Amy, and Mitzi were all together, scouting locations. Correct?" There was enough muttered agreement from the participants for me to go on. "Gavin was back at the hotel, alone. Brigette was in her own room, resting."

"This vas according to the schedule," Brigette said as if I had accused her of abandoning her charge.

"Right, no problem," I said. "It had been a long day. You needed, and were entitled to, your rest. Lucy was sitting downstairs, waiting for Alan to return, right, Lucy?"

"I wasn't waiting for Alan, I was just waiting, you know. There's not much to do here, right? It's pretty boring."

"You asked the desk clerk to tell you the minute Alan came in," I said.

"Nooo," she said.

"That's what he told Detective Moser."

"Yes, ma'am," Moser said.

"Well, it wasn't like that, I was bored. And I wanted someone to talk to. I can talk to Alan."

"So you were waiting for Alan?"

"Well, I was, originally. Like in the first place. But then . . . But then I didn't see him. There, and you can't prove I did."

"Detective Moser has a warrant. To search your room. To see if we can find any traces of Alan's presence, a hair on your clothes, for example. Or the thing that's missing from Alan's room."

Choice tried to get my attention. I ignored him. Lucy turned a little paler and her nose began to twitch, like a cornered rabbit or a worried snow queen out on probation who couldn't even take a charge of possession of paraphernalia.

"Do you want us to search your room, Lucy dear, or do you want to tell the whole truth?"

"Well, like I was sitting there, bored out of my gourd. Face it, when you've seen one tree you *have* seen 'em all. And good ol' Fern came over. At least I know Fern and we started in to chatting away. You know, girl talk and well, you know what he said . . .''

"Tell us."

"All right, but you won't like it."

"Tell us anyway."

"Fern told me that Alan was sweet on you."

"Sweet on me?"

She rolled her eyes. "Well, maybe he said it more like you were the flavor of the week and he said, 'You know how Alan gets with new stuff, can't see straight until he's had it.' There, satisfied?"

"Is that all he said?"

"No, he said I would have better luck with Choice. Also that Dan Ginzburg was coming to location and I could do myself a lot more good being with Dan than with Alan. And that sounded like a good idea to me because Dan has been a friend of my dad's, and my mom's, for years and years, so I feel like I know him and it wouldn't be like being with a stranger, kinda comfy, you know. So I went for Dan and had a totally good time and we've been together ever since and I haven't had five minutes with Alan alone, even sixty seconds, even. So there. Leave me out of this."

"Let's continue. Mitch was in the production office, right, Mitch? And there are phone records to prove it."

"Yes," Mitch said.

"Angie was in her room, the suite she shared with Alan. She had Chelsea with her."

"Yes, precious to me is my time with my daughter. It goes by so quickly, the time when they are young like this. And now, tragedy. It is so sad, for one so young." She spoke as Angelique della Verona with her Eurotrash accent, not as Angie Getzevitch from Staten Island. Playing a role on stage, sustaining it for somewhere from one to four hours is strange; but playing a role, day in and day out, without the theatrical structure that strictly limits the number of surprises you must sustain, and keeping your character, must be vastly stranger. Or was this just an obscure but extreme variant on that which we all do, the constant creation of our adult selves, and it only seemed strange because it was so arbitrary and disconnected from her roots.

"All right, Alan had seen all the locations. He'd selected one. He returned to the hotel with Mitzi and Amy. Lazlo didn't return, he went to the location that was selected to stay and watch the light as the afternoon ended, evening began, and the sun went down. Lazlo?"

"The light, it is always the light that matters. Yes. I stayed."

"Derek followed the three of them," I said.

"What?" Derek said.

"You followed Alan and Amy and Mitzi back to the hotel."

"Did not." He stuck out a pugnacious jaw and flexed his chest. It was a very roosterish reflex.

"You followed them most of the day. You were seen by several people."

"Well . . . well, there's a lot of crevasses and stuff. Ledges and rocks and stuff. Somebody couldda got hurt. I wanted ta be there, if somebody got hurt. Rescue 'em."

"We'll deal with motive later. But you did follow them."

"I kept an eye on them."

"Fine," I said. "The three of them went to Alan and Angie's suite. Angie was already there with Chelsea. Amy left immediately, right, Amy?"

"Yes, I did. And," she added defiantly, "Derek was waiting for me right there in our room."

"No," I said. "He wasn't."

"Yes, he was."

"Amy, he was following you, which he just admitted, he wouldn't get there before you, would he?"

"He was there so soon it seemed like he was," Amy said.

She was standing by her man, but the equivocation was clear to everyone and I didn't need to argue about it. I went on to the next item. "Mitzi stayed in the suite for about fifteen minutes."

"We discussed the next day's shoot," Mitzi said in her businesslike tones, a dedicated lieutenant reporting duty done. "I took notes. Then I left."

"And did you see anyone in the hall as you left?"

"Yes, I did. I noticed it because usually people in the hall are doing something. Either coming or going. This person was doing neither. He was just standing around like a Teamster."

"That was . . . ?"

"Derek."

"Thank you," I said.

Derek, looking sullen and offended, mumbled something to Amy. I think he said, "I didn't think the witch saw me."

"As soon as Mitzi left," I said to Angelique, "you and Alan began to have a fight."

"I have told you all about that. I have nothing to hide," she said.

"Tell me, what did you fight about?"

"Oh." She raised her eyebrows. "This is not a thing I would think you would wish me to repeat. With all of these persons here, in front of them."

"Tell me anyway."

"It was over you. I did not want him going to you. It was to protect you that I said that. Though I think I should not care so much for you, you who was willing to go with the husband of another woman. But he insisted . . ."

"Is that when you got him another room?"

"He got the other room. So he could be free to be with whomever he wanted."

"You're lying, Angie," I said.

"You tramp, you," she said, standing up and sneering at me with great disdain. The sneer of disdain is the peak of the model's art form, what the aria is to an opera singer, and consequently Angela, who had practiced the expression assiduously for years, did it singularly well. "You are not one to be calling me a liar."

222

"Someone was in the hall, Angie," I said. "They overheard you."

"Who? Who?" she shrieked.

"And Alan didn't call the desk to change his room. You did. You called and booked him a new room. Then you tossed his things in a suitcase and tossed it out in the hall."

"How do you know that?" she said, sounding Staten Island again. "How do you know that?"

"We spoke to the desk clerk," I said.

"About the suitcase, you don't know that. You wasn't there. No one was there."

In truth, I had guessed. Which I shouldn't have done. But once I started visualizing the scene, it just slipped out because that's the way I imagined it. And apparently I was right. "It upset your son, who was in the hall, listening. It upset him a lot."

"Gavin," she said, not out of pity for his pain but in realization of who had betrayed her.

"Uh-huh," Derek said to Amy.

"And Derek saw him there," I said, picking up on his response.

"I left when I seen him," Derek said.

"OK," I said, "you left. Gavin went to Brigette. He told her what he heard. Right, Brigette?"

"I am the nanny. He comes to me."

"And you comforted him."

"Ja. I am doing that. My job."

"Then you told him you would take care of things. Then you left him alone."

"I only meant that I would talk to the parent. I would explain how important family is. That is what I would do. That is all. No more. No more. The father is the authority in the household. I am Swiss. I would not attack the authority. Only remind him of his duty. Duty. Duty."

"We'll get back to you in a minute," I said.

"You must not forget duty."

"You," Moser said, "I am the authority here. You keep quiet."

She growled deep in her throat, but she shut up.

"Meantime Alan goes downstairs. He gets his new room key, goes back upstairs to the new room with his one suitcase, which includes some clothes, some toiletries, his medication, his script, and his notes. He's there long enough to partially unpack, take a shower. Then someone came to see him. We have two clues. A partially smoked Sherman's . . ." All the smokers touched the places where they kept their cigarettes. Lazlo smirked. "And Alan's script and notes, both of which are missing." Choice Wardell fidgeted like a little boy who wants to leave the room to pee. "The Sherman's smokers are Lazlo, Fern, Lucy, and Mitzi."

"I didn't do it," Lucy cried. "I was in my room, alone, doing my own thing. I'm sorry, but that's what's what."

"OK, time to cut the crap," Choice Wardell said. He stood up. "I'm gonna solve this case. Me, Choice Wardell, P.I., ex-actor. Listen to me, copper," he said to Moser. "I'm gonna hand this one to you on a silver platter." He looked down at Mitzi. "Sorry, sister. But you shouldn't do the crime, if you can't do the time. Someone died here and someone's got to take the fall . . ."

Larry Rhinebeck looked at me, greatly distressed. "Do I sound like that?" he asked me.

I said, "Yes."

He said, "I'm sorry."

"It couldda been one of them, but they didn't do it, so that wouldn't be fair, and Choice Wardell, P.I., he's fair. That's part of his code. Code of the streets. Rough justice, but fair, see what I mean. She smokes them high-toned cigarettes, and she's got the script and the notes. She's the one. It'll be a long time till we meet again. Too bad, it was sweet while it lasted."

"You sonuvabitch," Mitzi said. "You came back to my room just to sneak a look and see if I had Alan's papers?"

"It's the search for truth. That's what—"

Mitzi kicked him in the shins. Speaking as a woman, I thought he deserved it. As he yelped she swung her pocketbook. He put up his hands to defend his head and she kicked for his crotch.

"Wait," I cried.

"Go to hell," Mitzi yelled.

"Help," Choice said.

Sonny, moving slow but sure, managed to get in between Mitzi and Choice. "He's scum," Mitzi said. "Slime of the worst order. I hate actors. Actors are the worst. Actors are puke. Our job would be so easy without actors. And you know what else?" She looked around at us all and said loud enough to be heard two floors down, "Choice Wardell is a lousy lay."

"You're going to have to tell us where you got the script, Mitzi," I said. "But the cigarette didn't belong to you. It belonged to a man, right, Mr. Davenport?"

"Yes," the forensic specialist from the NY State Police Bureau of Criminal Investigation lab said.

"Now the issue of who smokes Sherman's was confused by Lazlo Viktorska—who bought a whole carton, didn't you, Lazlo?"

"Well, my dear . . ."

"That's what the clerk says. His name is Greg. We took his deposition. He remembers it vividly. You came in. You were initially going to buy a pack. Mitzi showed up and you started to talk about cigarettes. You offered to buy her a pack. She said, 'No.' Then you turned to the clerk and bought the whole carton. Then you gave her a pack, which she accepted. Normally she smokes Carltons, is it?"

"Yes," Mitzi said, "or Gitanes."

"Fern came in. He entered the conversation. You gave him a pack also. Lucy Kohl was with Fern. She didn't want a whole pack because she's trying to quit. Or rather she only smokes when she's doing coke and she didn't have that much and knew it, right, Lucy?"

"Yeah. You are a busybody. A real witch. I don't like you. And I can do the part better than you can."

I wanted to tear her eyes out. I wanted it to be her that had killed Alan. "However," I said, "all of this took place after dinner, just about the time I found Alan's body. Neither Lucy nor

Mitzi normally smokes Sherman's. Fern, however, often does. Don't you, Fern?"

"No comment."

Choice Wardell sat stewing. He really wanted to be the hero, and his big scene, meant to be the climax, had turned out to be no more than a burp in midmeal. Gavin and Chelsea both fidgeted. Brigette tried to settle them down but the two of them being disturbed at once was a bit much for her. She took out a baby bottle as I spoke. She gave it to Chelsea, who accepted it but pouted and did not drink it. So, with a grim expression, Brigette picked poor little Chelsea up and carried her to Angie and said, "Your child needs you." Then she sat down with Gavin and held his hand.

"Lazlo would have us think that he was out watching the light. Did anyone see you, Lazlo?"

"I am afraid not. Just the native avian species and some white-tailed deer."

"Enough of this crap about cigarette butts and clues that don't count," Choice cried out. "Enough. You don't figure out whodunit that way. You figure out with your guts. You got to smell it. Who hated Alan enough to kill?" He looked around the room in a very theatrical manner. "Who was"—he paused—"a cuckold? Whose wife was Alan sleeping with?"

Derek turned white.

"Who's the muscle man who let the director do it with his wife? We all know. This case is as plain as the nose on a face."

Derek began going red, like a kettle that's overheating when the water's boiled away.

Choice walked right up to Derek. I don't know, maybe the idea that stuntmen would treat him gently and always lose to him was so ingrained that he had no idea that he was in danger. "You knew all along, didn't you, Derek. And you put up with it because it kept both you and your honey on the payroll. But when you found out that Alan was diseased and still doing it with your wife, that was too much, you lost it."

I didn't know how Choice had discovered that. But movie sets are gossip mills, and since no one gasped in shock at the revelation apparently the story had already made the rounds. However, Derek had gone purple. With a roar he rose and picked Choice up off the floor. He held him overhead like he was a toy, a doll. Then, snorting and with spittle foaming from his mouth, Derek marched to the end of the room and threw Choice out the open window.

We all rushed over to see what had happened.

Down and down Choice sailed, all three stories down and hit the lake with a mighty splash. Then he went under.

Both Sonny and Bob Moser had drawn their guns and held them on Derek. Derek, after the release of heaving Choice out the window, had become docile and quiet. He held his hands over his head. When Moser took out handcuffs, Derek held his hands out and let the detective cuff him.

Choice's head popped up. He looked up to see how big his audience was. Waving he screamed, "Don't worry about me, I can swim."

So we didn't. Everyone pulled their heads back in and we resumed where we'd left off. Amy was weeping. She had known all along how strong Derek was and how much potential for violence was leashed inside him.

"It's OK," Derek said. "I won't hurt nobody else."

Moser sat him down. He looked diminished with his hands cuffed in front of him and his shoulders hunched. Abashed, like a little boy in kindergarten sent to sit in the corner for pulling little girls' braids.

"Are you ready to talk?" Moser asked him.

"Yeah, I guess I am. Sure, why not? I didn't do nothin' wrong. Don't think I didn't think about it. I thought about it. I thought about it good. I wouldda, I shouldda . . . ahh, its almost like I'm sorry he died without me doing nothing."

"He's really a gentle person," Amy cried out. "Really, really, really. Of course he had those thoughts. Anyone would. With what, with what I did to him. But he never once hurt me. Or anyone else. You can't imprison him for thinking, can you?"

"Quiet there, will you, lady," Moser said. "Let your husband say what he has to say. Come on, son. Tell us everything, and we'll go easy as we can on you."

"She was right," Derek said, evidently referring to me. "I followed them. Amy said they weren't doin' it no more but, but Alan, he was a snake, see, and he could hypnotize her. But nothing happened. I was gonna make a confrontation with him. So I hung around in the hall outside o' Alan's room. Oh boy, did they have a fight. That Angelique of his, that's one nasty bitch. What a mouth on her. If my wife had a mouth like that on her, I would sock her one. One thing you gotta say for Amy, she's quiet and she don't talk back. And that Alan's son wouldda had to hear the way she was mouthin' off. Yeah, it was her wanted him out. See, cause he didn't think what was good for the goose was good for the gander."

"What exactly did they say?" Moser asked.

"I ain't gonna repeat it, not with the kiddies in the room. Bad enough they heard it firsthand."

"Can we get back to that, if we need to?" I asked.

"Sure," Moser said. "Then what happened?"

Derek looked at his cuffed wrists and sighed deeply. "I got a temper. I gotta admit that. I figured, I figured that if me and Alan ever got confronted, well, it would get . . . it would be something he would regret. So I didn't want nobody to see me makin' the confrontation. So when Gavin seen me loitering in the hall, I left. I didn't know that bitch Mitzi seen me too.

"So what I did, I went away to think things over. You gotta understand, things was hauntin' me pretty bad at this point, waitin' for the lab report. Jeez, that's the worst. So I was pacing back and forth and I decided to go up there and have it out. Man to man. So I went back up there, and I knocked. There was no answer. I listened at the door and I couldn't hear nobody inside."

"This was room 508. The suite that Alan and Angelique were originally in?"

"Yeah, that one."

"You're sure?" I asked.

"Sure, I'm sure."

"Go on."

"So I goes downstairs again. I didn't know what to do. I couldn't believe they just disappeared and I wanted my confrontation. So I called the room from the phone in the hall, you know the hotel phone. You can't dial those phones, you gotta ask the operator. So I asked for DeLucca and the operator asked if I knew the room number, so I says, 'Yes, that's 508.' A moment later she says that's not so. 'It's 437.' 'Are you sure,' I says. 'Yes,' she says, '437.' She rings it. Alan picks up and I decide not to say nothing. To go up there for my confrontation. I hang up and go.

"I go up there and before I can even knock I hear voices inside that're quarrelin'. Somebody else gettin' their confrontation."

"Do you recognize the voice?" I asked.

"Yeah, sure," Derek said.

"You want to tell us?"

Gesturing with both hands, Derek said, "Him."

We all turned and looked at Fern. The casting director.

"No, no, it wasn't me," Fern said.

"Did you overhear what they were fighting about?" I asked Derek.

"Sure. Could hear clear as day. These old hotels, crooked doors, you can hear in rooms pretty good if you wanna."

"Should Derek tell us or do you want to tell us?" I asked Fern.

"I knew you were bad news," Fern said to me. "The minute you walked into my office. I would never, ever recommend you for a part. You smell of trouble. You can never leave well enough alone. You don't know your place. That's your real problem. You don't know your place, that's why you can't get a part, because one look at you and troublemaker is written all over you. I still think you killed Alan. In spite of this circus."

"That's real interesting," Moser said. "But how about you tell us what happened between you and Alan."

"Well, certainly. Because we didn't have a fight. We had a discussion." The fat man reached into his pocket and took out his antique cigarette holder. It had Sherman's in it. He lit one with his silver lighter. "Alan and I go back a long way. We know how to communicate with each other."

"What did you talk about?" Moser asked.

"I had a project. A script. I wanted Alan to help me arrange backing for it. It was a reasonable request and I thought Alan would be amenable to it. After all, as I said, we've been friends for a long time. And when I left he was very, very much alive. As proof, he made it across the hall on his own two feet to Little Miss Troublemaker's room, didn't he? You had better look elsewhere than here for motive." He smiled with as much smugness as he could muster and cast his eyes around the room, from possible suspect to possible suspect.

"What a load," Angie, the Staten Island vixen, said. "It must've been tough for you, hatin' Alan the way you did, but having to work for him. He had to work for him because Alan was his prestige client. The main reason people used Fernando Howard Casting is because he did the casting for Alan DeLucca. If he ever lost Alan's business, the whole industry would know in a New York second and then he'd have to get clients on his own merit."

"I don't think . . . ," Fern began.

"Alan was a user," Angie said. "Here's the story of Alan and Fern. They were at NYU film school together. Fern was a very handsome young man at the time." I remembered the picture of the young Fern on the wall of Fernando Howard Casting. "Plus he had some money. As we all know, Alan has a great deal of charm. Alan charmed Fern. Fern fell head over heels in love with Alan, didn't you, Fern?"

"Yes. I loved Alan. More than you, bitch," he said to Angelique. "Or you, either," he said to me, sneering. "He was wonderful. And he cared for me."

I found this all strange and unsettling.

"Yeah, sure," Angie said. "Cared for you so much he got you to put your money in his student film. His first film. You were gonna be an actor. But there was no part quite right for you, so you were the executive producer. Anybody doesn't believe me go read the credits on Alan DeLucca's first film. God knows I have, I hadda see that film maybe a hundred times. Alan loved to watch Alan's work because Alan thought Alan was very clever and Alan loved Alan and nobody else.

"And when Alan got his first real film, and he owed Fern big time, what did he do for Fern? He got good old Fern the job of assistant to the casting director."

"The studio was calling the shots," Fern said. "He wanted to do more, but that was all they would let him do."

"Oh God," Angie said. "You can't still believe that crap. That's what Alan told you. The studio wanted him to be comfortable on his first picture. They said he could have anyone he wanted. What he wanted was to get as far away from his student film days and that bunch of amateurs as fast as he could. He threw you that bone, to keep you busy and keep you from suing him to get your money from the first film. Which, since he'd spent it, embezzled it, he would've had to pay out of his salary, which he was too busy spending to want to do.

"I'll tell you what they fought about," Angie said. "Fern hates being a casting director. It's made him fat and a drunk and a two-pack-a-day smoker. He wants to be a producer, at least, if not a director. He has an option on a script. It's a real piece of garbage. Or at least that's Alan's opinion. But Fern wanted Alan's backing, because Alan owes him. And Alan wasn't going to give it to him."

"Not at all," Fern cried.

"Yeah," Derek said, "that's what they fought about."

"We discussed, we didn't fight."

"Like two old queens," Derek said disdainfully. "I thought they was gonna go to hair-pulling and clawing each other with long fingernails."

"All right," Fern said. "We fought. Alan did owe me. I gave him his start. Without me he would've been nothing. Nothing. It was payback time and he wouldn't pay back. But . . ."

"But what?"

"I couldn't bring myself to hurt him. I couldn't. I'm . . . I still love him. What a beautiful talented boy he was. What wit. What charm. Grace and genius combined in one form. He had it still. He hadn't lost it. I have. I know what I look like now and what I looked like then, I'm a shambles, a flab-ridden wreck. But I loved Alan from the day I met him and I'll love him till the day I die. Which is more than anyone in this room can say. Isn't it, Angelique?"

"No it's not," Angelique replied, trying to stare him down. "Of course I loved Alan. I love him still."

"Liar," Fern said.

"You were having an affair with someone else," I said to Angelique.

"You're crazy."

"In fact, that's what you came up here for."

"I came to be with Alan."

"No," I said. "To be with your lover and, maybe, to flaunt it in Alan's face. It was Alan who insisted that you stay with him in his suite. Originally you asked for your own room."

"That's true," Moser said. "We got that off of the desk clerk too. Once we thought to ask."

"It was Alan who told Brigette to spend her time with Gavin and leave Chelsea with you. Your little girl was supposed to be an impediment to your seeing your lover. In fact, the minute Alan left that night, you left too. That's why when Derek went to your room nobody was there."

"I was possibly in the bath, or resting. I don't remember. It's all so traumatic now."

"Brigette, when you left Gavin and went to see his parents, where was the first place you went?"

"I don't remember exactly."

"Can I see your green card, lady," Moser said to Brigette. "Come on, cooperate with the authorities or go back to where they make the cheese."

"I am sorry, madam, but yes, I went to room 508."

"And what happened there?"

"Nothing happened," Brigette said.

"What does that mean? Nothing?" Moser asked.

"I knocked on the door. There was no answer."

"Thank you," Moser said.

"What did you do next?" I asked Brigette.

"I knew from what the poor little boy had told me that Mr. DeLucca had looked for a new room. So I went to the front desk and asked for the room number, which they gave to me. I then went to there, but he"—she pointed at Fern—"was inside. Fighting with Alan. As he has confessed. That's what I did."

"But you knew where to go to find Angie, didn't you?"

"*Ja, ja.* I knew."

"Come on, miss," Moser said. "Share it with us."

"To his room," Brigette said and pointed at the blushing Mitchell Du Bois.

"Aw, she's lying," Angie said. "Lying like a rug on the floor. Mitch is an old, old friend of Alan's and a business associate. There wouldn't be nothing between us."

"I searched Mitchell's room," I said.

Mitch and Angie turned pale. "What I thought was amusing was Mitchell's secret director's outfit. With his stopwatch and director's finder. Is that what you think it takes to make a director?" I waited. There was no answer.

"So what do you think, Annie?" Moser said. "He done it for the girl or he done it because he wants to direct?"

"The relationship between Angelique and I is one of complete propriety," Mitchell said.

I opened the bag beside me and I took out the silver silk underwear with the monogram. "Angelique's underwear. I found it in your room."

"That monogram, *ADB*," Angelique said. "That's not me. I am *AdV*."

"It is too you!" a small voice cried in accusation. We all looked around for the source of the sound but couldn't find it. Then Moser, going down on his hands and knees, peered under the stacked tables in the corner.

"Come out of there, you," Moser ordered. There was no reply. "Come out or do I have to go in and get you? The hard way or easy way, kid, it's up to you."

"I'm comin' out," Rain Popko said. A moment later he appeared from beneath the table. "Don't tell my mother, OK?" He was very dusty.

"Sure, kid," Moser said. "You got something to say?"

"Yes, I do," he declared, standing tall. "I saw those two kissing and stuff. And he said to her, *AdV will become ADB.*"

"Is that exactly what they said?"

"Nonsense," Angie said.

"Crapola," Mitchell said.

"It was a gift from Mitchell," I said. "By the time we go to trial we'll know where he bought it and where he got the monogram put on. It's a private joke..."

"Not a joke," Mitchell said.

"Pardon me," I said. "An endearment. That Angelique della Verona will become Angelique Du Bois. Right?"

"Yeah, that's it," Rain said. "Wow, that's cool."

"So, the minute Alan left," I said, "Angelique called Mitchell. Then she rushed downstairs. They undressed to some degree. They began to make love. Then Brigette came pounding on the door. Right, Brigette?"

"Yes," the nanny said.

"Did you yell anything?" I asked.

"Remember, this is an official police inquiry," Moser said. "And you were overheard from the neighboring rooms."

I wondered if that were true or if Moser was bluffing?

"Yes, I yelled," Brigette admitted. "I said, 'You must come out. For the sake of your children. I will not permit this,' I said. 'It is not proper.' "

"Go on."

"Well, then *Mrs. DeLucca* said, 'Quiet, I am coming. Be quiet.' I waited and shortly she opened the door."

"Was she dressed?"

"Yes, but she was not entirely correct. I think she had just put her clothes back on."

"That's her opinion," Angie cried out. "Who the hell does she think she is? The Swiss fashion editor for *Women's Wear Daily*? She knows about dressing three-year-olds, not grown-ups."

I held up the monogrammed silk evidence. "And this got left behind in the rush, right, Mitch?"

Mitch didn't answer.

"I said to Mrs. DeLucca, 'You must come upstairs. You have left your little girl all alone.' So she came upstairs. And I went back to Gavin."

"All right," Choice Wardell cried, "I'm back." And so he was, dripping on the carpet. "You got him cuffed. Good work, Moser." He looked around for applause or congratulations or *something*. "Well, he done it, right? ... Huh? ... Didn't I get it right?"

"Choice," Larry Rhinebeck said, "you probably should change before you catch a cold."

"Wait a minute, I want to know, I want to know—right now— are we going to nail this guy or what? I mean, come on. It gotta be him."

"Nah," Rhinebeck sighed. "Maybe, maybe not. It's still not done. Just be patient, and maybe change your clothes."

Choice looked very unsettled. He'd handled being thrown out the window with a great deal of poise, but not having solved the case unnerved him. "Maybe I could get a towel here," he said. He snapped his fingers. "Somebody get me a towel." No one did. He stood there, baffled.

"So, Mitchell," I said. "What did you do, when your girlfriend ran out? Did you go upstairs determined to settle this once and for all?"

"Wait a minute, wait a minute," Choice said. "I gave you two solutions here. Her"—he pointed at Mitzi—"she has Alan's notes and script. And him. He has the motive. And somebody get me a towel! Or heads are gonna roll on this picture."

"Why don't you sit down, Mr. Wardell," Moser said. "And shut up."

"You better tell us, about the notes and the script," I said to Mitzi.

"He left them with me," Mitzi said.

"No, he didn't," I said.

"You could be charged," Moser said, "with half a dozen things, even if you didn't kill him. Am I right, Mr. Costello?"

"Yes," the prosecutor said. "Obstruction of justice, interference with a public official in the performance of his duties, destruction or concealment of evidence. We could probably make felony charges stick. Even if we couldn't, you'd spend a lot of time in court and it would cost you a lot of money. I'd enjoy it. I don't like it when people interfere with the administration of justice."

"Just tell the truth and make it easier on yourself," Moser said.

"I didn't take them until much, much later," Mitzi said. "When all the fuss happened and I went to Annie's room and I saw that the scripts and notes weren't there. I tried Alan's room, just on the off chance, like when you go into a pay phone, you always check to see if there's a quarter in the coin return. The door was open. I saw the notes. Maybe I shouldn't have taken them, but dammit, I can complete this picture. I know I can. He can't." She pointed at Mitchell. "He doesn't know a 10K from a Steadicam. I paid my dues. I'm ready. I'm not a second-class citizen just because I'm a woman. I'm tired of picking up after men who are doing the job I should be doing. Do you know what it's like being the assistant to most of these jerks? It's worse than being their mother, going around picking up their socks and dirty underwear off the floor, telling them how to do what they don't know how to do without bruising their little-boy egos, fixing their screwups without usurping their authority. It was tough enough doing it for Alan, who had some talent, but doing it for Mitchell Du Bois of the Bronx Du Bois would be more than a human could stand."

"Pretty thin alibi," Moser said to Costello. He sounded eager.

"I say the evidence places her near the scene of the murder and I think she'd kill to direct."

"Do you have an alibi for the time of Alan's death?" I asked. I already knew she did.

"I was on the phone," Mitzi said, unintimidated and very buttoned up. "New York, and L.A. for two hours. From five-forty to seven-forty. The phone bill will back me up. And I have notes." She reached into her voluminous shoulder bag of things and unerringly pulled out the appropriate notepad. "In the instances where the calls were incoming, you can check with each person I spoke to."

"So tell me, Fern," I said. "How did it end up with you and Alan?"

"He said no to me. And finally I left."

"Did you see anyone in the hall when you left?"

"Yes."

We all turned to look where he pointed. Derek seemed to shrink even more in his chair, looking hopeless and lost. His wife buried her head in her hands and softly sobbed. "I didn't do it," Derek said. "I didn't. When Fern seen me, I ran away. I said to myself, something is telling me not to have this confrontation. Every time I got close, someone seen me. I swear that's the truth." He didn't sound like he expected anyone to believe him. Not even his wife.

The room grew quiet except for Amy's sobbing. Everyone was fascinated or relieved, depending on the degree of suspicion that had attached to them. Moser stood up but looked to Costello for a go-ahead.

"There's one more person whose story we need to get," I said, though as a matter of strict self-interest, I probably should have stayed silent because at that point Derek was on the hook and I was off it. But just as when I get a part, somehow I wasn't in it for the payoff, I was in it for the truth, some sort of truth. "I don't know what Mitchell did after Angie left. Maybe he thought it was time to have *his* confrontation with Alan. Maybe Angie was fed up. Maybe Brigette as the enforcer of Alan's double standard was the straw that broke the camel's back. And maybe something else happened."

"Jesus," Larry Rhinebeck said, "don't you ever stop?"

"Be quiet, Larry," I snapped, close to losing it. Maybe I'd stirred up enough mud to keep myself from getting convicted, but even a trial that proved me innocent would use up a year of my life, probably in jail, ruin my career, and bankrupt me. It was easy for Rhinebeck to be light and flip, he had nothing at stake.

"Sorry, Annie," he said. With respect. I liked that.

"What time was sunset, Lazlo?"

"Oh, I am not exactly sure . . ."

"Bull. You know to the second when it went down in this time zone and what time it appeared to go down from the location. That's your job, and you're good at it."

"All right, yes. It was down at six-forty-two, below the horizon, at the location, from camera position."

"And you stayed until then."

"A few minutes more."

"You headed back, say six-forty-five, six-fifty?"

"Yes, this is true."

"That got you back here in ten minutes."

"I am not timing the walk, the time of the walk, this can be estimated."

"That's OK. Several people saw you come into the hotel."

"Yes, of course. I have nothing to hide."

"You figure that you can direct this picture now, from Larry Rhinebeck's director-proof script, don't you?"

"If it were necessary, I think it could be done. I don't know that I could live up to the great DeLucca, but, for the sake of all . . ."

"For years now, you've watched all kinds of incompetents and fools and drunks and drug abusers direct films, while you've saved them with your cinematography and your knowledge of what will cut and of creating action with the camera, isn't that true?"

"To say no would be, what is the expression, fake modesty."

"And you've told Larry, any number of times, that with his script and your ability, Alan DeLucca was superfluous. Didn't he say that, Larry?"

"Yeah, he did," Rhinebeck said. "To kill to direct. I like that. That's what Art is about."

"I did not kill Alan DeLucca."

"What time did Alan die? Mr. Davenport?"

"He died at seven-oh-five, give or take five minutes," the forensic expert said.

"To get from the lobby to your room you would have had to walk right by my room, wouldn't you, Lazlo? What used to be my room, the one where Alan was killed."

"Yes. Of course. This is true."

"What did you see?"

"I saw nothing."

"You're the one person I can positively place at the scene at the time of death," I said. "Right, Detective Moser?"

"Yes, I think that's true," Moser said.

"All right. Yes. I was there. It was five minutes after seven." He sighed. He took out a cigarette and lit it.

"So what did you see?" I asked.

"Or what did you do?" Moser asked.

"Yes, all right, I saw something," the cinematographer said. "I am not knowing that what I am seeing is important. Then when all these other things happen I think I am better with silence. I come from a place where everyone is guilty even after we make proof of innocent. To be tangled in the courts and the police, this is not my desire. My family, we know what police can do. Yes, we have had much tragedy . . ."

"What did you see?"

"I saw Alan go into Annie's room. There was someone following him. And she went in, oh, a moment or two later."

"Who?"

"That one. The Swiss nanny."

"I didn't kill him," Brigette cried. "I would never kill the master. I only wanted to recall him to his duty."

"All right," Moser said. "I guess we got you now." He smiled at Costello. "Told you we could do it."

"I did not touch him," Brigette yelled. "I did not. When I walked in, he turned. Then, he just fell right over. Right over, like a chopped-down tree in the forest. No bending or putting out the hands. Right over. His head hit the metal thing in the fireplace. Please, somebody, believe me. Please, please, please." She fell to her knees, hands clasped in prayer, like a painting of a dumpy saint.

"Shit," Moser said loudly.

"I knew you were wasting my time," Costello said.

"What?" I asked.

"That's exactly what the forensic evidence indicated," Davenport said. "Especially after you found the drugs that he was taking. That was the only question. Why would he fall over in a faint? The drugs, in combination with his condition, could easily do that."

"Dammit, I wanted it to be murder," Moser said.

"You knew this?" I said. I was incredulous.

"Forensics aren't that exact," Moser said.

"Maybe not," Costello said, shaking his head. "But juries love 'em."

"It's a possible explanation," Moser said. "Just possible. What if someone had pushed him. I still don't know if I believe that Swiss psycho. She's pretty weird. But it's Mr. Costello's opinion . . ."

"You bet it is," Costello said.

". . . that without a confession and with access to what our own experts say . . ."

"Which we would be required to disclose to the defense," Costello said in a rote manner, as if repeating the cool public version of a heated private argument.

". . . that if the defendant told a story similar to what the nanny just told, we wouldn't have a case."

"We wouldn't even get out of a prelim," Costello said.

I had a sudden thought. "I bet you even have a witness that saw me, waiting by the dining room."

"Yeah, yeah," Moser said. "We found a couple of them."

"I can't believe you did this to me." I was incensed. "This was incredibly amoral. Vicious. Are you aware of the pain and distress you caused me? As well as all these other people. Did Derek and Amy need their private agony exposed in public? And even Fern, even if I don't like him, I didn't enjoy breaking him down in front of other people. What kind of person are you? This was outrageous. I'm going to sue you for false arrest and whatever else I can think of."

"Well, we didn't arrest you, did we?" Costello said. "We just brought you in for questioning and we released you. What's the big deal?"

"You lied to me. You made me think I was your main suspect."

"Well," Moser said, "I'm a cop. And if it turned out someone did kill him, I would hate for them to walk away to enjoy the unjust fruits of their crime."

"You used me."

"Yes, I did," Moser said. "I was stuck. According to the autopsy there was only one place on the head that was struck. Even, probably, just one blow. It fit the cast-iron grate in the fireplace. So either he fell—like the nanny says—in a dead faint, or someone hit him with the fireplace grate, then laid his body down so it looked like he fell, or he was hit with something real similar and then slammed his head down in the exact same place. And," he pointed with his forefinger, "just like I told you, none of these people would talk to me without a lawyer. And, I had nothing on any of them, not evidence, or motive, or nothing. All I had was you, and you had motivation."

"What a terrible thing to do to a person," I said, angry and hurt.

"You did a great job," Moser said. "You should be proud of yourself."

"Absolutely," Costello said. "That was masterful."

"Thanks," I said sarcastically. "I thought it was your job to protect people. Not to use and abuse them. Which is what you did and you made me part of it. That's what I can't forgive you for, you made me part of your unnecessary dirty work."

"Hey, you don't regret this a bit more than I do," Moser said sadly. "Celebrity murder, gorgeous suspect—if it was you, I mean—or even some of those others. Lots of sex and money and glamour and dirt. It would have been a hell of a case."

"Hell of a case," Costello said. "Too bad it wasn't murder."

EPILOGUE

I was lucky in one sense. When I got back to New York there was a job waiting for me. But not as an actress. As a detective.

Rudi Dietz, the rich German businessman, was still with the feckless Elissa. He was very impressed with my work. But now that she was going out with Stephen and probably his twin, Harold, he wanted me to resume my friendship with her and get all the details. All the details. I could even go back to Rudolpho's and charge it to the case.

I went out with Larry Rhinebeck. I managed to overcome my distaste for his eating habits. I just tried to avoid food dates. He was beginning to grow on me when we went to see Oliver Stone's *JFK*. I thought it was fascinating and brilliant. Larry fell asleep. I didn't mind that. But he began to snore. If our relationship was ever going to come to anything, I would, eventually, be with him at a time when he slept. I have a problem with noises and I cannot be with a man who snores. I just can't. I got up from my seat and left the theater without waking him. Which put an end to that.

Mitchell Du Bois convinced the money people and the distributor to let him finish the movie. They agreed, with one change only: the return of Lucy Kohl, of course. The picture was completed and then disappeared. There is a kind of cult yearning to see it—Alan DeLucca's last unfinished epic—but rumor has it that it is so bad that it cannot be released—even on video.

The best thing that came out of it was that I made a friend. A real friend, and those are rare. Rain somehow overcame his mother's anger at me and she let him visit me and then hang out with me from time to time. His real name, it turned out, was Rain, but because it had been his father's choice his mother was trying to change it to the more normal Raymond. He jokes that I'm his substitute father figure because I'm a detective who survived against great odds and because I have things to teach him about acting and stuff.

"What stuff?" I asked.

"Well, I dunno . . . ," he said in that kid way that meant he did know but didn't know how to say it. That male way that meant it was something emotional and he didn't want to say it.

"What?"

"You know what you are, Annie? You're a stand-up guy and I like that."